# GO SADDLE THE SEA

'Ye've run yourself into a real nest of adders, here, lad,' Sammy whispered.

'I know they are smugglers,' I began protesting. 'That was why the fee was low. But I could take care of my – '

'They are worse than smugglers, lad – they are Comprachicos,' he breathed into my ear.

'Compra – c-comprachicos?'

At first I thought I could not have heard him aright. Then I could not believe him. Then I *did* believe him – Sam would not make up such a tale – and, despite myself, my teeth began to chatter.

# Joan Aiken

## GO SADDLE THE SEA

RED FOX

A Red Fox Book

Published by Random House Children's Books
20 Vauxhall Bridge Road, London SW1V 2SA

A division of The Random Group Ltd
London Melbourne Sydney Auckland
Johannesburg and agencies throughout the world

Copyright © 1977 by Joan Aiken Enterprises Ltd

5 7 9 10 8 6 4

First published in Great Britain by Jonathan Cape Ltd 1978

Red Fox edition 1997

Typeset in Sabon 11 on 12 pt by Intype London Ltd
Printed and bound in Great Britain by
Bookmarque Ltd, Croydon, Surrey

THE RANDOM HOUSE GROUP Limited Reg. No. 954009

Papers used by Random House Group Limited
are natural, recyclable products made from wood grown in
sustainable forests. The manufacturing processes conform to
the environmental regulations of the country of origin.

www.randomhouse.co.uk

ISBN 0 09 953771 0

# Contents

*Go saddle the sea, put a bridle on the wind,
before you choose your place.*

Proverb

# 1

The sheep had been brought down from the mountains, because the year was dwindling; winter would soon be here. That's how I know it must have been around September, my saint's month, when Pedro came and rattled my door at black of night.

You could hear the sheep a-crying and a-calling, near and far; the dark night was riddled by their thin, peevish voices, even louder than the wind – and that was loud enough. The sound kept me wakeful. Also my bed was cold as a marsh, for there had been weeks of rain before the weather turned wintry. I had not even thrust my feet down to the bottom yet, so I had no particular objection to getting up again. But I did wonder what brought Pedro to this part of the house. He was the cook's great-nephew, and he slept on a shelf in the kitchen, which was a good ten minutes' run from my quarters on the upper floor.

I had a whole room of my own – lucky Felix! – with two windows that pierced clean through the city wall, and looked southwards towards the mountains, the Sierra de Picos de Ancares. For sure

I was lucky: I had a room, and a mule to ride, and learned Latin and the Lives of the Saints from Father Tomas, and was Don Francisco's grandson. But, no question, Pedro had the snuggest crib. He was fourteen, two years older than I, and six inches taller.

But I was heavier, and could throw him on the floor, three times out of five.

'What's the row?' says I, pulling on my jacket – I hadn't taken off my shirt, it was too cold to go to bed naked.

I padded across the massive, creaking boards in my stocking feet to open the door. Always sleep with your door locked – if you're fortunate enough to have a door – was one of the things Bob had taught me. Bob had been dead four years and the French had been gone for eight, but you never knew; maybe the French had invaded and come back, burning and snatching. If not the French, there was always a chance of armed brigands or *guerrilleros*, on the scavenge for anything they could pick up. There were plenty of queer culls in the mountains.

'It's me – P-Pedro,' he called, shivering. 'Santa Maria, am I glad I'm not you. Fancy having to sleep in this ice-house!'

'Why the devil did you come, then? Doña Isadora would have your skin off.'

I had thought my bed cold, but the air was much colder.

'Great-aunt's dying. She wants you.'

'*Dying*? – How do you know?'

Bernardina, his great-aunt, had been cook in my grandfather's house ever since I was born. And long before. She was a huge woman, quick on her feet as a bull, with a bull's little red eyes and neat ankles. She could rage like a bull, too, when she was drunk, but, most of the time, she was laughing, roaring out songs, cursing, hoisting huge trays in and out of her oven, giving a stir to all her pots; I found it hard to believe that she had even been taken sick. And as for *dying*, that seemed impossible. Could she have run her head against a stone doorpost, whilst chasing one of the maids with a skillet?

'I wouldn't tell a lie. It's true enough,' whimpered Pedro, pulling at me to hurry me. His hands were shaking, and all he did was unbalance me as I tried to stamp into a shoe, so that I put my foot down heavily, and a splinter from the floorboard ran into my toe.

'*Estupido*!' I snapped, but instead of taking offence, he said,

'Father Tomas is with her, hearing her confession.'

That settled it. Bernardina would never confess before she had to. No point in upsetting God, she said. And shovel-faced Father Tomas was not to be hoisted from his bed for a simple case of colic; she *must* be dying.

But she had been in good health the evening before; had thrown a pan of onions clean across the kitchen because, she said, they were not hot enough to serve to Don Francisco for his supper.

11

And she had also threatened to tell my grandfather what she thought of Dona Isadora's tale-bearing ways. I do not know if she would really have done that, though. Perhaps it was having to keep a rein on her indignation that polished her off at last.

A great cold fright took me. What'll I do when she's gone? In all this freezing barracks of a house, big enough to hold an army, filled with richness and silence, Bernardina was the only one who ever laughed or sang, the only one who ever gave me a friendly word, who looked as if it mattered to her whether I walked into a room or left it.

No, that is not quite true. My great-aunt Isadora's nostrils twitched, whenever she saw me, as if she smelt bad fish. And the kitchen brats muttered rude words under their breath when I came in to talk to Bernie – not aloud, any more, since I had knocked out three of Pedro's teeth.

If Bernardina goes, I might as well go too.

But where?

Down the stairs we crept. Not much need to worry about making a noise – the stairs were solid stone, wide enough to take a horse and carriage. Besides, all the old people, my grandparents and great-aunts, slept on the far side of the courtyard. Still, I went quietly. For three days I had been confined to my room as a punishment. I had tied the cord of Father Agustin's habit to a lamp-stand in the chapel, so that he pulled the lamp over when he tried to stand up. Beaten by Father Tomas and no food until Saturday. It hadn't been worth it, really. But you have to do *something* to keep your spirits up.

Pedro had brought a candle with him but it wasn't wanted now. Bright moonshine scalloped the cloistered side of the courtyard, where we stayed under the arches, for the wind was like a dagger; then alongside the chapel entrance, where a lamp always burned in a red glass shade; through a black-dark passage, then round the cloisters of another court, for the house was built around two, like a double-four domino.

Pedro did not stop at the door of Bernardina's clammy little room, which always smelt of the goose-grease she rubbed on her chilblains, and the raw onions she ate for her complexion. I said, 'Where is she?'

'She took a fancy to die on the stairs.'

'On the *stairs*? Why there?'

Bernie had always maintained that she was too fat to walk up and down stairs; which was why she chose to sleep on the ground floor; if the conde or the condesa or any of the senoras wished to speak to her, let them come down to her level, she said.

'She thought she'd be nearer to God; or it would be easier for Him to find her; I don't know,' Pedro said, sniffing.

So we went up again.

Quite a steep little flight, this was; we were now in another section of the town wall (my grandfather's house took up one whole corner of the town of Villaverde); and you could climb right up on to a walkway that led along the wall, or into a turret which looked out to where the French or the English might be coming to carry off all the poultry and mules, and drink all the wine.

Bernie was not as far as the top, though. She had got herself perched about ten steps up, like a whale beached by a big wave at Finisterra. She was wrapped in a cloak and her feet, in felt slippers, stuck out like an untrussed pullet's.

Father Tomas was there with his sacred things, and the place, besides the usual draughty smell of cold wet stone, breathed strangely of incense and holy oil.

Bernie shone like one of her own chickens she'd been a-basting.

The minute I saw her I knew that Pedro had spoken the truth. Light from the full moon came through an arrow-slit, and Father Tomas had brought a rush-light in a holder, and by the mixed illumination I could see that she looked dreadful. Although she smiled at me and gave me a wink, I felt my heart open and close inside me, with a pain as bad as when Bob died.

Father Tomas was mumbling Latin over her like a ball of string unwinding, but she interrupted him.

'Oh, give over, Father, do, *muchas gracias*! You've done your best for me; if God wants a good cook, He knows where to find me. And if He doesn't, I'll hire myself somewhere else! Run along, now, Father; I daresay you've greased the way into heaven for me so I'll slide in somehow. And I'll put in a word for you if I get there. But now I want a private word with Senorito Felix.'

Father Tomas spared me a glance cold as a slice of tombstone. 'What's that boy doing here?' says he peevishly. 'You are supposed to be confined to your chamber for impertinence and sacrilege.'

'*Vaya, vaya*, you can't refuse a dying woman's wishes, Father,' Bernie objected, heaving herself up like a sack of fodder, so that she nearly rolled off the side of the steps, which had no rail.

Father Tomas gave a squawk of alarm.

'Be careful, woman! Oh, very well – very well; Senorito Felix may approach and bid you goodbye. But you are not to be long, mind, and then he must return to his room immediately.'

'Si, si, si! Now go and tell your beads somewhere else, Father, and take that little sniveller with you,' Bernie said, pointing to Pedro.

I have seldom seen a look so full of annoyance as the one Father Tomas gave me while he slowly collected his sacred things together and retreated down the steps. Then he went a-gliding away over the flagstones, with his black woollen robe swishing around him; you could always tell when he was near by that sound, and the smell of old greasy wool and the wintergreen ointment on his rheumatic knees.

A couple of kitchen girls, Rosario and Isabella, had been fussing uselessly with bowls of hot water and towels; Bernie sent them packing too.

'Is there any wine left in that jug, boy?' she said to me. 'Yes? Good! I've a fancy to die drunk, just

15

in case there's no wine where I'm going. Give us a tot. Now come closer.'

So I climbed up another step or two. She groped about among the folds of the tent-like wrapper, and passed me a little bundle.

'Wh-wh-what's that?' I asked. I stammer when I am upset; it is a stupid habit that I can't shake off. It was horrible to see her lolling on the steps in that unlikely way, her face all grey and shiny, looking so different from the Bernie that I was used to find in the kitchen, tossing her fritters and roaring out wicked songs.

'Things of your father's,' Bernie said. 'Bob gave them to me when he died.'

'Why didn't he give them to *me*?'

Bob had been my father's batman. After my father – who was a captain in General John Moore's army – had died at Los Nogales, Bob somehow made his way over the mountains to Villaverde, where my grandfather's house was. How he did it, no one ever knew, for he, too, was terribly wounded: one leg shot away, one arm useless, a bullet lodged in his spine, so he was all doubled up. The journey took him months and months. But he managed. Bob was the bravest person I ever met. He managed the journey, and even lasted some years after that, hobbling about the stables, doctoring the horses, and telling me stories of my father. He died when I was eight. He'd been very good to me. I still hated for him to be dead.

'He said to keep these for you till you were

16

grown,' croaked Bernardina. 'He said, no use to burden you with them till you were a man, and able to fight for yourself. But I can't do that, can I? I shan't be here. And there's no one about the house that I'd trust; those aunts of yours are a lot of canting old snakes in sheeps' clothing – that Isadora would put poison in your *garbanzos* as soon as look at you! So you must just have the things now. There's a lot of written stuff, but I haven't read it, not I!' She chuckled. I knew that she could not read a word. 'Then,' she said, 'you will just have to decide for yourself.'

'Decide *what*?'

It was all too much for me to bear; in spite of gritting my teeth, clenching my fingers, and holding my breath, I could feel a great sob snap in my throat. Tears came bursting out of both eyes.

'Oh, Bernie, *please* don't die!'

I was bitterly ashamed of myself. However much Father Tomas beat me for bad Latin – or for letting loose the pigs – or greasing the stairs, so that Dona Isadora slipped on them – I used to take pride in the fact that I never blubbered. Not even when Dona Isadora kept on and on about my being a Bad Seed and the death of my mother.

'I *must* go, my poor little pumpkin,' Bernie whispered hoarsely – her breathing was very awkward, her words came in bunches. '*I'm* not wild about it, either, to tell you the truth – but when they call you, you've got to flit. And there's a bad thing in my heart, I can feel it – it's not beating as it should. The question is, what are *you* to do? You don't

17

belong here, any ghost could see that. Bob always said that, if he'd been in better shape, he'd have taken you to England to your father's folk. But he knew he'd not last the journey. He did try to write to them once, but with his right hand gone and his left hand crippled, he could hardly scratch out the words; likely the letter never went where it should. No answer came, that I know. Anyway, Bob used to say that a cold home was better than none.'

Bob had been English, like my father; the English I speak I learned off him. But luckily he spoke Spanish as well, like a native, besides having such a wonderful gift with horses that, in spite of his one crippled arm, Don Francisco was glad to keep him on in the stable. Bob believed – he was the only one who did – that my parents really had been married. As they were both dead, *they* had no say in the matter. All my relatives in the big house were quite sure in their minds on the opposite side. My grandmother looked at me as if I gave her a pain, and Dona Isadora, my great-aunt, had masses said every single day for my mother who had died, they said, in a state of sin, after having given birth to me.

Bob said that my father was Quality. 'Captain Brooke wasn't his real name,' he told me. 'Don't you let those toffee-nosed Cabezadas put you down. Pooh to el senor Conde! An English baronite is worth half a dozen Spanish counts any day. You are as good as they are, Master Felix, and don't you ever forget it.'

18

'Perhaps these things of my father's will tell me where to find his family,' I said to Bernie, feeling the little bundle, which was wrapped in stained linen, thin and brittle with age and hot weather. My thumbs itched to untie it, but I felt it would be more dignified – as well as more polite – to wait till I was back in my own chamber.

'Maybe – they will,' wheezed Bernardina. 'And my advice to you, *hijo*, is, not to stay here, where you're despised. Leave this place and find your father's kin. You've a right – to choose – where to hang your hat. You know what I always say – go saddle the sea – '

She stopped speaking. A look of pure concentration came over her face – as if she were trying to remember some important name; or as if – I thought stupidly – she found herself obliged to dig out a bit of gristle with her tongue from between her back teeth –

'*Manolo*!' exclaimed Bernardina suddenly.

She lifted herself up, looking past me.

I twisted my head round, thinking someone must have walked up silently behind my back. But nobody was there. Then I remembered that Manolo was the name of Bernie's baby, who had died long before I was born –

One of the kitchen girls, coming back with a hot brick in a cloth, screamed piercingly and dropped the brick on the flagstones.

I turned my head again in time to see Bernardina topple slowly and heavily off the step on which she was balanced; it was like seeing a great log, which had been floating down a millstream, suddenly up-end itself and go over the milldam.

Isabella flung herself forward; I scrambled back down the stairs. But we both knew that what we were doing was no use. I think Bernie died before she fell. There she lay, on the granite flags, her great mouth open and her small eyes staring, still with that look of surprise. Dead as the stone on which she lay.

Father Tomas swished back, tut-tutting irritably, and pushed us aside.

'Go to your room, boy! And you, girl, fetch the others – fetch some strong women, and the porter, and one of the gardeners – tt, what a way to die – '

I went away quietly. There was no point in staying.

Taking a different passage, I walked into the big kitchen, where Bernie had been mistress all my life long. It was a grand room. The walls and floor were covered with shiny red tiles, decorated by little blue-and-white diamonds and crosses. The fire burned on a wide platform, the step up to it marked out by more tiles, green-and-white ones, these; and a two-foot-wide shelf ran most of the way round the room. There was still plenty of fire in the hearth, and some candles burning, but nobody in the room; I daresay they had all run off to lay out Bernie and say prayers in the chapel. I pulled up a stool to the fireside and sat there shivering. I couldn't believe yet that Bernie was dead. Every minute I expected her to come roaring in through the door, calling out, 'Hey, boy! *Hola*, my

little tiger! You want a *merienda*? Glass of beer?
Bit of bread and chocolate? Just a minute, then – '

It looked as if she had been making herself a
merienda just before she had been taken ill. A
pestle and mortar stood on the big scrubbed table
with some chocolate in it she'd been pounding,
and a platter held a pastry-cake sprinkled with
salt, my favourite food. Maybe she was going to
sneak it up to me in my room. Now I couldn't
have touched a crumb of it. I kept thinking: 'She's
sure to come in soon. No she isn't, she's dead.
She's sure to come in soon – '

I listened for her loud, slapping footsteps, for
her cheerful bawling voice. They didn't come.
Instead, to my horror, I heard a slow, measured,
double clack-clack: the sound of two elderly ladies
in high heels. If I'd had any sense I'd have run like
a hare – but I hated to leave the warm red kitchen;
besides, up to the last minute, I couldn't believe
they were really coming here. They hardly ever set
foot in the kitchen. But they did come in, one
behind the other, stepping stately and scrawny, like
a couple of old moulting guinea fowls with their
long necks. Dona Isadora and Dona Mercedes.
They were in their usual black bombazine dresses,
black mantillas, grey lace shawls wrapped round
their shoulders, and black mittens on their hands.
Each carried a fan, and Dona Isadora gave me a
rap on the ear with hers as I scrambled to my feet.

'What are *you* doing in here, Felix?' she
demanded in her high angry voice, that was like a
saw biting through stone. 'You are supposed to be

21

confined to your chamber. Why do we find you here?'

I could see dislike in every line of her long, thin, sour face, with the V-shaped upper lip overhanging the one below. She was my grandfather's sister and she hated me worse than poison. And I hated her back.

'Shall I summon Father Tomas to beat him, sister?' she suggested to my grandmother.

'Later, Isadora. We had better go on now, to Bernardina's bedside.'

'You're too late,' I gulped. 'She has just died.'

I couldn't help thinking how very unwelcome they would have been at that strange death-bed on the stairs. Bernie despised both of them.

'You have not answered my question,' said Dona Isadora coldly.

'Bernie wanted to see me before she died.'

The two old ladies looked at one another.

'A *wholly* unsuitable friendship,' complained my grandmother. 'Between the cook – the household cook – and my grandson. But what can you expect? God only knows who or what his father was. Yet born to my daughter – a Cabezada, who could trace her ancestry back twenty generations to the Conquistadores!'

'Is it to be wondered at that he prefers low company?' muttered Dona Isadora.

'Bernie wasn't low!' said I angrily. 'She was kind. She wanted to give me some things of my father's – '

'What things, boy?' said Dona Isadora sharply.

She was ten years younger than my grandmother, and much more forceful. Dona Mercedes
often drifted off into vague memories of her lost
sons.

'I don't *know* what things. I haven't looked yet.
This bundle . . .'

'You had best open it directly.'

I hated to open it under Isadora's supercilious
stare, but there was no way of refusing. Slowly I
undid the stiffened knots of aged linen, which,
I now saw, was stained with streaks of brown –
bloodstains, very likely – and spotted with grease
too. It smelt as if Bernie had kept it alongside her
chilblain ointment.

Inside I found another cloth, not a great deal
cleaner, but softer and easier to undo. And inside
that, a wad of folded paper, covered with faded
writing. And inside *that*, a small brittle black
plume and a few gilt buttons.

'What have you there?' inquired my grandmother in her vague way.

'I think it must be a plume from an officer's
shako – '

'Not that, idiot!' snapped great-aunt Isadora.
'The letter.'

I unfolded the paper. There were several pages
of it. Dona Isadora twitched it out of my fingers
and held it close to a candle – for a moment I
feared she was going to burn it. But she peered at
it with her short-sighted eyes. I noticed that her
hands were shaking. In a moment, though, she said

disgustedly – but as if this were no more than she had expected –

'It's nothing but gibberish! It must have been written by a maniac! The blessed saints themselves couldn't make head or tail of it. And furthermore,' she added spitefully, 'it is all covered with grease. The drunken old woman probably carried it about in her pocket for the last four years.'

'Let me see the paper, please, Isadora,' said my grandmother.

But she could not decipher it either, and at last it was passed to me. I resolved to make it out, if it took me the rest of my life. But not in front of those two hateful, cribbage-faced old hags.

'Go to your room, Felix,' my grandmother said. 'You shall be dealt with in the morning. Come, Isadora; we had better go to the chapel.'

And the two of them went slowly clacking away.

After waiting till they were out of sight I picked up one of the candles – which I was not supposed to take – and took a different route back to my room. I crossed the main hall, where all the weapons had once hung – but they had been taken away during the French wars, and never brought back. None of the decorations had been left, except a huge spotty mirror, brought back from Venice many years ago by my great-great-uncle Carlos. The candle's reflection in it caught my eye, but I looked away because I did not want to see myself there. I knew only too well what I looked like: short, rather plump, and yellow-headed as a duckling, with a round face, a pointed chin, and blue,

24

angry eyes; wholly unlike the portraits of black-haired, lanky-faced Cabezadas, with their hook-noses and hollow cheeks, that hung in the dining-room and all the way up the stairs.

'How *can* that boy be one of us?' Isadora had said a hundred times, peering at me in her beady-eyed, short-sighted way. 'It's hard enough to believe that he was Luisa's child – even though I myself was present at his birth – '

I hated my own looks. Bernie used to call me Tigrito, her little tiger, because of my yellow hair, and because I fought such a lot, but that was no consolation. I longed to be dark, six foot tall, with a scar on one cheek, like my great-grandfather, El Conde Don Felipe Acarillo de Santibana y Escurial de la Sierra y Cabezada, whose portrait hung in the dining-room. What a hope! I would never be like him, if I lived to the age of ninety-three.

Returning to my room, I locked the door. Then, putting the candle on the chair, I unfolded the papers that my grandmother had reluctantly given back to me, and tried to make out the scribbled words on them.

Not one word could I understand.

It might have been written by a demented spider which had fallen into pale brown ink and then staggered drunkenly to and fro across the greasy sheets of thin grey paper. I stared at every line in turn – every word, every stroke of the pen – until tears came into my smarting eyes, tears of grief and rage as well as eye-strain.

What was the use of the stupid paper? I would

never be able to read it. I might as well throw it away.

I almost did. But then I changed my mind. It *was* a relic of my father, after all; this soiled paper, scrawled with unreadable words, and the pitiful little plume, and the tarnished buttons, were all I had of him, things he had once touched. I wrapped them all carefully in the linen once more, and then clambered back into my cold bed.

Hours went by before I fell asleep. I thought of Bernardina's last words: 'Go saddle the sea.' She had stopped in the middle but I knew the rest of the proverb: 'Saddle the sea, put a bridle on the wind, before you choose your place.'

Put a bridle on the wind . . . I could hear the wind wailing outside, hurling itself against the massive stone walls, rattling the casement. And mixed with it, the crying of the sheep, like sad, lost souls. Where was Bernardina now? Was her soul in Purgatory, or had she gone to provide the angels with her baked butter cakes, chicory salad, beans with smoked pork, and semolina balls in syrup?

Trying to say a prayer for her, I fell at last into uneasy, dream-threaded slumbers.

When I woke next it was high daylight. The room was full of sorrow, which seemed to have stolen in like a mist. There was a real mist outside, too; when, as was my habit, I clambered up on to the stone window-seat and looked out towards the Sierra, all I could see was a short stretch of pale stony plain, huddled with sheep in their damp

26

coats. The distant snowy ranges were out of sight. I could feel their icy breath, however, in the wind that came through the fog, and I pulled on a thick sleeveless vest over my shirt and under my black jacket.

Bernardina has died. What am I going to do?

It was late, I knew and didn't care. Presently Father Tomas came to reprimand me for not attending early Mass.

'But grandmother said go to my room and stay there – '

'Don't answer back, boy!' he snapped. 'Come along now, you are wanted in the saloon.'

Dismally, I followed him down the stairs. I was only ever summoned to the saloon, now, when I had done something wrong.

The saloon was a large, handsome room, freezing cold, like all the rooms in that house except for the kitchen. My grandparents and great-aunts were all so old that I suppose they had ceased to feel the cold; they wrapped themselves in a few more shawls, that was all. Occasionally in the depths of winter my grandmother Mercedes would have a charcoal brazier placed beside her chair.

The walls were hung with linen wall-hangings in dove-grey and gold, and the furniture was all upholstered in grey satin. Marble side-tables were protected by fringed damask cloths. Enormous walnut cabinets against the walls were filled with treasures of china and silver, which my grand-mother and great-aunts polished themselves because the servants could never be trusted not to

27

break things. The pictures, in thick gold frames, were of dead hares, great slices of water-melon, cut salmon, and bunches of grapes painted so realistically that you expected the fish to drip. They were supposed to be very valuable, and so were the ornaments of Toledo steel over the fireplace. So were the gilded leather-bound books in the library, and the heavy chairs of studded leather, and the grey curtains interwoven with gold thread. Everything was a treasure in that house, and for years my grandparents lived in terror of the French, who might arrive and burn it all – or the English, who were just as bad. It was a piece of luck that Villaverde was such a high-up, tiny, unimportant place that all the armies had missed it completely in their various comings and goings. For years the silver had been hidden under clay and sacking in the stables, the pictures perched on rafters in the barns. But now the various valuables were all back in their places. All that the house lacked was sons – my grandfather's four sons, Manuel, Carlos, Juan, and Esteban, who had died in the wars, one after another, at Talavera, and Albuera, and two at the battle of the Bidassoa. And his daughter, Luisa, who had died giving birth to me.

The old people were sitting in the saloon, silent as the painted fish in the pictures, munching their breakfasts: fried eggs, cups of chocolate, and toast, which they dipped in the chocolate. I preferred Bernardina's crispy *churros* to the dry bits of toast, but nobody was offering me any breakfast.

'Boy! Come here!' said my grandfather.

I went, trying not to look humble, trying not to look cocky, and stood in front of his invalid chair, which was made of oak, steel and damask. The Conde was very lame, and had to be wheeled everywhere in this contraption, which was equipped with a side-table, a writing-desk, a lamp, and a mirror.

He was a handsome old man, my grandfather; his legs might be useless, but his back was straight as a musket. Smooth grey locks, eyes like chips of coal, a beak of a nose, a grey satin jacket, striped satin waistcoat, and a snowy cravat. His face, much lined, was the same colour as his jacket – like pewter. He looked at me as if I were a weevil that he had found in his toast.

'You were to be confined to your room for three days. Yet you left it without permission.'

'She *asked* for me – she was *dying* – ' I began hotly. I had meant to keep my temper, but injustice always put me in a passion.

The Count raised his hand.

'That is not all. Father Tomas tells me that he found in your school-room a disgracefully impertinent poem that you had written about him, and a drawing so outrageous that I ordered him to tear up the paper before your grandmother or any of your great-aunts should chance to set eyes on it.'

I couldn't help half a grin at the thought of their expressions if they *had* seen that drawing, but the Count added coldly, 'Father Tomas has done so.'

Miserable old pig, I thought. Trust him to go

rooting about among my schoolbooks and papers whilst I was shut up.

I hope the poem stung his thick hide.

'Also,' continued my grandfather, 'when Father Agustin returned from his visit to the monastery at Lugo and retired for the night, he found among the coverings of his couch a dead fish. I have no doubt that it was you who put it there – such disgusting pranks have been all too common.'

'I did *not* – ' I began indignantly. Father Agustin was rather stupid, and I had not been able to resist the trick with his dangling waist-cord, when it occurred to me, but I had no real grudge against him; at least the subjects he taught were a little more interesting than the prosing of Father Tomas; and he had once showed me how to make a kite.

'As if I'd put a fish in his bed! What a stupid notion! Besides, how could I? I was in my room.'

'You have played such tricks before. And what reason have we to believe you?' said my grandfather coldly.

All the old great-aunts – six of them had flocked to this house, from every part of Spain, during the French wars, and had stayed ever since – nodded their mantilla'd heads up and down and hissed to one another: 'Disgraceful, disgraceful! The boy's little better than a savage. But can you wonder? Poor Francisco – how I pity him, having such a troublesome charge.'

Moan, moan, mutter, mutter, mutter. Isadora directed a particularly mean stare at me; I daresay she was the one who persuaded my grandfather that I must have put the fish in Father Agustin's bed; she was always carrying spiteful tales against me.

'I don't tell lies!'

'Hold your tongue, boy!' said my grandfather wearily. 'It is the height of impertinence to speak to your elders until you are requested to do so.'

'It isn't fair!' I burst out in a real rage. 'I am the only person in this house who is not allowed to speak when I have something to say. Every soul about the place despises me. And yet I am your *grandson*!'

'Oh, how outrageous to address his grandfather in such a way,' muttered the old ladies behind their fans.

My grandfather, turning his face away as if he could not bear the sight of me, said to Father Tomas who was standing by him looking like a hungry raven.

'Take the boy away and beat him. Three strokes for leaving his room without permission, three for the poem and the drawing, three for the fish in Father Agustin's bed, and three for his impertinence to me. Twelve in all.'

'Doesn't Your Excellency think he ought to have a few more strokes for the poem and the drawing?' said Father Tomas, obviously disappointed. 'After all, he was not only ridiculing *me* – as if I should care for a boy's insults – but was making fun of Holy Church in my person!'

'Twelve will be sufficient,' said my grandfather.

'You may do it in the dining-room. Then take him back to his chamber.'

'You're a lot of old fossils!' I yelled, as Father Tomas dragged me away by my ear. 'You and your silver plates and your china jugs and your dead-as-dust treasures. *That's* what I think of you all!'

Father Tomas was hauling me past a leather-and-gilt table on which there was a little alabaster statue of a boy. I snatched the statue as we wrestled past, and flung it on to the stone floor, where it broke into three pieces.

A hiss went up from all the old ladies.

'Oh! *Look* what he has done now! The monster! Why, he must have the *devil* in him!'

But my grandfather only said,

'Three more strokes, Father Tomas, for the statue.'

The dining-room had a huge polished table, and more chairs of studded oxhide. Father Tomas tied my hands to one of the chairs with a cord from his pocket, and beat me with vigour. There was plenty of room for him to wield his cane – you could have fitted a couple of farm wagons into that room as well as the table and side-board. I pressed my lips together so as not to make a sound; I could picture all the old things in the next room pricking up their ears as they sipped their choc-olate, hoping to hear me blubber. When Father Tomas had done, he pushed me back to my bedroom and this time bolted me in, shouting through the keyhole,

'There you stay, until your grandfather decides you can come out!'

'I *prefer* to stay in! I don't want to see *any* of you, ever again!' I shouted back, and then I went and lay on the bed, on my stomach. I wondered if the whole world was as hateful and wretched as this house. I could not call to mind one single thing that seemed pleasant or cheering – so, in the end, I went to sleep for a couple of hours. When I woke, feeling very hungry and stiff, I went back to poring over the papers Bob had left me, for something to pass the time. By daylight it was easier to see the shaky scratches, but no easier to guess at their meaning. I worked all the way through, line by line, wondering if the words were English at all – maybe they were French – or some strange script. Arabic or Moorish? But then, on the last page, after a lot of thought, I decided that I recognised some English words. One was *the*, another was *and*. Hurray! I thought. With two words, I am on my way. The sentence in which they occurred was printed out more carefully than the rest, in large wavering spidery lines. Probably, I thought, the person who wrote these pages – my father? – wanted to make sure that whoever read them would understand this at least.

I stared and stared, and at last, after perhaps another sixty minutes of utter concentration, decided that those particular words were 'The Rose and Ring-Dove'. But, given that was so, the words made no sense to me, nor did they help me in deciphering the rest of the message, which remained wholly cryptic.

The Rose and Ring-Dove. What could that mean? Was it the name of a ship? A book, a play, a poem?

I had gone as far as this when there came a tap on the door, and the outer bolt was cautiously pulled back.

'Who is it?' I growled. Yesterday it would have been Bernardina. Today, there was nobody I wanted to see.

'It's me, Pedro.'

'What, again? Haven't you got me into enough trouble?'

'I am very sorry,' he said, coming in. He carried a handful of fritters, a bag of nuts, and some slices of ham, which he put on the stone window-seat. He said,

'It was I who put the fish in Father Agustin's bed.'

'Do you think I didn't guess?'

'It was good of you not to tell.'

'What would be the use? They would have beaten me anyway. Thanks for the food. Now, get out!'

'I don't blame you for being angry,' he said dejectedly.

I threw a shoe after him as he left, but my aim was half-hearted. It missed, as he slammed the door hurriedly. I had an idea that he had forgotten to shoot the bolt – or perhaps he had left it undone on purpose.

My first act was to eat the ham and fritters. Then I put on my riding-jacket, found my hat, took a little money which I had saved up in a box, and the nuts, and the bundle of my father's things, and a book, and put all these things in a canvas bag. Then I tried the door. As I thought, it was unbolted. I walked out, and bolted it, just to puzzle them.

Then I went down to the stable. No one was likely to be about at this time of day; it was mid afternoon, siesta time.

On my way to the horse and mule stalls, I passed the little harness room where Bob had always slept. As I invariably did, I opened the door and put in my head. The room was just as Bob had left it – blanket folded, a few clothes hanging on a hook. Bob had died in the stable one night, doctoring a colicky mare. His body had been found next day.

'Bob?' I said softly, into the empty room. I did not expect an answer. I don't know *what* I expected. Only, the room still held such a memory of him that it comforted me to say his name there.

'Bob, I'm going. I'm going to try and find my father's family.'

There was no reply from inside the room. Only a mew, from the stable-yard behind me.

I closed the door again and walked over the cobbles to the horse-boxes. Old Gato was waiting for me, as he always did when I came to the stable. He was the stable cat, really, but I pretended to myself that he was mine, because he seemed to like me best. He was stripy ochre colour, with big yellow eyes. Old, and rather lame, but a clever mouser.

'A tiger, just like you, hijo,' Bernie said once, laughing. 'No wonder you are so fond of each other.'

I picked him up and pushed my face into his sweet, hay-smelling fur. That nearly did for me – I could hear his rumbling purr, so loud.

But you can't stay in a place just because of a cat.

'Goodbye, old Gato,' I said. 'Be a good cat. Catch plenty of mice.'

I set him down, and clicked my fingers over his head. Immediately he did his trick for me, rising up on his hind legs in a beautiful flowing movement, like a Mameluke-trained horse, to rub his jaw along the side of my hand.

'All right, that's enough, now!'

I saddled and led out a mule, one I sometimes rode. She was a lean, haggard animal, rather savage and morose in her nature, but with an amazingly fast trot, which she could keep up for hours on end. I thought she would be able to carry me, not as far as I meant to go, but at least a fair part of the way. Mules are not so nervous as horses, they are nimbler in mountain country, braver if attacked by wolves, and better able to bear the fatigue of travelling on day after day. I led my mule softly out of the stable yard and was about to mount her at the block, when a voice behind me said,

'Where are you going?'

I spun round, thinking, 'All's up!'

But it was only Pedro.

'Never mind where I'm going,' I said. 'You had better forget that you saw me.'

'Can't I come too?'

'No, you cannot.'

He turned away discontentedly, kicking a stone; but then picked a sprig of rosemary from a bush that grew out of the wall, and gave it to me.

'Here, put this in your hat-band. It will protect you from witches and dangers.'

'Very well. Thank you, Pedro.'

As the mule's hoofs clopped under the big arched gate through the town wall, I turned round. Pedro was still standing in the empty cobbled street outside my grandfather's house, watching me.

I called,

'You might give a dish of milk to old Gato now and then,' and he nodded.

Then I rode off into the mist.

# 2

I kicked the bad-tempered mule into her fast trot, and she let out a series of grumbling snorts, throwing up her head and shaking it from side to side. After five minutes of this, however, she settled down and went swinging along very well, of which I was glad, for I wished to put as much distance as possible between myself and Villaverde before the mist lifted.

Next to the town wall there was a strip of cultivated land, about a mile wide, but beyond that, wild, bleak downs stretched for twenty or thirty miles in every direction, to the jagged points of the encircling mountains; the road ran over sandy flat ground and, apart from a scrubby kind of thorn-bush, no higher than my knee, and a great many rocks, varying in size from a cobble to a cottage, there was no cover along the road. If the mist should chance to lift, I could be seen for miles from the walls of the town – which was why I had chosen to leave in such a hasty and precipitate manner, while the road lay hidden. Turning to make certain of this after half a mile, I saw with much relief that the little town on its lopsided hilltop had quite vanished from sight; nothing could be seen of the small stone redroofed houses or my grandfather's great mansion, all girdled by the encircling wall.

Goodbye to every last one of you, thought I, with fierce satisfaction; you won't be seeing the little tiger again. Never! They would have to drag me back by my tongue to get me inside the town wall. But no one will miss me – except old Gato – Grandfather will probably rejoice to be rid of such a disagreeable burden. – He will be angry about the mule, though.

However, I was obliged to acknowledge to myself that in my hurry to escape, I had come away very ill-provided with necessities for the journey. My clothes were tolerably warm, to be sure, but my black jacket and breeches were too conspicuous; wearing them, I would hardly be taken for some country boy on his way to the next village. Also it was a great regret to me that I had been unable to supply myself with any kind of weapon; I had a small knife, true, but what I needed was a pistol or musket, for besides wolves, wild boars, and wild dogs, I might very possibly encounter brigands or *rateros*. I had not dared go to the armoury, though, for fear of encountering the steward or one of the servants. Likewise I lacked a proper carrying-pouch – I had hoped to find saddle-bags in the stable or in Bob's room, but had seen nothing suitable. I must therefore contrive to remedy these deficiencies in my equipment as soon as possible, but how? My stock of money was very low, and it would be needful to keep as much as possible for the latter part of the journey; furthermore, if I attempted to buy clothes or weapons at any village within twenty miles of Villaverde, a report of this would surely find its way back to my grandfather, and he would know in which direction to send a pursuit.

Exercising my mind, fruitlessly enough, over these problems, I rode on for several hours. – In spite of which, I was happy to be away, and free. I sang sometimes, whistled, and even laughed aloud at the thought of their faces when they discovered my absence.

The air became colder and colder. A fierce nipping blast swept down from the mountains, causing the mule to put back her ears and me to button my jacket up to the neck. By degrees, now, the mist began to lift, but by this time, fortunately, my road had commenced a descent from the wild and desolate upland regions where Villaverde lay perched, and plunged between cliffs which, in some degree, protected me and my mount from the wind, and, more to the purpose, from the view of any person in our rear. I lost sight of the mountains, in their horrid rocky nakedness; luckily the highest lay behind me, but I knew that five more ranges at least rose between me and the coast. I hoped, however, that since these ranges ran in a north-easterly direction, it would be possible for me to follow the valley of one of the rivers between them, the Eo or the Navia or the Narcea, which would lead me northwards to the sea, the Mar

Cantabrico. And then, surely, it would be no difficult matter to find a ship bound for England, which lay on the far side of that same sea.

Such was my plan.

I had a fair notion of England, from the tales that Bob had told me, and from a book belonging to my father which he had managed to preserve, somehow, on his journey from the battlefield, and which I had always kept, and carried with me now. From diligent reading in it, as from my talks with Bob, I had achieved a certain proficiency in the language, though my speaking of it had become somewhat rusty since Bob was gone.

The book, *Susan*, was an odd tale about a young lady and her quest for a husband; to tell truth I wondered what my father had seen in it, that he had even carried it with him into battle; I found it rather dull, but since it had been my father's I kept it carefully (his bloodstains were on the cover); story-books were few at Villaverde, most of the volumes in the library being treatises on religion or the management of crops, while such tales as were there I was generally forbidden to read. In such a case, any book is better than none, and as I rode along I was glad that I had thought to bring mine with me, to while away the time in the evenings of my journey. I did not know how long it might take me to reach the coast but feared it would be upwards of two weeks – perhaps three – I had never been farther than three or four leagues in this direction, and had no very exact notion of the distance to the sea.

My longest journey from Villaverde had been when I was four-and-a-half years old, a pilgrimage to Santiago de Compostela, which had taken two weeks. Grandfather, Grandmother, and two of my aunts travelled there in September of the year 1813 to pray for the preservation of my uncles Juan and Esteban, who were alive at that time, fighting in O'Donnel's company ( – alas! to no avail. Our prayers were unanswered, for both my uncles were killed three months later). This journey was the most remarkable thing that had yet happened to me and, although so young at the time, I had remembered many details of it most clearly: the rolling hilly country with golden gorse and purple heather and berries on the briars, which I was allowed to pick while we rested the horses. In those days Grandfather had been much more active and less severe; his infirmity had not come upon him and he still sometimes played with me and would talk to me kindly. I was in the care of Bernardina's niece Angustias (who had since left to get married) and enjoyed myself mightily. I remembered Compostela – the vast main square, all paved with stone, the mysterious face of St James's statue in his silver hat and breastplate, the glare of what seemed like a thousand candles, the steep stair we had to climb to place our own hats on his head; and the pillar at the front of the great, dark church, where Angustias banged *my* head quite hard against the smiling face of a small gnome-like stone figure carved on a pillar, saying, 'There, little tiger! That's Master Mateo, who built this church – let's hope that a portion of his good sense will find its way into your obstinate skull!' and Grandfather had laughed, and agreed. How different he had become after the deaths of my uncles Juan and Esteban – there was no pleasing him; sometimes it seemed as if he could hardly bear the sight of me.

However the memories of that journey, with two coaches for the family and servants, and another for the baggage, with coachmen, outriders, and provisions, over easy rolling country to the west, would in no way help me now on my solitary course northwards through the mountains.

The mule and I had now come out of a steep narrow pass, where high slaty cliffs rose on either hand, while the stony track was continually soaked with rills of water, which made it smooth, slippery, and dangerous. Ahead of us I could see the road winding and looping downwards into a lonely valley with no habitations in it. There were some cultivated fields, though, and a haystack, so I thought there must be a village not too far away.

Observing that the track encircled a brilliant green meadow, I turned the mule to cross it, rather than waste time taking the long way round. To my astonishment she refused to budge, and stood with head down, ears back, eyes rolling, forelegs firmly planted, snorting in the most obstinate manner possible.

'Why, what is the matter with you, thick-head?' cried I. 'You are not generally so particular about riding over cultivated land. Vaya, estupida!'

But move she would not, and at last I was fain

to dismount, and try to drag her by the bridle; I wished very much to show who was master, right from the start of our journey, otherwise I feared we might have continual battles.

'Come along, imbecile! There are no wolves or serpents here, or anything to frighten you,' I urged her, taking a step forward on to the bright grass.

But what was my fright and amazement to find myself sunk immediately up to my knees in soft mud, and all the time sinking deeper. I yelled aloud in my terror, and, the mule bawling at the same time, we made enough noise between us to summon all the inhabitants of the valley, if any had been there. But nobody came.

By the great mercy of providence I had retained my hold of the mule's bridle-rein. She, affrighted, was already rearing backwards, trying to keep away from the brink of the morass into which I had plunged.

'Pull, daughter of an ass!' I shouted. 'Pull, pull!' and, thanks to her pulling with all her strength, I was presently hoisted, black to the waist and dripping with stinking swamp-water, from the bog which I now knew it to be. I had heard about such quagmires, but never before encountered one, the soil being all hard and dry in our upland.

Vastly relieved at my rescue from such a frightening pass, I gave the mule a hug, and told her that she was a fine beast.

'I am sorry that I called you estupida, and will do so no more! You have saved my life and I am truly obliged to you. Another time I will pay greater heed to your opinion. But come! Dusk is falling, and we had better quickly find somewhere to sleep.'

I remounted and we continued on down the winding road. This adventure shook me deeply for it showed me, in some measure, how ill-prepared I was for the perils of such a journey as mine and how little I might rely on my own judgment; but for the good sense of the mule, indeed, I must have perished in a most foolish and useless way before the trip was barely begun; it behoved me to be much more heedful and vigilant in future, and to keep my wits about me.

I remembered Bob saying, many and many a time:

'Don't be in such a pucker, Master Felix! Take things steady, steady and slow; that's how Old Douro wins his battles.' How often I was to remember that before the end of the journey.

Arrived at the bottom of the valley, I observed that the road forked; the wider and better-used track continued on downwards, while what seemed like a small footpath led away round a fold of hillside. I thought this looked like a path used by farmers or shepherds, and that it must lead to the haystack I had sighted from above; so, not wishful to pass a night in a village so close to home, I resolved to sleep in the shelter of the stack. There would be forage for the mule, and bedding for me.

Sure enough, to my great satisfaction, after two or three twists of the valley, the path led us to the stack, which was situated, conveniently, at the top of a sloping meadow and close beside a steep cliff face; by pulling out some of the hay I could make myself a snug and sheltered nest between stack and cliff.

I allowed the mule to refresh herself by rolling, as mules are accustomed to do, gave her a truss of hay for herself; and watered her at a little brook which came dashing in a cascade out of the cliff face and then ran down to join a larger stream in the middle of the valley. How to tether the mule had me in a puzzle at first, but the haystack was secured by stakes, a large one at the core and smaller ones all round. I borrowed one of the latter and, hammering it into the turf with a stone, tied her bridle-rein to it so that she, too, would be in the lee of the stack. She was weary enough – for we must have covered some twenty miles – so that she showed little disposition to stray.

I was weary too. Nevertheless I found it hard to compose myself to sleep. Uncertainty, excitement, and all manner of fears and imaginings about the unknown regions that lay ahead went whirling through my mind and kept my thoughts in a buzz. Also, now that I came to lay me down in this high, strange, lonely, silent valley, I could not help, in some measure, regretting the comforts of Villa-verde; thinking of my thick flock mattress and coverlid, the cup of hot chocolate that Bernardina often prepared for me at bedtime, and my old Gato looking for me in the stable. Was God angry with me for leaving my grandfather's house, I wondered;

was that why He had led me into the bog? But then I reflected that He could quite easily have left me there, instead of directing the mule to pull me out; in any case it was too late to turn back now, I told myself; besides, everybody must leave home sooner or later, and go out into the world. So, feeling more cheerful about my situation, I recited the rhyme that Angustias always used to sing over me when she put me to bed:

> Cuatro esquinas tiene mi cama,
> Cuatro angeles la guardan
> Dos a los pies, dos a cabecera
> Y la Virgen Maria a la delantera.

and began drifting towards slumber.

I could have wished, though, that my first bed out in the world had not been quite so prickly: thorns and thistles continually worked their way through my shirt, small creeping creatures discovered my warm self and made haste to become acquainted with my skin; while every time I shifted, the hay parted and let in a piercing shaft of cold air.

About halfway through the night, as I was endeavouring to patch a cold spot with a handful of hay, I heard the mule give a shrill, nervous snort and stamp her hoof uneasily.

'What's the matter, *nina*? Why do you cry out?' I called to her, having more respect for her judgment now than formerly.

She snorted again more loudly, and, rousing up,

I saw, by the half-light of a moon drifting behind the mountain mist, a cluster of small black dots down in the middle of the valley, and heard a high howl which made my heart go pit-a-pat, for I knew the dots must be wolves or wild dogs.

Now indeed I cursed my lack of a weapon!

Before, I had been reluctant to kindle a fire for fear of advertising my whereabouts, but in this danger I lost no time pulling out steel and *yesca*, and kindling a small blaze; unfortunately there was no brushwood, for the valley was quite bare of trees, therefore I was obliged to feed my fire with hay, despite feelings of guilt towards the farmer whose fodder I was destroying; but if my life were to be weighed in the balance against his cattle's winter feed, I had no hesitation as to which I thought the more valuable!

The wolves circled, howling, but kept their distance, while the mule snorted and stamped, and I, from time to time, let out a shout, to show the enemy that I was not of a kind to surrender tamely. Nevertheless they came in as close as they dared, and often I felt a chill of dread at the pit of my stomach: I could see their green eyes shining, their hackles bristling, and their bushy tails uplifted. I flung handfuls of stones among them and they would retreat, but they returned again and again.

At last, however, when dawn was heralded by a faint streak of red in the sky at the valley-foot, they decided that there was no good to be got out of me, and took their departure.

Capital, thought I; let me but take ten minutes' nap, and then we had best be on our way.

*Ay de mi*! What did I do but fall into a deep slumber. And when I awoke, to my horrid dismay, I discovered that a spark from my small fire must have sprung across to the haystack, for a great black bite had been burned out of its side and only, I suppose, due to a sharp rain which was now falling, had the whole stack not been consumed, and very possibly the mule and myself as well.

With feelings of guilt and anger at myself I beat out the last embers, gave a truss of hay to the mule, and ate a handful of my nuts. Then we both refreshed ourselves at the brook and started on our way – I, stiff, cold, wet, muddy, and not much the better for my night's repose. The mule, too, seemed morose and balky; however when we had gone a mile or so, she perked up and proceeded at her usual lively pace, and I, too, by degrees, became warmer and less low-spirited.

Arrived at the point we had reached yesterday where the tracks joined, I chose the wider one, which turned into quite a well-made *carretera*, or carriage road. After a mile or so I could see small mud-and-slate dwellings ahead.

Not wishing to encounter the villagers, I struck off to the right, and took a wide course around the houses; my way, fortunately, was screened by a wood of chestnuts and oak trees. I was thus able to avoid notice – and also the danger of being marked down as the vagabond who had set light to some farmer's store of hay. My conscience was tender on this point: I remembered a time, a couple of years ago now, when, my grandfather having refused to allow me to attend a *feria* which was being held outside the walls of Villaverde, because, he said, I would rub shoulders with a horde of gipsies and *canalla*, I had been so enraged that I had deliberately set fire to three of his haystacks, and had watched them burn with the greatest satisfaction. At the time I had thought this a great joke and a just reward for his unreasonable tyranny.

At least – I thought now – my grandfather, one of the richest men in the province, could afford the loss of three stacks; but a mountain farmer was a different case. However there was nothing I could do for the farmer except apologise to him in my thoughts, and I made haste to put the village behind me.

There were big lumpish hills, now, all about, half-hidden behind the rainy mist; it was most wretched weather. After a long while, though, the mist began to lift, the rain ceased, and a mild autumn sun beamed out, illuminating a wide and noble scene ahead. A ravine, which I had been descending, gave on to a spacious valley whose sides, though steep, were cultivated. The harvest had been gathered and only stubble was left in the fields. Willow trees marked the course of a stream in the middle of the valley, high blue mountains reared their peaks on either side, and another village with a church could be seen in the far distance.

Although by now hollow with hunger I judged

it prudent to avoid that village also. This was not so easy, for it lay full in the lap of the valley and whichever side of it I passed, I must be visible among the sloping stubble-fields. However the village lay farther off than I had reckoned, and by the time we drew near it was the hour of siesta; no creature save a couple of stray dogs and a wakeful rooster seemed aware of our presence as the mule and I went quietly through the stubble, she snatching up a barley-ear now and then.

Beyond this point the valley took a turn and became, of a sudden, much steeper. Above us a black, frightful crag hung at an immense height over the road, which here drew close beside the river. This, now large and full, dashed roaring among huge rocks, carrying with it great mats of leaves and branches of trees – probably broken off in some tempest among the higher hills – and knots of yellow foam. There were, however, silent pools to be found now and again, and in one of these I was lucky enough to be able to catch a couple of trout, with my hands, in a manner taught me by Pablo, one of my grandfather's shepherds. These, cooked over a small fire of willow-twigs, appeased my hunger – and seemed to me, indeed, the best food I had ever eaten.

Greatly heartened by this wayside banquet, I sprang on the back of the mule – who, meanwhile, had feasted too, on the juicy grass at the river's edge – and we continued on our way at a good pace.

Now we had to thread a long, wild region, rocky

and forested, with no dwelling; the only sign of life was a rare, solitary stag, crashing through the underbrush, or a hare, sitting bolt upright in the track ahead. Many times I wished that I had a fowling-piece – or even a bow and arrow – with me. The stags of these parts are too strong and coarse to eat, though their skins are used by the farmers, but the hares are thought a great delicacy and I thought I could make shift to roast one if only I had the means of catching it.

Most of the day had gone before we reached another village, which lay at the foot of a deep glen. The house-roofs, here, were made of huge slates and came down almost to the ground, as a protection from the mountain rains. Up above the houses, on the sides of the mountain, almost like cloths hanging on a line, were the small fields, with cattle grazing; they seemed so steep I wondered that the cattle did not fall down the chimneys. A little church, up above, clung to a crag like a stone-martin perched on a cliffside.

I asked a woman whom I saw carrying a pail of water from the river if the village had an inn (thinking myself now far enough from home to risk notice); she stared at me in surprise, as if quite unused to strangers, and asked if I came from San Antonio? When I, having no idea why she asked the question, answered no, she directed me onward to a small *venta* at the end of the village street.

I rode along, tethered the mule to a tree outside the building, and entered. The place, inside, was one large room like a stable, with heaps of straw on which a number of rough-looking fellows were seated. Some slept, some drank wine from wooden cups, others were sharing a great bowl of stewed hare. A fire burned on a stone hearth in one corner, where travellers might cook their own food (there was no other provision). Another corner was partitioned off for the owner's family.

I was told by a dirty, weary-looking woman that I might stable the mule in a cowshed at the rear, and I obtained some grain (not barley, but maize, which, however, the mule consented to eat). There seemed no prospect of purchasing food for myself, but, retracing my way through the village, I was lucky enough to see a woman milking her cow, and obtained a drink of new milk from her. Thus refreshed I returned to the venta and laid myself down on one of the piles of straw, reflecting that my last night's bed had probably been cleaner, if more exposed to rain, wind, and wolves.

The men eating the hare, travellers like myself, had already gone to sleep, but the wine-drinkers were still drinking and talking; their voices prevented me from falling asleep.

'It is a great insolence,' one of them was saying, 'that he should come to our village! For my part, I think that we should blow his head off – or at least, throw him down from a precipice.'

All in a moment, at these words, I was wide awake, for I thought they were speaking of me, and I trembled in my heap of straw.

'Yes, but, Isidro, he is bringing his daughter,'

objected another voice. 'We can hardly throw a girl off the side of the mountain.'

Then I knew they could not be speaking of me.

'It is of no consequence what happens to the girl,' said Isidro. 'We can leave her on the mountain. Someone from San Antonio will doubtless come looking for her. Or if not, let her perish! She is only a sick girl. But I say that no man from that place should be allowed to set foot here! They are all rogues.'

'That is the truth!' struck in another voice. 'We all know how abominably they behaved over the grazing rights. And about Manuel's ox!'

'And the wild boar that Juan shot!'

'And the sheep that fell into the river!'

'Well, then is it agreed among us?' demanded Isidro.

'Yes, agreed!' came all their voices.

'Where shall we wait for him?'

There was some argument; then the one called Isidro said, 'Let us wait at the top of the path where it comes round the crag above the church. We know he must come that way. And there we may toss him into the next world without the need for fire-arms, and so save ourselves money now and trouble later. If carabineers or *alguacils* should come investigating, what can they find? A broken neck is a broken neck.'

To this they all agreed, and trooped from the building. One of them, passing by me in my corner, said, 'Who is that?' and I made believe to be fast asleep.

'That? Nobody,' said another voice. 'A stranger boy. He came from the south. He is not of San Antonio. I know every soul in that accursed village.'

They went out, and left me wondering very much what was afoot.

To be sure, it was none of my business, but I could not help puzzling about it. Why should they be so resolved upon the death of this man from San Antonio – wherever that was? I recalled the woman in the road who had asked me so suspiciously if I came from there. What fault had the natives of San Antonio committed?

Presently the sad-looking woman who had shown me the cowshed came in, carrying a great bundle of wood. Discovering that all the men had gone, she looked about anxiously, crossed to one of the sleeping voyagers, shook him awake, and asked in a trembling voice,

'Senor, where are all the men who were here just now?'

'May the devil fly away with me if I know,' he growled, not at all pleased, 'and may the devil fly away with *you*, for waking me!' and he burrowed his head back into the hay.

'Ay, Maria purissima, where can they be?' she murmured turning irresolutely towards the door again.

She seemed so distraught that, in spite of some intentions I had had not to meddle in what was no affair of mine, I could not help rising up, and softly following her outside. Bernie always used to say that I was too inquisitive for my own good.

'Senora! I can tell you where the men went,' said I, in a low voice, when we were a few yards from the door. 'I heard them say they would go up the mountain to the church, to meet some person who is coming from San Antonio with his daughter.'

There I stopped. Even in the moonshine I could see her pale face had become even paler, and great drops stood on her wrinkled forehead.

She gripped my wrist with both hands.

'Oh, Dios mio. Are you telling the truth, boy?'

I said certainly I was.

'He is my brother! Bringing his afflicted child! I begged him not to – I sent a note ... Oh, the monsters, the devils! But what can I, a poor woman, do about it?' She wound her sackcloth apron between her hands. 'To think of seven of them setting upon one – and he bringing a poor child who has neither moved nor spoken for three years! How *could* they be so wicked?'

'Well,' said I, 'why are they doing it?' For I could see she knew full well what they planned. 'What did your brother do to them?'

'*He* has done nothing! It is just that he comes from San Antonio. Anybody from that town is sure to be killed if he comes here.'

'But you come from there?'

'Oh, I am only a woman. And they took me by force.'

'I do not understand at all.'

'There is a feud! It all began long ago,' she said

impatiently, as if that were not important. 'They said we took a holy relic from their church – or *we* said *they* took it from ours – nobody remembers any more. But now there are many more grievances – about grazing rights, and somebody's ox that strayed and trampled somebody's crop . . . When did they say they expected Jose?'

'I do not know, senora. Tonight – that was all they said. They are going to wait above the church. But why does he come, if there is such danger? Why does he bring a sick child? Is there a doctor in this village?'

'No – yes, there is,' the woman said distractedly, still twisting her apron. 'But it is not that.' Her eyes kept flying about, she turned her head as if listening for some terrible sound. 'No, you see it is the Saints' Walk. My brother must have hoped that as nothing else helped poor little Nieves – *Hark*, what was that?'

'It was only a dog barking. What is the Saints' Walk?'

'It is a walk taken to heal illness,' she said rapidly. 'There is a relic of San Antonio here, and one of Santa Teresa over yonder – ' She crossed herself. 'It is a pen she wrote with, kept in a box. And they say that if you walk from one church to the other, over the mountain, fasting, and without speaking to anybody, in one night – it is like bearing a message from one saint to the other – it makes them glad, and their virtue will pass through you and heal you of your trouble.'

I thought of Bernie, and wished I had known about the Saints' Walk.

'How far is it between one church and the other?'

But the woman said, 'It is thirty miles, along a very steep mountain path. Few have done it in one night. And some have fallen over the cliff trying to find their way in the dark. Ay, my poor little niece!'

No, Bernie could never have done it.

I said, 'We had better go up to the church. Perhaps we shall think of some way to stop them.'

She stared at me. 'What could *you* do? You are only a boy.'

'We can't just stay here,' said I.

'But they will kill you too.'

I had considered that also, but still – seven against one! And a sick child! I knew what Bernie – or Bob – would say about such dealing.

'Never mind, senora,' I said. 'You stay here. Just show me the way to the church.'

'The path is very s-steep.' Her teeth were chattering with terror. But she came with me.

It was steep indeed. A narrow alley ran between two houses, and almost straight up the precipitous hill behind, climbing in steps, turning a little one way, a little the other, then up, up. The track, slippery from rain, threaded between trees whose roots were useful for foot- and hand-holds.

Presently the trees grew fewer. Ahead in the moonlight we could see the little church, nestled on a kind of shelf which just held it. In front grew

58

a great chestnut tree and by its trunk I thought I saw a moving clump of darkness, blacker than the shade round about.

'It is they!' breathed the woman. 'There! I saw a spark as one struck his yesca.' She halted and said, 'I cannot go on. My heart is dying within me.'

'What of your brother? Your niece? You will let them be killed?'

'I will go back and pray. That is the only thing I can do. If my husband found me here. – He is with them!'

'You are afraid for yourself,' said I, thinking poorly of her.

'Yes! No! It is what he would do to the children!'

'Oh, very well, go, go!' I heard her give a whimper, and then she slipped away down the hill among the trees.

By now I could distinguish the group of men clearly enough; they were standing, squatting, and lounging in the shelter of the tree, certain that their quarry must come that way. I could see that the path led on round an overhang on the mountain-side, with a steep drop down below. It was only just wide enough to walk along, where it approached the shelf on which the church was built.

I felt sorry for the man from San Antonio, carrying his sick child.

There would be no sense in my going forward and confronting the men. They would kill me or laugh at me; I did not know which would be worse.

I wondered if it might be possible to creep along behind the church and so reach a point up above the group. Pursuing this plan, I turned off to my left, quitting the path and scrambling up through the trees – which were pines, here; more light came through the branches, but the ground below them was treacherous as glass because of the needles. I had to crawl on all fours, gripping the ground with my fingers, but this proved lucky, for one of the men, hearing some sound, discharged his gun in my direction, and the shot went over my head.

Then I heard Isidro's voice:

'You fool! Why did you do that?'

'I heard a twig snap – a bear perhaps.'

'Dolt! Suppose Jose heard you?'

'Oh I daresay he is nowhere near us yet.'

Now I had put the church between myself and them and the sound of their voices died away. Thick brushwood had grown up behind the church and I had the devil's own trouble making my way through, and was in fear all the time that one of the men would hear me again. But they were still arguing, I suppose, and at length I made my way through a mass of prickly gorse bushes and found myself on the steep slope above the group, but screened from their view by the bushes.

Here, as chance would have it, I could see a good stretch of the path by which the man from San Antonio must come, and I bethought me that it might be possible to intercept him, and give him warning of what lay in store for him, and persuade him to turn back.

However this plan did not sit at all comfortably in my mind.

To tell truth, I could not abide the idea that these hateful wretches should successfully turn back a poor fellow who had made his way thirty miles over a dangerous mountain track for such a piteous purpose. So I squatted among the gorse-roots, whittling a piece of pine-wood that I had picked up, and cudgelling my wits for some means of preventing their horrid deed and allowing the man to complete his pilgrimage.

Presently I stole upwards again, beyond the gorse cover, to survey a longer stretch of the path. And there I saw what put a notion into my head.

Above the belt of gorse-bushes the mountain-side lay bare and steep as an elbow, save for a number of boulders, amazingly big, scattered over the slope like lumps of salt on pastry. If only, thought I, one of those could be loosened, so as to roll it down . . .

But if I roll it, they will come looking, to see who set it moving. How can I make them believe that the hand of Providence is against them?

Suddenly a thought came into my head which caused me to chuckle out loud. And I blessed the habit which always inclines me to carry a spare length of cord or two in my breeches pocket.

Crawling like a lizard over the mountain-side I found a boulder which was right for my purpose – big as a mounting block, but so insecurely poised on a smooth slab of rock that it was a wonder it had not rolled away before now. One stout heave, thought I, should suffice to dislodge it from its base.

Having chosen my boulder I returned to the shelter of the gorse and whittled away again at my pine-stave, cutting a hole through one end of it and a row of notches along the side, and a groove round the other end. This done, I wound my cord tightly round the groove and tied it, leaving eighteen inches dangling free. I also removed the stiff leather lining of my hat, which I pressed and moulded into the shape of a cone.

Thus prepared, there was nothing for me to do but wait, hugging my ribs with anticipation. Oh, how I wished Father Tomas had been among the group of men down by the church. I could hear them, from time to time, talking in low voices.

'He is long enough coming!' said one impatiently. 'I wish I had thought to bring a handful of roast chestnuts.'

'Be silent, idiot! A good ambush is better than a hot dinner.'

Becoming impatient myself, I crawled back to the edge of the gorse and strained my eyes, looking along the side of the mountain, which in the moon's bright light shone like a silvered nutmeg at Twelfth Night. And far off, on that silvered surface, I thought I perceived a moving dot, coming slowly but steadily along the track, dragging something behind it. After staring steadily for a few more moments I was certain, and my heart began to thump so hard that my hands shook.

'Come, Felix! Don't be a cow-hearted clunch,'

said I to myself, and, returning with all speed to my cover, I took up the notched piece of wood and commenced whirling it round and round at the end of its cord. It made a wonderfully loud roaring sound, like a furious bull a-bellowing, or a great roll of thunder sounding among the trees, and I heard the men below me cry out with fright.

'Ay, Dios, what is that sound?'

Then, still whirling the wood with my right hand, I held the leather cone to my mouth with my left hand, and, through it, bawled at the top of my lungs:

'BEWARE, SACRILEGIOUS PROFANERS! Let him beware, who setteth an ambush against his brother! Beware, bloody murderers who hinder the will of the holy saints!'

My voice, through the leather cone, buzzed and boomed like the howl of a ghost – I could hear one man fairly whimpering with terror, and others calling on heaven to protect them, and even on the saints.

'CALL NOT ON THE SAINTS, YE PROFANE DOGS!' I bawled. 'The saints will not help those who lie in wait against unarmed men – ' and then I was obliged to stop, for I was bursting with laughter at the thought of what Father Tomas would say if he could hear me making such use of the language he had poured out on me, day after day.

Quick as a monkey I ran up the hillside, bent double, and dislodged my boulder from its rest. It went bounding and hopping down the hillside, in a zigzag course, with a great roaring, rumbling, and crashing – and, even better than I had expected, it dislodged several others in its course, which all burst through the gorse cover and out among the assassins in front of the church. I could not see what befell them, but I heard their yells of surprise and terror as the first boulder landed. Then, from their running footsteps and fading voices I concluded that ghostly fright had overcome them and they had bolted for home.

I heard the frantic cry of one left behind:

'Miguel! Jorge! Help, help! The rock has broken my leg! Do not leave me here!'

Grumbling, two of them returned and assisted him down the hill, which was just as well, for I did not at all wish my presence discovered.

No great time after their dispersal I began to hear another sound – a slow, dragging footfall, weary and limping; also the rattle of wheels over stony ground.

Stealing close through my covert I beheld the arrival of the man from San Antonio. If I had not known about him beforehand I might myself have believed him a ghost – so skeleton-thin, dusty, and gaunt did he seem, poor soul, toiling along the last stretch of the path to the church, and pulling behind him a handcart made from plaited osiers, on which lay a small huddled form.

He looked round him in a puzzled and fearful manner as he neared the church – he must have heard some echo of all the creaking, crashing and shouting that had passed so soon before; but he did not speak, and I, mindful that his pilgrimage must be made in silence, did not reveal my presence.

Halting by the church door he lifted the sick child off the cart and, carrying her in his arms, passed within.

He remained in the church a long time and I did not disturb him. While he was in there I had ample leisure to unwind the cord from my bull-roarer (which I buried under a heap of pine-needles) and replace the leather in my hat. Then I knelt on the pine-needles and said a prayer myself, that his weary walk might be rewarded. It could do no harm. And I thanked God for helping me in regard to the boulders, and mentioned that I hoped He had enjoyed the joke as much as I had. He must have, I thought – after all, He put the plan into my head.

When at last the man came out, he was still carrying the limp form of his child, which caused a check in my flow of spirits. He laid her back on the cart with a sigh, and then stood dolefully scratching his head, as if he did not know what in the world to do next. It was plain to me that he had not the strength to begin on the return journey, yet did not dare linger where he was.

I had not intended to discover myself to him (curiosity as usual had kept me there) but, seeing him at closer quarters, I felt sorry for his plight, and came out from my hiding-place.

'*Buenas noches, senor,*' I said.

He started with terror.

'Who are you?' he gasped. 'Are you from the village below?'

'No, senor, I am a wayfarer. But I have met your sister down below. And I have a message to you from her. You are to descend to the village, go boldly into the venta, and say that the saints have told you it is their will that the feud should be ended.'

He was amazed.

'Did my sister really say that?'

'That is her wish,' I said. 'Shall I help with your cart down this hill? It is very steep.'

He seemed irresolute still, but the child behind him made a soft whimpering, like somebody who awakens from sleep, and that appeared to decide him. He murmured to himself, 'If the saints wish it, I must not stand in their way,' and so we half-dragged, half-lifted the cart with the child on it down the zigzag path: a most difficult task, for she was far heavier than I had expected.

When we reached the gap between the houses I said,

'I will leave you now, senor,' for I feared that if I were seen with him, somebody in the village might begin to suspect the truth. Therefore I slipped round the other side of the house and ran like a hare to the cowshed at the back of the venta, from which a door led through into the main room. I passed through this, and so into the street. I found that every soul in the village appeared to have gathered on the flat piece of ground in front

of the venta, where they were all talking in low
amazed voices and crossing themselves repeatedly.

I noticed the innkeeper's wife in the crowd and
made my way to her without attracting attention.
When I reached her side I plucked her sleeve and
said softly,

'Senora, your brother is coming. He has been
protected so far by the saints.'

Her mouth dropped open when she saw me. She
began to say,

'Was it *you* – ?'

'Hush, senora! Not a word!'

At that moment a kind of gasp went through
the crowd, and a lane opened to show the dusty,
skinny figure of Jose from San Antonio, dragging
his little cart across the ground towards the inn
building.

There was total silence as he limped along, and
for a moment I felt great fear. Suppose the muttering crowd were to fall on him and stone him to
death? Burn his daughter as a witch? Oh, what
have I done? I thought. It was impossible to judge
their mood.

Then somebody shouted,

'Why does not the child walk? If she has been
healed in the church, why is she still in the cart?
Let her walk!'

And they all cried out,

'Yes, let her walk. Let the child walk!'

I trembled.

Her father said to her in a low, pleading tone,

'Can you walk, Nieves?' But not as if he

expected that she would. He halted, however. And then, in the middle of the silence, she whispered,

'I will try.'

Slowly she stretched up a hand to him. He took it. And she began, inch by inch, little by little, to drag herself upright, with the slow, unaccustomed movements of somebody who has been lying still for years. I was astounded when I saw how tall she was – no wonder she had seemed so heavy coming down the hill! Why, she must be almost my own age! I had thought her a child of six or seven.

At last she was standing, balanced perilously on her thin legs, holding her father's hand, while he gazed at her, his mouth open, almost petrified with fear and astonishment, it seemed.

I thought she might fall when she swayed and, as no one else seemed ready to help her, I went forward to take her other hand, saying in as matter-of-fact a voice as I could muster,

'Come along then, Nieves, you must be hungry! I will help you walk to your aunt's house.'

Though heavy in the cart, she seemed now, balanced on her stick-like legs, as light as a flower of angelica. Guided by her father and me she moved along slowly – but she was walking herself, we were only helping her to keep her balance.

A kind of sigh came from the crowd, and grew louder and louder, until by the time we reached the venta they were cheering their heads off, shouting, '*Ole, ole!*', throwing their hats in the air, embracing each other, and weeping. Dozens of

68

candles were lit, people ran to their houses and fetched stools and chairs and bottles of wine; there was a feast in the street; you would never have guessed that half an hour before every man in the place had cherished the notion of tossing the father of Nieves over a cliff.

In the venta Nieves was given a bowl of milk. Very soon a dignified white-haired man came bustling in. He wore a suit of black and a three-cornered black hat; he, it seemed, was the doctor, much esteemed in the village. He expressed great interest in the recovery of Nieves but said,

'She should rest; all this excitement will be bad for her. Let her pass the night at my house. My housekeeper will look after her.'

This being agreed to, he asked for three helpers to carry her in a chair to his house, which was at the opposite end of the village. Being close by Nieves at the time, I was chosen for one of the helpers, and we walked with her slowly and carefully. The moon had gone down by now, but people were dancing in the street, which was lit from end to end by candles and rush-lights.

I heard the doctor muttering to himself as we walked along:

'Eh, well, the feud is over and *that* is a good thing – though no doubt they will find some other excuse for killing each other soon enough.'

He sounded like a man who had lived too long to believe that people would easily change their ways.

I thought that the doctor's house was most likely

the best in the village, for it was stone-floored, furnished with chairs and tables and book-cases, a great contrast to the earth floor and piles of straw in the venta.

'You may sleep in my shed if you wish, boy,' said the doctor, noticing, I suppose, my wistful glance around his room. 'You'd get little enough sleep along *there*; they'll keep on drinking till day-break, very probably.'

'Thank you, senor. That is kind of you.'

While his housekeeper was heating bricks for the bed and fetching a bowl of whey with warm wine in it for Nieves, the doctor asked a few questions.

'How long is it, my child, since you were able to walk and talk?'

'I don't know, senor,' she said. 'I feel as if I had been asleep a long, long time.'

'I believe it was three years,' said I, remembering what the girl's aunt had said, for the father, abashed by the grandeur of the doctor's house, had gone back to the venta.

'And what was the last thing you remember?' asked the doctor.

'I saw my mother and my little sister washed away when the river came down in flood. Oh, it was dreadful! – the snow and the black water and the trees tossing like sticks.' Her eyes were huge in her thin white face as she remembered.

'And since then you could neither move nor speak?'

'I – I suppose not, senor.'

'Well – well, it is a very interesting case,' the doctor muttered to himself. 'Hysterical, without a doubt.'

Now the housekeeper took Nieves off to a back room and I slipped away to the shed. The doctor was eyeing me too attentively for comfort. I certainly slept better on his hay than I would have at the inn, where, to judge from the sound, every soul in the village drank and sang till daybreak.

Next morning I was up early and went along to feed and tend my mule, for I wished to set forth. Not another soul was abroad; looking through the open door of the venta I saw it layered with snoring bodies, fowls roosting on the rafters, a baby asleep in a horse-trough, even a man lying outside, sunk in slumber, with his goat tied to his leg. Potato sacks, pumpkins, and even pigs were being used for pillows.

But at the back, when I fetched the mule, I found the aunt of Nieves, talking to her brother.

She must have come to some conclusions during the night, for when I offered to pay for the mule's stabling, she put her arms round me and nearly squeezed me to death.

'Take money off you? Not if I had eaten my last crust! I would *give* you some if I had any – I do not know what you did, but I am sure it was you who – '

'Hush, senora!' We both glanced round, but nobody had heard us. I added modestly, 'It was nothing – a trifle! But still, if you had an old saddle-bag – '

71

'That you shall have!' And she fetched a pair of *alforjas*, and placed in them bread, cheese, fruit, and a bottle of wine.

Jose, her brother, on learning that I was travelling northwards, suggested that we should go together, since that was his direction also. He wished to return to his other children as soon as might be, and I too wished to leave without delay. So, having saddled the mule, we returned to the doctor's house to pick up Nieves.

The doctor came out in his nightcap to say goodbye, and gave me a very keen look.

'Where are you from, boy?' says he. 'By daylight your face seems familiar – though I can't call it to mind exactly – '

'O, my grandfather has a farm at Los Nogales,' said I very fast – for now it came back to me that he had been called in to cure my great-aunt Barbarita of a quinsy when the doctor at Villaverde was away on a visit. I hoped he would not remember where he had seen me, and made haste to drag away Nieves in her little cart.

Luckily at that moment his housekeeper screeched from indoors that the chocolate was hot, and it would spoil if he did not come directly, so he gave us a wave, thrust a couple of coins into Jose's hand, and left us.

It had been arranged between us that we should take turns to ride the mule and pull the hand-cart; so, without more ado, Jose mounted and we left the village.

# 3

I was happy to have the company of Jose Lopez and his daughter on my journey that day: firstly, because the weather was foggy and the way confusing, all set about with precipices and chasms, so that the mule and I would almost certainly have been dashed to destruction had we travelled without a guide; but even more because Don Jose, when the cloud of fear and trouble was lifted from him, proved to be a very kind, wise man, with whom it was a pleasure to converse. He was a miller, I learned, and had two more children back at home, a boy, Mario, older than Nieves, and a girl, Anita, some years younger. Being a widower, he had felt much distress in his mind as to what might become of Nieves if he should die, and had therefore undertaken this dangerous pilgrimage as a last hope of curing her dumbness and paralysis.

When we had gone several leagues from Cobenna (which was the name of the village where we had spent the night) Jose inquired of me,

'Tell me, my boy, was it not you who threw down those boulders on the assassins?'

(For, during the festivities of the previous

evening, he had easily discovered what had come to pass before he arrived at the church.)

'Yes, Don Jose, it was I, and I also shouted threats at the men through the lining of my hat. I will not show you just now how I did it, for fear of frightening the mule,' said I – for we were at that moment skirting the rim of a fearsome precipice – 'but at all events it served to scare off those villains, and I am heartily glad of that.'

'God's ways are mysterious,' he said. 'I daresay if the people of Cobenna had learned this morning that it was you who threw the stones, and not San Antonio himself, they would have changed their minds about the miracle and torn us to pieces, all three; yet I see it as God's will which brought you to that place at that time.'

Looking at the matter in this light, I thought he was probably right, and I felt very friendly disposed towards God, Who had put this notion of scaring off the murderers into my head, and Who must have enjoyed the joke as much as I had. It now struck me that Father Tomas, who told me so often that God hated my wicked ways, very likely had a wrong notion of God altogether; and I wondered this had not occurred to me before, since Father Tomas had been wrong on many other points. And it struck me, too, how often a dark, dismal, and frightening idea is believed above a cheerful and hopeful one. Why this should be, I cannot say.

However, Don Jose, having achieved the cure of his daughter, was now as cheerful and hopeful as a man could be, and enlivened the way by telling me about the work of his mill and the people of his village. I asked how it had come about that the two villages of Cobenna and San Antonio were at such deadly feud; he said the original cause was now lost in the mists of the past, but he himself thought it might be because the natives of the two towns were descended from different races: he believed the men of Cobenna had as forefathers the Moors, who had once overrun the whole land of Spain; whereas the people of San Antonio were descended from the Goths.

'You saw how dark and scowling the folk were in Cobenna; but in San Antonio they are fair and grey-eyed, and much taller.'

Don Jose asked me about myself, why I travelled alone at my age, and where I was bound. Having taken such a liking to him, I was loth to tell him a lie, and so said frankly,

'Senor, I have left my home, which was not a happy one; my parents are dead, and my grandfather disliked me; so I am on my way to England to seek my father's kin there, for he was English. But I will not tell you my grandfather's name, or mine, in case he sends out men searching for me. Then, if they should come your way, you will be able to say that you know nothing about me.'

'But,' said Nieves, lifting up her head from the cart, where she had lain sleeping for the first part of our journey, 'if we do not know your name, what shall we call you?'

I thought a moment and said, 'A friend at my home used to call me Little Tiger.'

'*Bueno*; we will call you that. And it suits you well,' said Don Jose, 'for your hair is just the colour of a tiger's belly-fur.'

'And his face is round, just like a tiger's,' said Nieves, laughing.

By daylight I could see that she was not a bad-looking girl, although her skin was so pale, through having lain indoors on a bed for the last three years, that she was well-suited to her name of Snows (from Our Lady of the Snows); but her hair was a beautiful glossy brown, and her eyes, now that she was awakened, sparkled with interest at all she saw. I was curious about the long silence through which she had lived, while she had been dumb, and asked her if she could remember nothing of that time.

'No, friend Tiger; or not in a way that I could make plain in words. I can remember colours – which were like sounds; and scents and tastes that I seemed to see; and music that touched me like a wind; it was a long, strange, dreamlike time.'

'Thank God you are awakened from it,' said her father.

Now she wanted permission to walk, saying we should not have to pull her, since she was cured; but this he forbade, because the way was so dangerous, and she so newly recovered, her legs still weak and thin; so she remained on the cart. Indeed, at times we were obliged to fasten her to it with a leather thong, along the worst parts of the way, for fear she should be thrown off; and Jose pulled her then, saying that he was more accustomed to the mountains than I; it was true that sometimes I was obliged to turn my gaze from the giddy edge lest my head should begin to swim and I topple headlong over. Jose made me ride the mule who, like all her kind, cared nothing for the heights by which we passed, ambling on her way without the least objection, often treading so close to the brink that, if I had dared look past my foot in its stirrup, I should have seen nothing below it for thousands of feet.

Nieves, like the mule, seemed unaffected by the precipices; she felt sure, she told me, that she had not been woken from her silence only to fall down a cliff. She had a simple, plain way of speaking – like that of a much younger child – which pleased me greatly. Yet she could be thoughtful too.

'Tell me about England!' she said.

I was obliged to admit that I had never been there; yet related all that I could remember from Bob's tales.

'They eat their meat half-raw; beer and cider are drunk mostly, for wine is very dear; the bread is abominably bitter; the hedges are mean and insignificant, being full of nettles, thistles, and thorns instead of our oak and vine; they burn a black, shining stone everywhere instead of wood; their candles are made of tallow, very coarse and stinking, for wax is too dear; their clothes are not gay or colourful, as in Spain, but mainly grey or brown; there are no goats in England; they have no aqueducts or wayside fountains; their streets are wide, for the sun never shines, and they need no shade; their night-watchmen cry out every half-hour all through the night, telling the state of the weather – a needless service, for it is always raining . . .'

'Stop, stop!' cried Nieves. 'You are mad to go to such a place! Why should you wish to do so? Why not remain here, in beautiful Spain?'

'I wish to find my family. Besides, I have a curiosity to see other lands.'

'And how do you plan to get there?' inquired Don Jose.

'I shall go to the coast; I have heard that from the port of Villa Viciosa many ships sail to England at this season carrying cargoes of filberts; my intention is to take a passage on one of these ships.'

'But how will you pay for your passage?'

'I have a little money saved; and shall hope to earn more. I can sing quite well; I shall sing in the streets; or work, and run errands for people.'

Don Jose looked thoughtful at this, and said that since the French wars people were not very free with their cash.

'Oh, well, I can make wooden tops, and toys, and pipes for children to play on.'

I had learned these arts from the shepherd who taught me to fish; it was he who had shown me how to make the bull-roarer that had scared off the assassins.

'Can you make pipes?' cried Nieves, delighted.

'Oh, make me one, if you please! I should like to play on a pipe that you had made.'

I promised that I would do so when we reached the mill. Meanwhile, discovering that she dearly loved any kind of song or music, I cudgelled my brain to remember all Bernie's songs:

'Este pobre nino, no tiene cuna, su papa es carpi-ulero, he hara una . . .' and others of the kind. She joined in, Jose did likewise, and between us we made so much noise that ravens and wild hawks flew shrieking from their rocky perches, and at length Jose said we had better desist, or we might start an avalanche rolling down the mountain. This was indeed a most dismal and craggy region through which we were passing, with black rock, steep as the side of a church, on every side, and scarcely a tuft of green to be seen.

How Don Jose managed to travel that fearsome path at night, on his own, pulling the hand-cart behind him, with Nieves on it, inert as a corpse, I shall never comprehend. That was the real miracle! But he said that, when he was a young man, he had lived much in the mountains, before taking to the mill-business.

At last we came to a gentler country, of wide grassy mountain valleys, with many waterfalls like white plumes above us on the hillsides; then, always descending, we made our way through a great pine forest, and at last came out of the trees into a wide, gracious vale, where the grass was of the brightest possible green, the fields still had maize growing in them, the trees were palms, or apple-trees still laden with fruit, and beautiful blue flowers grew by the sides of the road, or climbed to the eaves of the houses. These were thatched; and often stood on stone legs, entered by ladders; I wondered if this was for defence against wolves, but Don Jose said no, more from the damp. Now we were within ten or twelve leagues of the Western Ocean, where the air, blowing inland, is so heavy with moisture that the ground becomes like a sponge. Much rain falls; and even the oxen here wear great caps of fur, gaily decorated.

Dusk was falling by the time we reached a small village at the foot of a ravine which entered the valley halfway down its length.

'Now I wish to get down and walk!' exclaimed Nieves. 'I would like everybody to see that your journey was worthwhile, dear father!' and she was so insistent that at last he agreed to let her walk slowly up the village street, while he took one of her arms, I took the other, and the cart rode on the mule's back.

It was a mild, misty evening, with a great moon rising, and several people were out strolling up and down the village street. News of our coming spread like a stubble fire:

'Look, *look!* As I'm a living woman, it's the miller's Nieves, walking on her own two legs!'

'Hey! Here comes Don Jose with his daughter – walking just like any girl! And a strange boy!'

'The miller has come back with his girl and she's *cured!* And they have a boy with them whose hair is yellow as barley-straw! *He* can't be from Cobenna!'

People came running and exclaiming and clapping their hands, embracing both Don Jose and his daughter (even I came in for a few hugs) – and we had much ado to keep Nieves on her feet as they pushed around us. By the time we reached the mill, which was at the upper end of the village, we had a whole procession on our heels.

Don Jose rapped on the door of the mill and a shrill voice from within called, 'Who's there?'

'It's I, Mario – your father!'

'Papa – at last!' The door was instantly pulled back, and I saw a brown-haired boy, rather taller than myself, still clutching an enormous blunderbuss which must have held bullets weighing a half-pound at the very least, while his small sister, who had unbolted the door, cried,

'Oh, how long you were away. We thought you were never coming back!'

Then he saw Nieves and let out a squeal that you could have heard across the valley.

'*Nieves!*'

Both the boy and girl hurled themselves at their sister, he dropping the blunderbuss – which exploded, burying its bullet, fortunately, in a heap of flour-sacks that lay against the courtyard wall. I noticed this with one part of me, while, like all the inhabitants of San Antonio, I was laughing and crying, and repeating over and over again,

'She is cured! Thanks be to God!'

When the family had embraced each other

enough, we, and all the rest of the village, went along to the church to say a prayer. And then Don Jose said,

'Neighbours . . . I thank you for your wonderful welcome – ' His voice was breaking with happiness, it sounded like a stream full of pebbles; he went on, 'And I have much to tell you about my visit to our enemies in Cobenna – but tonight my daughter Nieves needs rest, for she has had a long journey and is weary; so is my young friend here who has been of sterling help on our journey,' (which was kind, but hardly true, for it was he who had helped *me*); 'let us all meet again in the morning. For now, I will bid you goodnight.'

So the village people drew off to the *posada*, to celebrate the recovery of Nieves, while Don Jose invited me into the mill.

'But, senor, you will wish to be alone with your children – ' I said.

He pushed me inside, saying, 'You must be there too! I am sure you are hungry. And I can smell that Anita has made something savoury for our supper.'

'No, it was I, father,' said the boy, Mario. 'I have made a stew of meat and tomatoes.'

'But I made the macaroons!' cried Anita, who looked a well-grown nine – she was almost as big as her sister.

'Come in, friend Tiger!' said Nieves softly.

So I went in and shared their supper in the big mill kitchen, where a fire blazed on the hearth, and strings of onions dangled from the rafters.

I was even given a bedroom to myself, and slept for nine hours without stirring, on a flock mattress as wide as a carriage-way.

I spent three days with the family of Jose Lopez. Indeed, they all begged me to stay longer, and I would have been glad to do so, but feared if I did not then go on, I should never be able to tear myself away at all. That mill was a pleasant place! The family were so frank and friendly with each other! And so fond of one another. The children heeded what their father told them, and ran to obey his wishes, but they did so from love, and because they saw the sense in what he asked – not just because he said *I order you*. He showed me that a man need not bawl in a loud voice, nor utter threats, to make himself respected. Thin, quiet, grey, dusty with flour, Don Jose Lopez had far more authority than Father Tomas – or my grandfather's steward, who was always shouting and banging his gold-knobbed stick on the floor.

Besides respect, there was laughter and fun. They made jokes, they teased one another, they laughed and sang, they were endlessly happy to have Nieves restored to health and speech. If ever I have a family or children of my own, I vowed, our life shall be like this. And I wondered if most families acted thus – whether it was only in the great house at Villaverde that life was so silent, grim and wretched.

This is a thing you discover when you set out

into the world: looking at other lives, you begin to see your own in a new light.

On the fourth day I said I must go.

I had made Nieves her wooden flute (and a top for Anita); I had gone fishing up the millstream with Mario and caught six trout; I had helped plough the barley-field and pick the walnuts from the great tree which grew in the courtyard. I had also attended a banquet in the village, held to celebrate the recovery of Nieves and the end of the feud with Cobenna; for an emissary had arrived on the second day to propose peace between the villages. There were several sick people in Cobenna, it seemed, wishing to make a trial of the Saints' Walk in the other direction, and anxious to be sure of a civil reception when they came to the end of their journey.

'Must you really go?' said Nieves, not at all convinced of the need for my journey, as, dressed in some outgrown clothes of Mario's (a long loose tunic of coarse ticking, over a jerkin and short velveteen breeches, with woollen stockings – I kept my own shoes and hat, for his did not fit me) I prepared to mount the mule.

'Indeed I must go on,' said I, 'though I am very sorry to leave you at all.'

'Come back!' they all cried, and I promised that I would, some day, if it lay within my power to do so.

'Also, write to us from Inglaterra, to tell if you find your family,' cried Anita. 'A letter to the Miller at San Antonio will find us.'

84

'And if you cannot trace your family, come back and take this one for your own,' said Don Jose kindly.

I jumped on the mule, for I could see tears in the eyes of Nieves and I feared that if I remained another minute, I, too, would burst out a-crying. So I kicked the mule's sides vigorously, and we galloped away down the valley; but still I could hear them calling,

'Remember! Come back! Come back again!' until I was out of sight.

The mule was fresh from three days' rest and went at a lively pace. But I had ridden a long way before I was able to persuade myself into a cheerful frame of mind.

At length I said to myself,

'Come, Felix! Fie, for shame! What would Bob, or Bernie, say to see you so? Why should you ride along grieving, with a heart like a waterfall? You are a thousand times better off than you were two days ago! You have come through some dangers, you have gained a little sense, you are halfway to the Mar Cantabrico, and, best of all, instead of being solitary and miserable, you now have a whole family of friends. Added to which, instead of being horribly ill-equipped for your journey, you are now fitted out as well as any traveller need wish to be.'

It was true. The Lopez family had loaded me with gifts. Besides Mario's clothes, I had a pocket pistol, which Don Jose had given me, a bag of raisins from Anita, who had dried them herself, one of walnuts shelled by Mario, and a tinder-box, besides a wonderful old cloak which had belonged to Don Jose's grandfather. It was made from goats' felt, and was so thick that it would keep out almost any weather – rain, hail, or snow. It would serve as a blanket for me, or a horsecloth for the mule. I had it packed into one of my saddle-bags, for the day was warm and mild – a red autumn sun was beginning to climb out of the mist – and the other bag had been packed full of bread and olives by the girls.

So at last I shook off the sorrow of parting and looked about me.

Don Jose had drawn me a rough map, for, he said, even though I was now but twelve leagues from the coast, such a complicated network of mountains and valleys still lay between me and my goal (some of the mountains, moreover, being upwards of two thousand feet high) that even now there was every chance of my going astray and wandering miles out of my way. He had therefore written down for me very explicit directions. He told me my best course was to strike eastwards at first, along a track he pointed out to me, which would presently bring me out on the highway that ran south from Oviedo to Leon, and so on towards Madrid; this was one of the main roads from the capital to the coast, and so was well used. I must travel northwards along it, for, to reach my desti-nation of Villa Viciosa, I must first pass through Oviedo, which lay about four leagues inland.

Accordingly, climbing out of the valley of San

Antonio, I followed Don Jose's road eastwards into the red eye of the sun, through a village called, I think, Barzuna, or some such name, and then over a tremendous pass, from where, it seemed, I could see all the kingdoms of Spain, and even the sea itself, far away.

My spirits bounded up, at being so high, and at the immensity of the prospect before me, ranges of snowy peaks following one another into the distance like waves of the sea. Father Agustin had taught me that the world was very big, but up to now I had had no clear notion of its true vastness. And this was only Spain!

However the air up here was bitterly cold, and, moreover, so thin that both I and the mule began to cough; therefore I made haste to urge her on her way, and we began descending.

We had passed through snow at the summit, knee-deep, but this thinned off by degrees, and then I saw a beautiful sight: across the scanty grass of the bare mountain slopes, for miles on miles, farther than I could see, there spread a carpet of small flowers, a pale lavender in colour, clustered so thickly that they gave their bloomy hue to the whole hillside. And in among them, here and there, sparkled a different one, a deep dark blue, that of the sky just before the stars come out. I wished that Nieves could have seen this marvellous sight.

I was still lost in wonder, gazing around me at the flowers, and riding with a loose rein, when I heard a shout ahead of me. Much startled, and cursing myself for my careless lack of attention, I looked to see where the noise came from.

By now I was descending a great pass whose bare sides, all misted over with the purple flowers, curved together like the sides of a cup. About half a mile ahead of me I saw two men clad in black cloaks. At first I thought that they must be brigands or rateros, guarding the way, but then it struck me that their behaviour was not that of brigands; they seemed to be shouting at one another, not at me; they were standing on opposing sides of the valley, facing one another, while their hobbled horses grazed at a distance.

It was plain that they had not expected to be disturbed by any other person, up on this lonely height, for they gazed at me with astonishment as I on my mule came clip-clopping down the road, and when I reached a point midway between them, they both strode down to accost me.

In spite of their brigand-like cloaks, they seemed to be *caballeros*; the younger was handsome, with flashing black eyes and a white ruffle to his shirt. The hair and beard of the elder was somewhat grizzled. Both faces were alert and weather-beaten; they might be soldiers, I thought, or, anyway, used to living out of doors.

'Hola, boy, what are you doing here?' demanded the older man.

I replied civilly that I was travelling towards Oviedo.

'Hmn – he speaks well,' remarked the younger man. 'Not the country oaf you would think him from his clothes.' His brows flew up as he surveyed me, and I thought that *he* looked like a young king-hawk. He added, 'Shall we ask him to see fair play?'

'If you wish,' replied the other, shrugging. 'He can drop the kerchief.'

Seeing my puzzled look, they gave me to understand that their reason for repairing to this high, silent spot was because they intended to fight a duel, and duelling was frowned on by the authorities of Oviedo.

'The cause of our dispute need not concern you,' the younger man said haughtily.

I said I had no wish to pry into their affairs and, if they wished it, would continue on my way and forget that I had ever seen them.

A glance passed between them at this. I read it as, Can we trust him? but there was more to it than that, as I would soon learn.

'No; you can be of use to us,' said the older man. 'You shall stand here with this kerchief while we measure out thirty paces.'

They began doing so, very seriously. At first, in my alarm I had wondered if all this could be merely a scheme for shooting *me*, but I soon understood that such was not the case.

When they had established their positions on the sloping valley floor and marked the spot, each with a white stone, one of them called out, 'A moment!' and came striding back to me.

'If by chance I should be killed,' he said to me a little breathlessly – it was the elder of the two, the grizzle-bearded man – 'I should be greatly obliged if you could have this note delivered to my step-daughter who is a novice at the Convent of the Esclavitud in Santander. It relates to some property of her mother's which will come to her at my death.'

He handed me a scrap of paper. I was on the point of telling him that I had no intention of going anywhere near Santander – but you can hardly refuse such a request, made at such a moment. And I supposed that I could find means to have the note despatched without visiting the place myself.

It fills me with wonder, now, looking back, to think how much depended on this slight-seeming occurrence. My whole future life, indeed.

I pocketed the paper and the grizzle-bearded man, having thanked me, returned to his position. I glanced towards the younger man – in case he had a like request to make; but with a haughty lift of the head he intimated that he had no wish to delay further. So I bade them see to their priming and then asked if they were ready. Upon their answering yes, I dropped the kerchief, and both pistols went off together with a sharp echoing crack.

My eyes flew from one to the other. For a brief moment I hoped that neither had been hit, for they stood still and upright – but then the younger one turned slightly, as if he heard a noise behind him; his knees began to bend; then he slid to the ground, where he lay motionless.

It was not grief I felt, exactly, for his youth and

handsomeness, but a kind of awe at this terribly sudden change, which had taken him away for ever.

'Vaya!' said the older man, having walked over to examine him. 'He is dead; we can do nothing more for him. You may go on your way.'

'And leave him *there*?' I looked to where his black-clad body lay among the flowers.

'Oh, the hawks will soon pick him clean,' the other man answered calmly. 'Two days, and he will be white bones. We saw enough of *that* when Soult was chasing Moore over the mountains.'

Observing that I was troubled, however, he added, 'Don't concern your mind over it, boy. He knew what he was about when we began. If *I* had lost, I would not have complained.'

'I suppose not, senor; but then, you would have been dead!'

At that he grinned, and, taking a flask of *aguardiente* from the horse's saddle-bag, offered it to me. On my declining, he drank from it himself and returned it to its place. It seemed to me that he was in a strange state of mind – elated, hopeful, amazed, excited.

I said, 'Senor, since you have survived the duel, you will not now wish this note delivered. I will give it you back.'

But to that, after thinking, he replied, 'No, for the dangers ahead of me are as great as any that I have come through. The *gente de reputacion* will be on my trail like bloodhounds. I will add a line, saying that if she hears no more of me after two months, she is to assume that I am dead.'

This he did and then, looking up, seeing, I presume, my look of curiosity, he smiled and said,

'You wonder what this is all about, I daresay?'

'It is none of my business, senor.'

But of course I did wonder. Who could help it? And he, made talkative by his victory perhaps, or the drink, lit a cigarillo and explained,

'There were ten of us, you see, who knew the whereabouts of the treasure.'

'*Treasure?*'

'One of the ten was *there*, that snowy night, and barely escaped with his life. But then, later, he became drunk – drink is a terrible hazard, boy – and he let out the secret to the other nine men who were with him in the wineshop. Fool, sot, idiot that he was!'

Despite the matter-of-fact way in which he brought this out, I found something very frightening about it; perhaps the source of my fear lay in his strange composure. I said faintly,

'Are you sure you should be telling me this, senor?'

'Oh, it is all long ago now. Have you not heard that when Baird and Fraser were retreating with the English forces from Villafranca to Corunna, with General Soult hard on their heels, they were obliged to toss twenty-five thousand pounds' worth of gold dollars down a mountain-side, because their baggage-oxen had all died and they had no means of dragging it with them?'

Dumb, I shook my head. Vaguely, I remembered hearing from Bob how, when General Moore had to run from the French across half north Spain, his army suffered from terrible losses of men and material – but all this was a long time ago, 1809, the year I was born; surely whatever lay on that snowy mountain-side had long since been discovered and taken away?

'Not so,' said the bearded man. 'Somebody who was *there* – he saw it stowed in a safe place. Aha! He kept his wits, while everybody else was running and screaming and shouting that the French were half a mile away. He thought he might be able to get back one day. But then the fool had to get drunk and blab it all out to nine others. So what then? He makes a plan. Twenty-five thousand is fine pickings for *one*, but what use among ten? A bare two thousand apiece. So, 'Let us ten split into five pairs,' says he, 'each pair fight, the winners fight one another, until there's but one left. And *he* scoops the pool.' This was agreed – we fought – something told me that I should survive – and I was right. *I'm* the one that's left!'

'Ay de mi!' I murmured faintly. There seemed something so terrifyingly cold-blooded about this scheme – whereby nine men should die in order for *one* to succeed – that I could hardly believe it. But yet the duel I had just witnessed did convince me. This bright-eyed, brisk-spoken man in front of me, smoking his cigarillo in quick puffs, must indeed be the winner of the murderous contest.

What would he do with his twenty-five thousand

pounds' worth of gold dollars? I wondered. Supposing the gold was still there. Supposing he found it.

Then a thing occurred to me.

'Senor, you seem to know much about Baird and Fraser's forces – '

'Yes, boy?' he said, dragging on his cigarillo so hard that it made him cough.

'Perhaps you were with them yourself?' At his nod, I asked, 'Did you ever come across a Captain Brooke?'

'No, I do not remember the name,' he said, to my great disappointment. 'But why do you ask?'

'He was my father.'

'Hey?' he said, coughing again. 'So you are English?' He spoke in that tongue and I also replied in it.

'Yes, sir. But my mother was Spanish.'

'Ah, I see. Plenty of that kind about. Well, well! So you're half a Johnny Anglais. When I first laid eyes on you I wondered where you got that yellow hair!'

He puffed again, coughed again, and said abruptly,

'You look a decent lad – I've taken a fancy to you.' And he added in a mutter, half to himself, 'As well leave you the cash as poor little Annunciata, mewed up in her convent. – Would you care to bear me company through the mountains? Help me dig out the treasure?'

At his words I was seized by a peculiar excitement – half-avarice, half-dread. Who was this strange

94

man? I asked myself. And if I went with him – if we should chance to find the treasure – in whose existence I did not really believe – what would he do to me *then*? Would he make me fight him for it?

I did not know what to make of him.

I said carefully, still in English,

'No, I thank you, senor. It is kind of you to make the offer to me – but I go to the sea, and then to England, to seek my father's family. I go north-east, not south-west.'

He answered, rather slowly, and heavily,

'Going to England, are you? Lucky, lucky young devil!'

He seemed to speak with such a strange bitterness that I inquired, curiosity overcoming my fear of him,

'You too are English, senor? But you do not go back there?'

'Can't, curse it,' he said. 'I was in Baird's division, you see; slipped my leash on the way from Astorga; rompé'd off before Johnny Crapaud caught up – and there was one or two unpaid accounts back at home, where I was a night-hawk by trade – if ever I was to show my face in England, they'd hang me up from Tyburn Tree. Otherwise, Lord love ye, I'd ha' been home long agone. As it is – well, it's been a long haul, but now I'm on my way. With twenty-five thousand gold 'uns in my knapsack, I should be able to find me a snug little crib somewhere in Spain.'

'Why did it take you so long,' I could not help wondering, 'to go after the treasure?'

He coughed, and winked. 'Ah, well, d'ye see, boy, the gente de reputacion were interested – where there's gold, the vultures gather. We had to lay a long, slow trail – You're *sure* you won't join me?'

I shook my head and he said, sighing,

'Well, I won't say I don't wish I was going your way. Whereabouts are you bound for?'

'That I do not really know, senor. All I know is that my father's name was Captain Felix Brooke – as mine is, too. I shall just have to ask my way.'

He looked doubtful at this, but, seeing that I was resolved, said,

'Eh, well – good luck, in your search – if you won't come with me.'

'And good luck to you, too, senor,' I said politely.

He winked, coughed, and went for his horse; threw a leg over it, then turned to say,

'You might as well take poor Manolo's nag; I've no use for it in the mountains where I'm going. You can sell it for a good sum in Oviedo; it's from Andalusia, there's no better breed in Spain.'

Indeed it was a beautiful horse: dark brown, with a small intelligent head, fiery eyes, a broad chest, straight legs, and fine shoulders.

'Very well,' I said – there was no sense in leaving the poor beast in these mountain uplands, where it might die of cold and hunger, or, more likely, be pursued and brought down by wolves.

He sat on his steed watching as I caught the horse and then mounted my own mule. Waving his hand, he was about to depart, when I bethought me of something, and called to him,

'Senor?'

'Well?'

'Have you heard of a thing – I do not know if it is a house or a ship, or a place in England – its name is The Rose and Ring-Dove?'

'Why, yes,' he said at once. 'I've heard of it – who hasn't? It's a tavern – a famous inn. I never was there myself, but I've heard of it. It's as famous as the Mitre at Oxford or the Boar's Head in Eastcheap.'

'Where is it, senor?'

'Why, at Bath – is that where your folk live? Ah, you don't know. Well, Bath is a fine town. I hope you find them.'

'And I hope you find your treasure, senor.'

But I felt sure in my heart that he would not. He would perish in those savage mountains, between here and Los Nogales. I felt certain of it.

But he, riding up the valley without looking back, again waved a carefree hand; while I, leading the Andalusian horse, turned my mule's head north towards Oviedo. Once or twice I glanced back, at the tiny black spot, which was the dead man, lying in that great curved field of lavender flowers; and I said a silent prayer for him. But I gave up looking back, for great birds had begun to hover over the spot where he lay.

I wondered about him as I rode on: whether he, too, had a daughter in a convent somewhere, or a *novia* – for he seemed quite young – who would go on hoping for his return and wondering why he did not come. Then I reflected that I had by some means to despatch the other man's letter to the Convent of the Esclavitud at Santander, which I knew lay well to the east of where I was bound. Well – I thought – I would take the letter as far as I was going, and then find means to send it on from there.

After several hours, always descending, the road came within sight of Oviedo, which is a very ancient town. It is situated between two mountains, one of them high, rugged, and covered with snow. The other is of a gentler shape, and its sides are all planted with vines. The tall tower of the cathedral may be seen from miles away.

I entered through a crumbling gateway in the high town wall; as rain was falling in torrents, and it was now dusk, I did not loiter to admire the streets, but asked the way to an inexpensive posada, and was directed to a very old-looking building where I found accommodation for myself and the two beasts.

The cattle and horses were housed on the ground floor, I on the floor above them; such is the habit of these parts. The house was built around a court so that I could, if I wished, step out on to the gallery outside the door of my room, and look down to satisfy myself that all was well with the animals.

This posada also had a public dining-room upstairs, but I did not wish to eat there, being unused to such places, and also wishful to save my money. Besides, I still had much of the food the Lopez family had given me. I therefore munched bread and olives sitting on the floor of my room (for there was no chair, although the room was huge, and cold as a barn). It struck me as I squatted there, wrapped in my great cloak, that this was only my sixth night away from home – yet already I felt as if a whole lifetime had passed since I quitted Villaverde. The people of that place – now that I was away from them – seemed like people in a dream, without reality; and, considering them from this distance, I found that I felt quite calm in my mind towards them, and bore them little ill-will – even spiteful Dona Isadora, with her tale-bearing ways, even mean-minded Father Tomas, with his love of punishment. How little they know about what takes place outside the four walls of that house! thought I.

But, though I had lost my hate, I felt inexpressibly glad to be away from them.

Concerning my grandfather I had different feelings.

While I had been at the mill, Don Jose had asked me one or two questions concerning my grandfather's treatment of me, and then, sighing, had said,

'Ay de mi! Poor old man! To lose all four sons – and his daughter too. That is a heavy blow. I hope *your* loss will not grieve him too much.'

'Not likely! He will be glad to be rid of me,' said I.

But now I wondered if I had been quite right.

Perhaps he might be a little sorry that I had left: I did not know. He was a silent man, who kept his thoughts to himself.

I said a prayer for him, that he might not be grieved by my going, and then many more for the Lopez family. Indeed, I missed them a thousand times more than my own kin, and felt such a sorrow in my heart, when I thought of that happy place, that I was fain to go downstairs and purchase a rush-light from the ancient limping man who was the landlord. For I did not think I would be able to sleep yet awhile; if I shut my eyes, I saw the dead man stretched in the field of flowers, and the carrion-eaters hovering over him.

Returning to my chamber I distracted my sad mind by reading a chapter in my father's book.

This (as I think I have mentioned before) was a tale printed in two small volumes. The title-page, as well as the name, *Susan*, also gave the information that it was writ by An English Lady of Quality, and that it had been printed in the American city of Philadelphia for the publishing firm of Crosby, Norris & Jones. How my father had come by a book which was printed in America, I do not know; but *why* he carried it with him, I now, since meeting the bearded treasure-seeker, began to comprehend: for the adventures of Miss Susan in the tale mainly took place in the English city of Bath. If, as the man had suggested, my father came from that city, it was no wonder that he should delight in a story that brought its streets before his eyes.

Indeed, I now found myself reading it with a greater interest, when the book mentioned Pulteney Street, or the Pump Room, or Union Street, or Cheap Yard, wondering whether my father had visited these places. Though I still thought that Susan, the heroine, was a sad, nonsensical girl, always falling into blunders, blind to all the tricks of her supposed friend (a most detestable girl, on the catch for Susan's brother) and prone to fancy all kinds of absurdities about the people she met: as, that they had committed strange crimes and were haunted by remorse. What *could* my father have found in it to admire, apart from its taking place in Bath, I wondered, and, putting it away, I crept into my chilly bed and fell asleep.

Next morning I rose betimes. The ancient landlord was nowhere to be seen, but I found a starved-looking boy of about my own age, who promised to bring me a breakfast of stewed fowl in a few minutes. Since no other guests were about, I did not fear to go into the upstairs dining-room, which was furnished with a huge table and high backed chairs, all of them three hundred years old, the boy said. I did not know whether to believe him, so, by way of showing that I was not too impressed by his tales, I pulled out a wooden pipe, which I had made for myself at the same time that I made hers for Nieves, and proceeded to play tunes on it while I waited for breakfast.

The boy, returning, was greatly delighted. He cried out, 'Musica! Musica!' thumped down my dish of stew upon the table, and began to hop about like a mad thing, waving his arms and snapping his fingers until I was almost doubled up with laughing and could play no longer. Then, since he was out of breath, he fetched me some dry bread to eat with my stew, and a bowl of chocolate, which I did not greatly relish as it had large greasy lumps of goats' milk floating on top.

When I had finished eating the boy begged for more music, and, I believe, would have been happy to dance about all day to my piping, had not his master limped, scowling, out from some dusty nook, thumped him with a staff, and bade him get about his work.

Since I proposed to sell the Andalusian horse without delay, I then asked the boy to direct me to a beast market. He gave me instructions and I set out, after asking him to mind the mule for me, and promising to play him some more music when his master was not by. This had fortunate consequences, as will be heard later.

Now that morning had come, and the rain had ceased, the streets of Oviedo amazed me by their bustle and gaiety. It is a large town, greater than Santiago de Compostela (which was the only other I had seen) since it stands at the junction of four great roads, leading to Santander, to Gijon, to Santiago, and to Madrid. Also, it is the capital of Asturias.

The streets were lined with shops – tailors, glove makers, peruquiers, hatters, mantua-makers, bookshops, jewellers, and tobacco shops. I longed to enter the bookshops, but durst not leave go of my horse, who followed me biddably enough, though he kept shaking his head up and down fretfully as if, poor beast, he wondered what had become of his master.

I could not help a shudder when I thought of that wretched fellow, stretched cold and stiff on the bare mountainside.

At length I came to the *mercado*, a great arched place of two storeys where I am sure every kind of provision in the world might have been found for sale. In one corner were fruits – grapes of many colours, figs, apples, pears, oranges, and nuts; another section was set aside for cheese, others for meat, fishes of more kinds than I had ever seen, olives and oil, dried meats and sausages – besides cakes, pastries, and great loaves of bread. Our little market in Villaverde was not a tenth of the size.

I could have amused myself for hours just watching the people choosing and haggling, but I judged it best to be on my way, so walked through to the section of the market where beasts were sold. Here sat old farm-women with poultry tied by the leg and cackling; eggs and chicks in rush baskets; frightened calves bawling for their mothers; *burros* braying; massive bulls tethered tightly to posts; and horses of every age, colour, and description.

I went up to a gipsyish-looking fellow, dressed in a jerkin and wearing a high-crowned hat with a scarf tied round it. He had a number of horses in a lead, and I asked if he was interested in purchasing mine. He looked it over, examined its teeth, its forefeet, its hind feet, pulled its tail, pinched its windpipe, and finally offered me ten dollars, which I thought much too low; hardly the price of a donkey. I therefore shook my head and moved on, looking for a better buyer.

In a moment, however, the gipsy came up with me again. 'Stay, boy, the horse, though past its best, might do for an old man I know who wants a quiet mount. I will give you sixty dollars for him.'

'Sixty? I would not take two hundred and sixty.'

'Well, I will give you two thousand reals.'

'You must be joking!'

In the end he offered me three thousand reals* which I accepted; he paid over the money, and led the horse away into a canvas enclosure.

Now I felt rich indeed! Much pleased at my successful bargaining, due to which I thought I now had quite enough money to pay for my passage on a ship to England, I could not help loitering a little about the market, examining some fine steel weapons from Toledo, which were displayed at a stall near the entrance – and this was my undoing, for a mean-looking fellow, wearing a round black hat, a black coat and pantaloons, and carrying a brass-tipped staff came up behind me, tapped me with his staff on the shoulder and commanded me to follow him at once to the office of the *Corregidor*.

---

* About £30 at the time in England.

'Why should I? Who are you?' said I, my heart sinking horribly.

'I am an alguacil.'

'And why should I follow you? I have done nothing wrong.'

'You are suspected of horse-thieving.'

'I have done no such thing!'

'That we shall soon see.'

I had half a mind to run for it, but did not remember the way back to the posada clearly enough to be sure that I could get there ahead of him.

He led me across the Plaza Mayor, the wide main square, to the city hall, an ancient stone building, where I was obliged to sit on a bench in a dark cold ante-chamber, watched sharply by one or two carabineers.

My thoughts were not happy, as may be imagined.

In due course, that is to say, after about two hours, during which time I kicked my heels most miserably, I was summoned to the *alcalde's* office. The alcalde sat behind a huge desk. He was the most severe-looking man I ever saw; beside him, my grandfather would seem like a guardian angel. His nose was an eagle's beak, his face thin as a lamp-chimney, made, it seemed of parchment stretched over wood; his eyes sat in deep hollows, and his hair was black as charcoal-dust.

'Boy,' said this terrifying personage, 'how did you come by that horse, which you have just sold for three thousand reals?'

I was terrified. For all I knew, if I related the tale of the duel, I should not be believed, but should be accused of murdering the haughty young man. Or I might cause the other, the grizzle-bearded man, to be pursued and arrested, for he had said that the authorities in this province frowned upon duelling.

I therefore said in a shaking voice that I had found the horse masterless and wandering, up in the mountains – which at least was some part of the truth.

'*Where* did you find him?'

I replied that I had come from San Antonio, and had found the horse along the road between there and Oviedo. I was a stranger in these parts, and so could not give the precise location.

'And how could you tell that his master would not come back for him?'

'Senor, it was in a great wide valley, and there was no other living creature to be seen.'

'A likely tale!' broke in one of several men who stood listening – among them I noticed the gipsy who had bought the horse. 'It is well known that the horse belonged to the black-haired young man who has been lodging with Maria Diaz. The horse is an Andalou – all dark, with a white star on his brow – there is no mistaking him.'

'And where is the young man?' asked the alcalde.

'Your Excellency, he is not to be found.'

'Cause a search to be made for him. In the meantime, go through the boy's pockets.'

Two alguacils searched me, but got little good

for it, most of my belongings being in my saddle-bags back at the posada; all they found was the note to the man's step-daughter at the Convent of the Esclavitud, and my wooden pipe, and the three thousand reals, which were impounded. The gipsy who had bought the horse declared,

'Without doubt the boy assassinated that poor young man and stole his horse. He is a child of the devil – you have only to look at his face! Give me back my money.'

I guessed he had informed on me in the hope of getting both his money and the horse. However the alcalde said,

'Silence! We shall see what the search produces. In the meantime the money will be kept here. Let the boy be put in jail.'

So I was led off to the jail, which stood next to the city hall, and was entered by a worn flight of stone stairs. After passing through a massive door, on either side of which sat a turnkey, I was taken along a passage, then we descended as many steps as we had climbed, passed a large court where prisoners were taking exercise, and came at length to a huge vaulted dungeon, or *calabozo*, containing, I suppose, about a hundred people.

It was a wretched and disgusting place. Many of the prisoners there had hardly any clothes – perhaps they had been sold – but were merely wrapped in sacking or old rags. It was plain that they slept on the floor, apart from a few who were lucky enough to have a horse-cloth or piece of ticking to put between themselves and the stones.

'If you want food,' said my escort, 'you may send a message to your friends outside to supply you at visiting time.'

'How can I do that? I do not know anybody in this town.'

'In that case, go hungry!' replied the official, and, turning round, he left me in the calabozo.

I hunted about for a dry spot on the filthy floor, and sat down, a prey to the most dismal reflections. If Nieves and Don Jose could see me now! I was almost sorry that I had not accompanied the treasure-seeker on his wild quest. What will they do with me? I wondered. If a search is made in the mountains, they will discover the corpse of the man who was killed. They are not likely to find the other man – he will be far away by now. At best they will confiscate my mule and all my possessions, and I shall be left to rot in this hideous place for years. At worst, I shall be hung, or transported to the galleys at Malaga.

From Bernie I had heard fearful tales of those galleys.

Ay de mi! Now I wondered if it might not have been better to stay at Villaverde.

I spent the rest of that day in a very low frame of mind. Through my misery I began to observe how, at certain hours, the relatives of prisoners were allowed in, with food and necessaries for them. The best-served were a group of men in one corner, who, indeed, hardly bore the appearance of prisoners – their shirts were snowy white, their short waistcoats were made of velvet with silver buttons, they wore wide trousers and gaily-coloured scarves and sashes round their heads and waists. They laughed and talked and played cards with the greatest gaiety and unconcern, and, at visiting-time, they were attended by a whole troop of beautiful girls who brought them wine, fruit, bread, sausages, and all kinds of delicacies.

'Are those lords?' I whispered to my neighbour, an old man who lay propped against the wall on a kind of cushion, and who looked very ill.

'No, my boy, they are gente de reputacion – thieves, bandits, assassins.'

I was amazed. I had thought them to be nobles, perhaps imprisoned for political crime. It was plain that they considered themselves of superior consequence to all other prisoners there, for they ordered the rest about with the utmost arrogance. Even the turnkeys appeared to treat them with respect.

During the afternoon I was startled to hear a loud, deep voice at my elbow suddenly announce the hour:

'Three o'clock!'

Turning sharp around I saw that this voice came from a green parrot which sat composedly on the old man's wrist.

'That is Assistenta, my companion,' the old man said, smiling a little at my surprise. 'I taught her to tell the time by means of the movement of the shadows cast by the window-bars, and she can do it most exactly. Indeed she is now better than a sun-dial, for she seems to carry the hour inside her, and has never been known to make a mistake.'

I stroked and admired the bird, who turned her head about in a self-satisfied manner and chuckled.

'Would she like to hear a tune on my pipe, do you suppose?' I asked the old man.

'We should both enjoy it,' he said. 'She would, and I would.'

So I played a number of tunes, not loud, for fear of attracting angry attention from the other prisoners; though indeed there was such a volume of noise, each man talking to his neighbour at the top of his lungs, that I might have blown a trumpet without it being remarked. However my music pleased the old man and delighted the parrot, who stood up on her tiptoes, opening and closing her wings repeatedly at the sound of it.

Towards evening, greatly to my surprise, who should come towards me, carrying with him a loaf of bread and a big earthenware dish of peas, beans, beef, and bacon, but that same gipsy who had bought my horse and reported me to the alcalde! I could hardly believe he was making for me, until he squatted down beside me and said,

'Here, little brother. This is for you.'

'Why do *you* bring me food?' I demanded in astonishment.

'Why? Because you are a stranger in this town and have no friends. Eat, eat!'

I invited the old man, who seemed to have no friends either, to dip into my stew, but he said he was too old to be hungry, and that his grand-daughter would bring him some milk presently.

'Moreover I am not going to live long; food is wasted on me. But Assistenta would be glad to have some of your garbanzos.'

So the parrot sat on my wrist and had some peas. Meanwhile the gipsy squatting beside me said confidentially in my ear,

'Listen, little brother! I can get you out of this place if you will tell me your secret.'

'What secret? I have no secret!'

'Ay, Dios mio! You were with those two men, Senor Smith, the English deserter, whose step-daughter's address you carried in your pocket – I saw it, when the alcalde unfolded it – and the other, Manolo Candelas, one of the most notorious bandits in Spain, whose horse you sold me – and you say you have no secret! Why, it is common knowledge that those two men knew the where-abouts of a huge treasure lost by the English army on their way to Corunna – and you were with them and you say you have no secret! What kind of a fool do you think I am?'

'They did not tell their secret to me!'

Nevertheless for almost an hour he continued pestering and questioning me, asking over and over again where the treasure lay hidden. At last, however, he became convinced that I really did not know, and he stood up, very angry.

'I have wasted my time on you. You may stay here till moss grows over you, for all I care!'

He had hardly gone when an alguacil came to

111

conduct me to the alcalde. I followed, full of hope and fear.

This time I found myself alone with the alcalde in his office, and he came to the point at once.

'Boy: I have reason to believe that the man whose horse you sold had previously entrusted to you a very important piece of information: the knowledge of the whereabouts of the load of gold dollars which was lost during the English retreat to Corunna . . .'

'No, senor, he did not,' I cut in with a good deal of impatience. 'Nor do I know why anybody should think he did! I am utterly ignorant of the whereabouts of this treasure, and have no wish at all to know anything about it.'

'I do not believe you! It is your duty to lay that knowledge before the authorities.'

Just like the gipsy, the alcalde was most unwilling to believe that I could tell him nothing, and he questioned me with great skill and cunning, doing his best to lay traps for me, until I quite lost my temper.

'The good God knows why you should all think I have this secret! Is it likely that those men would tell *me* such a thing – the very thing they would wish to keep to themselves?'

The alcalde leaned forward, looking at me sharply. An angry spark burned in his deep eye-sockets.

'Have a care, boy!' said he. 'I could order you to be flogged for insolence.'

'It would make no difference. I do not know.'

After a pause he said more coolly, 'I begin to believe you. Only a simpleton would show such disregard for his skin. Take him back to the calabozo!' he shouted to an attendant outside the door, and to me, 'I warn you, you are likely to remain in here for a very long time.'

Burning with rage and injustice, I suffered myself to be led back. I remembered how I had felt when I lit my grandfather's hayricks. I would have liked to set fire to this whole place.

The old man nodded to me in a friendly way and I settled down again in the spot next to him, which he had kept for me, but I was not allowed to remain in peace for long. One of the rateros came over to say that the chief wished to speak to me.

This man was the finest and most elegant of the whole band, with a blue silk waistcoat, Turkish trousers, silk stockings, and soft black slippers; in contrast to all this foppery he had a long, savage-looking knife stuck in his scarlet girdle, and a terrible scar that crossed his face from brow to ear. He, too, wished to question me about the treasure, and was even more pertinacious than the other two had been; indeed the whole group stood round me in a ring, repeating their questions over and over, until I quaked for my skin.

At last I cried out roundly and furiously that they could cut me in pieces but it would do them no good, for I could not pass on information that I did not possess, even should I wish to. Convinced

113

at last by this – or apparently so – the ratero chief allowed me to return to my corner.

Visitors were now mingling freely with the prisoners, for it was the supper hour. Some were in the calabozo, others outside walking in the court. My old man, I saw, was being attended by a young, gentle-looking girl, his granddaughter no doubt. She had brought him clean linen, a towel, and a clean cover for his cushion. Out of delicacy I would have stayed at a distance, but he beckoned me to come.

'This is my grandchild, Frasquita,' he said. 'She is a good girl! Although she lives a league outside Oviedo, in the village of Lugones, she comes with food every day, and brings me clean linen twice a week. She keeps me as fine as any of those dandies over there.'

Frasquita smiled at him – she was a short, plump, round-faced girl, about my height – and said,

'Who would not, for such a kind grandfather?'

'Well, you will not have to do it for much longer,' he said, 'for I can feel my death overtaking me in swift strides. – You will not need to come again, my dearest child. Run along now, and God go with you.'

When he had kissed her and she had gone sorrowfully away, he looked at me and smiled, as if at his own thoughts. He said, 'I wished to see you standing beside Frasquita in order to be certain of something; and it is just as I thought: you could be brother and sister.'

I was puzzled.

'Senor, I do not understand you.'

'Listen, hijo,' he said, 'I can see it is not healthy for you here. I do not meddle – but I can see that too many people are after you for something that they think you have.'

'I do *not* have it!' I said angrily. Was he about to prove another of them?

But he said, 'As to that, I do not care – I am going to die tonight in any case. I feel Death in my bones – I know it is coming.'

Remembering Bernie I looked at him carefully and thought, with sorrow, that he was probably right.

'I am going to die,' he said, 'and I have a wish that my parrot shall not be left in this stinking hole without me. Somebody would probably eat her for breakfast! Listen – stoop closer – I asked Frasquita to leave her cloak and hood behind. It is a warm evening – I told her to wrap the towel round her shoulders instead of a cloak. Now, hijo, you squat down and put on the hood; no one is looking this way, they are all talking to their visitors. Very good: now wrap the cloak round you. Excellent! You could be a girl setting off for the market. Now: take the parrot on your wrist. Everybody knows Assistenta. Frasquita has often taken her out for an airing. Good: now run along! Keep quite calm; don't look to right or left but straight ahead; and good luck to you!'

'But, senor – '

'Don't delay,' he said, 'or the visitors will all

115

have gone and then you will be in trouble. At present many are going – you will slip out unobserved among them. Leave the parrot, if you will be so good, with Frasquita, who lives in the third house on the left after you cross the bridge into Lugones – '

'Oh, of course, senor, I will do that – '

'Good boy,' he said. 'Be off with you then. *Vaya con Dios.*'

So I left him, and walked out with the rest of the visitors, trying to look quite calm and unconcerned, though my heart was banging to and fro like the pendulum of the great clock in Compostela.

Nobody spared me a glance, however, and I got out of the jail without the least difficulty. Once out, and away from the main square, I ran like a hare back to the posada. There, by the goodness of God, the master of the house was from home, and only the skinny boy remained, sweeping the courtyard. He seemed startled to death at sight of me, and I remembered that I was still wearing the girl's cloak and hood.

'Why, it's *you*!' he gasped, when I took off the hood. 'The alguacils were here inquiring about you this morning, and they said you had been thrown in prison; luckily Master was asleep, so I did not tell them your mule was here or they would very likely have taken it. How did you manage to escape?'

I said that a friend had helped me, and I had

116

better leave the town straight away, and what was to pay for my and the mule's lodging?

'Nothing, nothing!' said he. 'Only play me another tune on your pipe!'

However, as the inn was his master's, rather than his, I persuaded him to take a few coins. Then, after leading the mule into the street – so as not to be caught in a corner – I played him three or four tunes, and he, as before, danced about like a lunatic, in an ecstasy of joy. At last I said I must go, tied on my saddle-bags – which he had hidden in the stable – and left him with his brow puckered and his cheeks hollow, trying to whistle the tunes that I had played.

Not daring to ask the way, in spite of my girl's hood, I had some trouble finding the right road out of Oviedo, which is a most confusing town. At last, by good luck, I chanced on a sign that said, 'Santander', and following its direction struck eastwards. I was greatly delighted at being re-united with my bad-tempered mule and my belongings, but very much saddened at the thought of the poor old man left to die in jail without even his parrot.

Also I was much alarmed by this false notion about the treasure which seemed to have become attached to me, and wondered if I should encounter any more dangers because of it.

After about an hour's ride I came to the small village of Lugones. By now it was dark: a mild, misty night. The mule clip-clopped across a bridge, the stones of which rang hollowly under her hoofs, and I could hear the gentle babble of a river below. The village was quiet and dark, smelling of wet thatch, wet stone, and horse dung. How sweet that seemed, after the stench of the prison!

I counted three houses on my left, and knocked at a door under which a faint thread of light showed golden.

When, after a pause, a frightened voice cried, 'Who's there?' I answered softly. 'This is a friend. I have brought Assistenta.'

The door opened suddenly, and I saw a woman standing outlined against the dim light.

'Ay, Mother of God!' she exclaimed, seeing the parrot on my wrist. The girl whom I had seen in the jail came swiftly up behind her.

'Senorita Frasquita: I have brought back your cloak and hood, and your grandfather's parrot,' I said to her. 'I am deeply grateful to you for the loan of all three. Without them I should still be in that jail, which I had done nothing to deserve, for I have not committed any crime.'

The older woman began to cry and wring her hands. She was a thin, doleful-looking person with scanty greying hair and a sallow, wasted face.

'Ay – ay – they are bound to discover that we played a part in his escape, and we, too, shall be thrown into jail!' she cried. 'Is it not bad enough that my own father must die in prison?'

'Mother, hush!' said the girl. 'Let the young gentleman come in and warm himself.'

But I thanked her and said I would not come in,

for I could see that the mother wished me at the other end of the world.

'Nor do I want that evil parrot!' she lamented. 'For if the alguacils come here inquiring about the boy, and they see it – '

'But why *should* they come here?' argued Frasquita. 'What is to connect the young gentleman with Grandfather? It will be thought that I brought the parrot home myself.'

However the mother was quite unreasonable and kept repeating,

'I do not *want* it, I tell you, it reminds me of our shame. Besides, who knows what wicked blasphemies he may have taught it?'

I did not at all wish to be encumbered with it myself, but as the mother seemed clean distracted by her terror, I feared the poor bird might have its neck wrung if it were left with her, and so finally I said that I would take it with me. At this Frasquita looked much relieved.

She offered me food – greatly to her mother's indignation – but again I declined, thanking her and saying that I had best be on my way, to put as great a distance as possible between myself and the town before day came.

Having very little money left, I gave Frasquita my bunch of raisins, and, as I took my leave, said to her in a low tone,

'If – if you should see your grandfather again – '

'No, I shall not see him again,' she said sadly but positively. 'He was very certain that he would die tonight. And I have never known him wrong about anything.'

I could restrain my curiosity no longer.

'He seemed such a good, kind man. Why should *he* be in prison?'

'Oh, he is the best man in the world! But he wrote a pamphlet which they said was seditious blasphemy – about the liberty of the individual and the properties of minerals and the laws of gravity – and many other things that I do not understand. So he was thrown into jail.'

I bade her goodbye and rode off, thinking how unjust it was that good men should be punished for using the wits God gave them in trying to puzzle out the secrets of the universe, while wicked men, who use their wits only for their own profit, seem to prosper in freedom.

Perhaps, I thought, it is some joke of God's, which He will explain to us later. But He had better have a good explanation!

As I had told Frasquita, I proposed to press on as fast as I could, and since the bad-tempered mule had been given a day's rest in the stable of the posada, I thought it would be no hardship for her to travel through the night.

Judging from the map that Don Jose had made me, I did not think that it could be more than eight or nine leagues from Oviedo to the port of Villa Viciosa, which, on a good road as this seemed, should not take the mule more than six or seven hours. As for myself, I was so happy to be out of the stink and misery of that prison that I would gladly have ridden thirty hours through a blizzard to put distance between it and myself.

However the night was fresh, mild, and damp, and I rode along it most happily, sniffing at the aromatic scent of the gum-trees, which grow plentifully in the valleys and *rias* of that region. The road, though well surfaced, twisted about very much, and climbed endlessly up and down, crossing or doubling along the side of innumerable creeks and inlets, all of which, I supposed, were making their way towards the sea.

For the first part of the night the moon, though veiled by cloud, showed me the road; and by the time the moon had set my eyes were accustomed to the darkness, and the mule, sure-footed as old Gato, proceeded confidently on her way. Meanwhile I was much entertained by my other companion, the parrot, who seated sometimes on my head, sometimes on my shoulder, announced the hour with deep gravity, in loud measured tones, every sixty minutes. And in between these announcements she diverted me with other scraps of information, as, that it takes two days to sail from Corunna to Santander with a following wind, five to six days if winds are contrary; that the resin of the eucalyptus and myrtle trees may be used to cure a cough; that the element mercury is obtained from cinnabar and the planet Mercury is nearest the sun; and many other useful pieces of knowledge. I resolved to increase her education myself, and began by reciting a list of the prepositions which in Latin govern the dative case; for, I thought, if I am lucky enough to find my English family, they will be glad to know that I have not forgotten all the Latin that Father Tomas took pains to beat into me.

So the night passed; and morning found us on a high, cultivated hillside, having crossed over the last and lowest ridge of the mountains that had lain in our way and cut us off from the ocean.

As the light increased I saw, with wonder, that same ocean, lying before me at a distance of some three or four leagues: like a long, shining steel knife-blade that stretched all the way across the horizon from right to left, as far as the eye could see. My heart filled with triumph and joy, for now all I had to do was pass over that water (though it would grieve me to part from the bad-tempered mule) – and then I would be in my father's country.

Below me, at no great distance, I saw what I took to be the Port of Villa Viciosa, which lay at the head of a wooded creek, about a league inland from the open sea. I made haste to descend towards it, and found it, on closer inspection, to be a small dirty town, scattered along its inland channel, which smelt abominably of salt mud and dead fish.

What was my dismay, on reaching the quayside and inquiring for boats to England, when I was told they had all sailed the previous week!

'It is the season for the *avellanas*, the hazel-nuts, you see, boy,' explained an old man whom I discovered sitting on a pile of nets. 'They have all loaded up with their cargoes and gone, since winds and tides were favourable. What a pity you were not here a week ago! For, after they return, it is not likely they will cross again this winter.'

'But what are all those boats I see anchored here?'

'Oh, they are just the small fishing-craft; they go out and return the same day; or, at most, sail along the coast to Santander or Corunna.'

'Then,' I said despondently, 'if I wish to cross to England, where should I look for a boat?'

'At Santander, my boy, or at Bilbao; there the craft are bigger and sail all winter long; there you will find something without much trouble.'

For a moment I considered inquiring whether any ships were sailing in the direction of Santander from Villa Viciosa during the next few hours. But it struck me that (as I had lost the three thousand reals from the sale of the robber's horse) I certainly had not enough money to pay for two sea-voyages; indeed it was highly probable that I had not enough for one; therefore I had better continue riding along the coast to Santander, which at least I could do for nothing on my faithful if bad-tempered mount. The distance might be about twenty leagues: less than I had come already, and a much easier road; it should not take more than three or four days' riding.

I delayed no longer at Villa Viciosa – which I found a most dismal and disappointing spot – but set out straightway eastwards on the road to Santander.

Now what beauties opened before me! The road

continued for a short time along the verge of the inlet, but then climbed on to a great shoulder of cliff, and from this height, which was all open, cultivated land, I was able to see for many miles along the coast.

Truth to tell, my first sight of the water, close at hand, in Villa Viciosa, had greatly disappointed me. But now I realised that was not true sea, merely an inland water; now the true sea, in all its majesty, lay before me, green and luminous like some great moving jewel catching the sun's light; here and there flecked with cloud shadows; hurling itself in smoking white plumes against the ribs of cliffs. I shouted with joy, and sang as we made our way along; the mule snorted as she filled her lungs with salt air; and the parrot gravely remarked,

'Six o'clock!'

However, the weather is very changeable in those parts, and all of a sudden the clear day clouded to mist, and then to a violent rain, so I wrapped the blanket-cloak over myself and as much of the mule as I could cover (tucking the parrot underneath my jacket, where she settled with her head under her wing) and so we travelled on. The road continually climbed and descended, passing over headlands and crossing estuaries; and still the rain fell in torrents.

At last, descending to one of these rias, I was dismayed to find it quite impassable. The river which formed it, swollen probably from rains higher up in the mountains, had flooded over the bridge and swept past in a furious, tossing torrent, carrying great hanks of hay and trunks of trees. The mule rolled white eyes, tossing her head, and backed away from the brink, so I knew it was useless to think of trying to swim that water. The only solution would be to go upstream, along the bank, until, perhaps, we reached a point where a bridge remained above water, or the river was narrow enough to ford.

A weary way it proved. Most of that day was spent in doggedly following the bank of the stream, which was more difficult because there was no road, sometimes not even a track; here and there we were obliged to push our way through close bushes, or to plod through marshy brooks; the mule became more and more bad-tempered and I more discouraged.

At last as dusk fell we were lucky enough to find, not a bridge but a deserted barn, raised on four pillars to keep it dry.

'Here we spend the night, nina,' I said to the mule.

The barn would provide good shelter for me and the parrot, but what about the mule? She could not go underneath, for it was only three feet above the ground on its stony legs. However, looking inside, I found some boards, long enough to make a bridge from the muddy ground to the entrance.

'Now, nina, you will have to be clever: come along – one foot after the other!'

The mule *was* clever (sensing, perhaps, that her cleverness would win her a dry stable); she came up my improvised ramp like a cat, and we spent the night huddled together for warmth on some prickly fodder in the dark barn.

Next day it still rained, and we continued our harassing way up the side of the creek. My spirits were very dejected; I imagined this long and tedious detour taking me halfway back to Villaverde.

But after an hour's scrambling we came to a man who was in an even greater state of distress and exasperation.

'My pigs, my pigs!' he kept lamenting. 'My old mother! My pigs, my pigs!'

I could not help but notice that he placed his pigs first, and seemed to value them somewhat above his old mother.

'Where are your pigs, senor? I see no pigs.'

'They are over yonder!' he wailed. 'On the island! Ay de mi! They will be swept to destruction!'

Walking closer to the flooded river I saw that here was another bridge, covered six feet deep in a swirl of floodwater; and that the wooded height which I had taken to be the opposite side of the estuary was in fact an island in the middle. I could just see that a second leg of the bridge led on from the island to the farther shore. The island, thickly grown over with young chestnut trees, was half-submerged, and it seemed possible that it would soon be completely covered with water.

Wringing his hands and tearing his hair the man informed me that he had sent his old mother across to the island that morning with his herd of pigs, so that the pigs might eat up the chestnuts before they were all washed away.

'Ay de mi! Never did I think the river would come down so fast! And pigs cannot swim! They cut their throats with their sharp hoofs!'

'Have you no boat?' I said.

'Yes, but it would be swept away! I dare not venture with it across that current.'

He pointed to a flat-bottomed row-boat which, fortunately for him, had been pulled a good way up the bank. The small thatched house on stone legs stood higher up. The man himself had evidently been off hunting while his mother minded the pigs; he carried a stout-looking bow and a sheaf of arrows, and a hare with several partridges lay where he had dropped them in his agitation.

Visited by a sudden notion, I said, 'Have you a long rope, senor? One that would reach across to the island?'

'Yes, in my house.'

'And a piece of thin cord the same length?'

'Yes, I daresay, but what will that avail? We cannot get the rope across to the island.'

Seeing his mother, poor black-clad old lady, now appear on the opposite bank, crossing herself and raising her hands to heaven as she looked at the water rolling down, I said,

'Well, there is no harm in trying! Let us make the attempt. Do you fetch the rope, senor, while I signal to your mother.'

She looked very much astonished when she saw me making gestures with the bow and arrow, but

127

at length I thought that she took a notion as to what I intended to do, for she nodded her head vigorously up and down very many times. The roar of the river was too loud for any words to be heard, though from time to time I thought I caught a snatch of the pigs' doleful squealing.

Nieves and Anita had equipped me with a reel of stout thread and a needle, besides a hunk of cobblers' wax – items I myself would never have considered necessary for a journey, but only see how wrong I was! For now I unwound a great quantity of the thread – having much ado not to let it become snarled – and tied a waxed end of it to an arrow, which I shot across the foamy river. It fell short, and the old mother threw up her hands in despair, but I gently drew back the thread and tried again. My second shot was more successful, landing in a clump of willow, and I saw the old lady hobble to the spot where the arrow fell and pick it up. I felt the thread – of which I held the other end – give a twitch, and I hoped she would have the sense not to pull on it too hard, or my scheme would come to nothing.

Luckily she proved both shrewd and dexterous; more so than her son, indeed, who, coming back with a coil of rope and a cord, stood gaping, quite unable to comprehend what I was at.

I now took the thin cord, and tied its end to the thread; then signalled the old lady to pull it in very carefully, which she did. This was the most apprehensive part of the business, and took some time, for she durst not pull too hard. But at last she had the end of the cord in her hand, and waved her kerchief triumphantly. By now her son had understood, and he made haste to fasten the cord to the rope, which was pulled across in its turn.

Now came another anxious moment.

'Will your mother have enough strength to tie the rope sufficiently firmly to a tree?' I asked the son, who muttered,

'We are in the hands of God. I do not know.'

However it was plain that God was on our side, for the valiant old lady wound the rope a great many times round a fair-sized chestnut tree and then made a great many knots; we meanwhile, did the same on our side; and then the boat was secured to the rope by another cord, doubled and knotted twice, so that we had a ferry rigged up, which was subject only to two possible hazards: that the trees at either end might be uprooted, or, more probably, that the rope might break.

Spurred on by hope, the man sprang into the boat, and said to me,

'You will come too? You will help me? It will be easier to catch the pigs if there are two of us.'

So, leaving Assistenta perched on the saddle of the tethered mule (whose nose I kissed, just in case I was washed away downstream and we only met again in Paradise) I embarked with the man in his boat, which was, in fact, of a good size, large enough to take five or six pigs.

The passage across the river made my stomach lurch, and my legs feel strangely weak; especially in the centre, where the rope dipped below water, and several rolling billows slopped over us as we pulled our way along; but we reached the bank of the island without mishap, and I used my hat to bail the water out of the boat.

The old lady was waiting for us.

'Thanks be to Maria Santissima! The pigs and I are saved!' she exclaimed, embracing her son. 'Though how the good God came to put such a clever notion into your head, I can't think!'

'Never mind that! Fetch the pigs!' was his reply.

I suggested, however, that she should get into the boat, so as to encourage any pigs who might be afraid to embark. Indeed we had considerable trouble with them, for although we could drive them to the verge, when they saw they were expected to jump into the wildly tipping boat, they attempted to escape along the bank with shrieks of terror. Pigs are stupid things! Give me a mule any day.

In the end we had to lift them in, one by one, while the old mother hung on to the rope, in order to prevent the boat slipping away into midstream.

I have never in my whole life handled anything so heavy as those frantic, wet, slippery pigs; they might have been stuffed with lead, instead of chestnuts.

And all the time I noticed that the water was rising along the bank, higher and higher.

There were too many pigs for one boatload. We had to go back three times.

While chasing the pigs around the island (which, now half-covered with flood water, was not much bigger than a small paddock) I had observed that the channel on the far side of it was much narrower than the one we had crossed in the boat; the second part of the bridge spanned it in a single arch. Nor was that bridge so deeply submerged, for the arch was higher.

Therefore, on my last trip to the island, I led my mule into the boat, where she stood shuddering with disapproval and horror, her nostrils raised, and her eyes staring. I gentled and soothed her, and bade her follow the example of the parrot, who was not in the least agitated, but merely informed us that the time was one hour after noon, and that foxglove seeds were good for palpitations.

The pig-farmer was so amazed to see me bring my mule on board that he had no wonder left over for the parrot.

'You're never going to try and get across the other channel?' says he, gaping.

'I shall try,' said I, 'for I am anxious to get to Santander. But if it should not prove possible, I beg you'll have the kindness to wait till I have made the attempt before you undo the rope.'

Going and coming with the pigs, we had brought over a second rope, passed it round a tree and taken the end back to the near side of the river; so now the first rope could be undone and the second one pulled in when he was safely back.

'Oh, very well, very well,' said he fussily, 'but I may tell you that I have a dozen uses for that rope and cannot leave it there for more than a short time.'

Reflecting that stupidity and ingratitude often seem to go together, I led the mule out of the boat and on to the island. Then I helped the man assemble his last levy of pigs and urge them on board; this took a shorter time than the previous boatloads for there was less of the island for them to run around. Once they were all in the boat and safely launched on their way, I mounted the mule and directed her nervous course to the half-submerged bridge.

'Now, nina,' I said to her, 'you must be a brave *macha*; be a brave *muchacha*; keep to the middle and don't let your feet be swept from under you. I'd lead you, but I think my weight on your back keeps you steadier. Just go steadily along – one foot after the other, that's the way – good girl – and if we get safe to the other side, you shall have the biggest piece of bread that's left in my saddle-bag, all for yourself.'

Slowly and steadily she pushed her way through the fierce, pulling water, which at times rose up to her shoulders. I had some trouble myself to keep steady on her back as the current dragged at my legs; and the last stretch was the worst, for a strong eddy swirled in under the bank, just where the curve of the bridge descended to its lowest point. However by good fortune and God's goodwill we struggled through, and up on to solid ground, where I dismounted and hugged the mule, then unsaddled her so that she could relieve her spirits by rolling and shaking some of the wet off her shaggy hide.

Having re-harnessed her, I rode down to a point from which I could signal to the pig-farmer and his mother that I had safely made the crossing, for the island would have impeded their view.

The old lady fell on her knees at sight of me and made signs of blessings with her hands. Her son was hard at work coiling up his rope, having pulled up the boat high on the bank. Looking back at the island I saw that I had made my crossing only just in time, for now it was completely under water; only the branches of the trees could be seen, bowing downstream with the current; and the bridge by which I had crossed was not to be seen at all.

I was about to turn away when I saw a sight that made me thank Providence even more heartily for my safe passage of the river.

Two men riding ponies had arrived at the far bank and were talking to the pig-farmer, gesturing and pointing over the water. They wore black hats and carried staves; they looked like alguacils. The man glanced across at me, and shrugged; his old mother spread out her hands and shook her head.

Whether they were saying that it was not possible to cross the river, or that I was a stranger and they did not know me, I could not guess, but I waited no longer; picking up the parrot, I kicked the mule into her fast trot, and made off along the road that led eastwards from the bridge.

# 4

Next befell me a very strange adventure, which makes me shudder, even now, when I recall it, so singular, so utterly uncanny were the circumstances, and so dreadful might the end have been, if matters had turned out differently.

After leaving the farmer rejoicing over his pigs by the swollen river, the mule and I turned uphill, on a steep winding road that climbed out of the ria through a forest of close-set beeches and gum trees, with all kinds of dense leafy bushes growing in between; so that we were soon out of sight of the water.

The mule and I were both fatigued – I from chasing and grappling with the wayward pigs, the mule from her valiant struggle through the flooded river – besides which, we had been travelling all the previous night – so I resolved that, since we must now be safe from pursuit while the river remained in flood, we might as well stop at the next village and find lodging for the night.

The rain still pelted down, which encouraged me to hope that the river would not be likely to return to its normal level for some time, but made me dismiss any notion of sleeping out-of-doors under a hay stack. Indeed, there were no hay stacks to be seen hereabouts; nothing but sodden thickety woodland.

By slow degrees the rain slackened off, but now a thick sea-mist added to the difficulties of our journey. All that could be seen was the wavering, white, indistinct shapes of tree-trunks along the verge of the road. All that could be heard – apart from the mule's footfalls – were the drips falling from the trees, the sigh of the branches, and the infrequent call of a pheasant through the woods. The road climbed and climbed; presently the forest changed from beech and gum to fir and pine, but by now the light was so bad that I would hardly have known this, had my nostrils not picked up the tarry, bitter scent of the pine-needles on the wet ground. Even the sure-footed mule was obliged to go more and more slowly in the fog, and she began to grumble and snort, as mules will, demanding, in her own way, when this interminable climb would be ended, and she given a dry stable and supper.

'I wish I knew, nina,' I said to her. 'I begin to fear that in the fog we must have strayed off the coast road onto some mountain track. But there is no sense in turning round; this path must lead *somewhere* if we only continue on it for long enough.'

The mule shook her head, as if she violently disagreed, but she did not rebel, poor thing; she was too tired for that; so on we went, I reciting

Latin verses, and anything else that came into my head, to her and the parrot, in order to prevent myself from falling asleep. Also I pondered in my mind about the pig-farmer and his stupidity and greed; he must have known the river was liable to flood, living by it as he did, so why had he sent his mother and the pigs to the island? If he wanted the pigs to eat the chestnuts before they were all washed away, why not take the pigs to the island himself, for he would be able to judge better how long it was prudent to stay there? Finding no clue to his actions, I thought instead about my grandfather, and decided that, if he had been a poor pig-farmer, he would not have sent my grandmother or Dona Isadora to herd his pigs, but would have gone himself.

The picture of Dona Isadora herding pigs made me chuckle, and I cheered myself for quite a long way by fancying her struggles as she tried to pick up the pigs and drop them into the boat. How they had squealed! – as if they thought their throats were being cut.

Then the remembered sound of squealing in my mind's ear changed to a real sound – the faint, far-away bleat of a goat. At this, the mule pricked up her ears. Presently the bleating was followed by the faint sound of a bell.

'Come, our troubles are over, macha,' I said to the mule. 'All you have to do is walk in the direction of that sound, and we shall find a bed for me, a stable for you, a big bowl of *estofado*, plenty of hay, and a handful of barley. Just go straight ahead.'

The mule, however, refused to make directly for the sound of the bell, but chose her own way, and I, remembering the incident of the boggy meadow, did not try to persuade her to do otherwise. She pursued a zigzag course through the fog, still ascending a steep track. To my relief, the sound of the bell continued to grow louder, and I thought hopefully,

'Perhaps it is some friendly monastery, built to supply food and shelter for the pilgrims to Santiago de Compostela. By now we must be on a high mountain-top, a long way from the coast.'

We had left the forest behind us, and the air was bitterly cold. The parrot, who, I thought, had been asleep, tucked inside my jacket, woke up and muttered something about the constellation Orion, in a hoarse grumbling manner, which made me laugh.

'If only we could see the constellation Orion, Assistenta, we should have been able to find our way to shelter long ago.'

No monastery did we discover, but presently found ourselves among a herd of goats – easily recognisable by their smell and their voices, and their shining eyes like candles in the dimness – guarded by a couple of ragged snarling dogs. The bell was attached to the leader of the herd.

'Come, we must be near *some* kind of habitation,' I told the mule, peering about in the icy fog, which was now moving and drifting on the back of a sharp wind. Then, among broken gliding layers of mist, I perceived objects which, at first, I took to be large round boulders, haphazardly grouped at either side of the track.

Looking closely, I saw that dim lights gleamed here and there among them. Also I smelt smoke, and dung.

Could they be dwellings? – huts? – the homes of human beings? Or were they the lairs of animals? They seemed too small for men to live in.

There was, however, the evidence of the goats, which the dogs had brought up among the huts. And now a dark figure came out, stooping, from one of the holes where a light showed.

When it was fully out, it stood upright and moved towards me. Through the floating mist, I saw that it was an old man, with scanty white hair falling to his shoulders. He wore some kind of dark, ragged garment, tied round the waist by a cord.

I said, and my voice shook a little, 'Buenas noches, señor. Can I get food and a bed in this place, for myself and my mule?'

His reply came after a moment's pause. He spoke in a strange, lisping voice, and in so strange and broad a mountain dialect that, for a moment, I did not catch his meaning. But when I did, it startled me to the marrow of my bones.

For he said, 'Good evening, señor. Welcome, welcome. We have been expecting you since sunrise.'

His words sent such a chill through me that I

had a strong urge to kick the mule's sides and ride on, wherever the path might take me. But the mule, tired out, had come to a halt; she smelt smoke, and goats, and fodder, and people; besides, from the other huts – for now, as the mist lifted, I saw that they were indeed tiny round stone huts, thatched, I think, with turf – more people were coming into view.

They all moved slowly, as if they were very old: ancient, white-bearded men, hobbling slowly; aged, bent, toothless women, with bits of rag tied round their nodding heads.

And they all said the same thing:

'Welcome, welcome, senor. We have been expecting you.'

They treat me as if I were a grown man, I thought.

'Come this way, senor,' said the old man who had first greeted me.

A dozen hands laid hold of my leg; the mule threw up her head and snorted affrightedly as they all pushed around her and almost lifted me from the saddle. Then they proceeded to urge me in the direction of one of those round huts, which were not much bigger than my grandfather's pig-sties.

'Wait – wait a moment! I must see my mule housed and fed,' said I – in spite of the cold, not in the least eager to enter that strange, cramped-looking shelter.

'His mule, his mule!' they all muttered, lispingly, to one another.

Now arose a difficulty, for it was plain that the

mule was by far too big to be brought inside any of their dwellings – but leave her out, exposed in the cold night on the bare mountain I would not; however after much muttering and disputation, they led me to a jutting outcrop of rock not far from the settlement. On one side of this an overhang projected, forming a kind of rude cave, which was further protected by hurdles. In this shelter, besides a heap or two of wretched mountain hay, stood one or two half-starved-looking little burros. Here I tethered the mule, strapping her into my felt cloak, with a truss of the hay and a pat on the nose.

'I am sorry to leave you in such dismal quarters, *amiga*,' I whispered. 'But as soon as we reach a bigger place tomorrow you shall have as much barley as you can eat, and a measure of wine too!'

I left her with one of the saddle-bags and brought the other with me. By now the old people were plucking at me impatiently to come away, so I suffered myself, at last, to be led into one of their dwellings. Even I – and I am not tall – was obliged to stoop double under the lintel, which I should judge to have been not more than seven hands high. Once inside, however, the roof rose higher, for the buildings were of a shape like conical beehives; but the air was unbelievably bad. It smelt thickly of human sweat, of dung, both men's and beasts', of rotten flesh, rancid grease, peat smoke, dried blood, and other things, all horrible. There was a little flickering light, from the embers of a peat-fire and a tallow candle, by which I could see that all the people I had seen appeared to have crowded into the hut, curious to inspect me, no doubt.

It was plain that their eyes were more accustomed than mine to seeing in this dim light.

The old man who had first greeted me issued an order to a woman somewhat younger than the rest, and she obediently fed the fire with handfuls of peat, and blew until flames broke out. I now saw that the fire was on a flat stone and that the smoke – a little of it – passed up through a hole in the roof.

The woman then fetched an iron pan from some cranny, and proceeded to fry eggs in it over the flames. Meanwhile I was invited to sit, and did so on the earth floor. As my sight grew accustomed to the dimness, I perceived that the dwelling also accommodated a couple of goats, and a clutch of scrawny fowls, perched on ledges in the circular wall, which was built of rocks and turf.

After a longish while the eggs were done, and were served to me on a wooden platter. A more disgusting meal I have seldom eaten, for before passing them to me the woman poured over them about half a pint of the same rancid oil in which they had been fried. However, I was too hungry to be very particular, and swallowed them down somehow, helped by fragments of stone-hard bread, which tasted principally of peat-ash.

I was then offered some drink, in a cup of leather so old that it had gone black and hard, like wood.

'What is this drink?' I asked with caution, for the liquor smelt strong and strange.

The old man who had first accosted me – whom I took to be the head man of the village, for the others treated him with great respect – replied with some word quite unknown to me. When I shook my head he went into a long explanation, ending with the words,

'*Brezo, brezal*,' several times repeated, from which I understood that the drink was prepared from heather.

It was sweet to the first taste, then very bitter; after two or three mouthfuls I put down the cup, for it was not at all to my liking. At this they all cried out, and pressed me to drink more of it, but I would not.

I then intimated that I would be glad to rest, laying my head sideways on my hand, repeating over and over again the words bed, sleep. The villagers looked at one another in surprise, it seemed, and perhaps affront; they burst into another long disputation among themselves. Being terribly fatigued, I did not pay much heed to this; although I feared I had offended them. Perhaps, I thought, strangers came that way so rarely that they felt cheated unless they had several hours of talk and information about the world that lay below the mountains.

'Tomorrow I will talk,' said I. 'Tomorrow. *Manana. Manana.*'

'Ah, *manana, manana*,' they all chorused, and

then moved outside, giving some instructions to the woman who had cooked my fried eggs.

She, with looks of civility, indicated a pile of rags and refuse against the wall, and I thanked her. As I moved towards this uninviting couch, the woman touched my hair with a wondering look, toothlessly repeating a word, which, after a moment, I recognised as,

'*Guapo, guapo.*' Beautiful, beautiful.

I suppose yellow hair was a thing unknown to them; all of them were black-eyed, and though most were white-headed with age, it was plain that their hair, when young, must have been black, as this woman's was. Out of politeness I touched her hair and said in my turn, '*Guapo*,' but she shook her head in a melancholy manner.

At this moment, the parrot, Assistenta, who had spent the last hour asleep inside my jacket, suddenly chose to emerge, stretching a sleepy wing, and croaking,

'Nine o'clock!'

The woman's face went wax-coloured with terror, and her mouth fell open, exposing the stumps of rotted and blackened teeth. She gasped and jumped back in fright as the parrot walked along my arm.

'Don't be frightened,' I said several times. 'It is a parrot – a bird. Only a bird. Look!' I picked up one or two crumbs of the bread left on my supper-dish and held them on my palm for Assistenta, who pecked at them greedily; when they were all gone she recited a list of plants with virtue for curing rheumatism, and then climbed back inside my jacket and went to sleep again with her head tucked under her wing.

Whimpering with fear, the woman retreated to the far side of the hut, where she crouched, watching me. I said again,

'She won't hurt you. She is only a bird – like a raven, like an eagle,' I said, naming two birds that one often sees in the mountains.

'Like an eagle,' she repeated doubtfully.

'An old man gave her to me in Oviedo,' I added. But I could see that the name Oviedo meant no more than if I had said, 'She was given me by the man in the moon.' The woman had probably never left this village in her life.

Wishing to relieve her mind and distract it from her fear of the parrot, I said,

'Senora – when I first came to this place, the old man said that I had been expected since sunrise. What made him say that? For I had no intention of coming to this spot. I came here by chance. I was lost in the forest.'

I had to repeat all this many many times, very slowly and loudly, before she understood me. But at length she came to grasp my meaning, for she replied, in her lisping way,

'Ah, senor – it is because tomorrow is the first day of autumn. On the eve of that day, a stranger always comes to our village.'

'*Always*? How can this be?'

'It is the will of the great father.'

'How curious! So you were not expecting me in particular? Just any stranger?'

She did not understand that, but replied,

'Yes, senor, we were expecting you. I am sorry, though, that it has to be one as young and beautiful as your Honour.'

This I found disquieting. What did they expect the stranger to do for them, on the first day of autumn?

'Is the stranger generally an older man, then? – What do you ask of him?'

But this she would not, or could not answer. She said merely,

'It is for the good of the village.'

'What is for the good of the village?'

'That the stranger should come. It is for the good luck of the bees, and the beasts, next year.'

'What is the name of this village, senora?' I asked.

'Name?' she said, puzzled. 'It is just *the village*. There is only the one, after all.'

It seemed as if she knew of no other place, in all Spain!

Wishing to thank her in some way for having cooked my meal, I wondered what to give her. Money, it seemed, would be useless in a place like this, where nothing was bought or sold. Opening the bag I had brought in with me, I gave her a big bunch of Anita's raisins, taking one or two myself, to show that she was to eat them. She tried one, gingerly, and then mumbled up the rest with relish, exclaiming,

'Bueno, bueno!'

Soon after there came a call from outside, and I lay down while she, laying a finger to her lips, tiptoed to the entrance, where she received some order from the old man. Returning she made the gesture of sleep to me, with cheek on palm, closing her eyes.

She had no need to make it, for I was drowning in waves of weariness. Two minutes, and I was lost to my strange surroundings.

It seemed to me, in my dream, that I had displeased Father Tomas. 'I shall have to take you before your grandfather!' he shouted. 'First he will reprimand you, then you will be punished most severely!'

In the dream I felt a horrid dread of this punishment. What could they be going to do to me? Father Tomas was shaking me by the shoulder, shaking and shaking.

But it was not Father Tomas. It was the woman, waking me. With some wonder, I saw that her eyes swam with tears.

'I am sorry I have to wake you, *muchacho*,' she snuffled woefully, 'but he is coming now.'

'*Who* is coming?' I felt so heavy and sodden with fatigue that I was sure it could not yet be morning; I seemed to have slept only for half-an-hour or so.

The woman did not answer, but laid peat and heather-stalks on the fire so that it blazed up quite brightly.

I saw that the old man, the leader, had come back into the hut.

'Now, your Honour, I have to tell you what we need,' he said.

'Yes?' I mumbled sleepily, not wishing to offend him. 'Why is that?'

'We need more bees, more goats, we need a warmer summer, less rain, we need more mountain hares, but above all we need more people. We need children! We are all growing old and we have no children. You must tell them that!' His manner was urgent; he pushed his face close to mine. I could smell his stinking breath, and see the sore places where his broken teeth had gouged his tongue.

He was squatting in front of me, staring at me intently. His eyes, under shaggy white brows, were like black holes in his face. It seemed as if I could look right through the holes, farther and farther back.

'Drink,' said the woman quietly, and passed me the leather cup full of heather liquor.

My mouth tasted horrible and my head ached. What I longed for was a dram of pure water. I took a sip of the heather liquid and then wished I had not, for it did my thirst no good.

'You must tell them of all these things we need,' the old man croaked.

'Whom must I tell?' I wondered if he meant I was to go down to the nearest town, to the mayor, perhaps . . .

'Drink, drink,' said the woman again, and

pressed the cup on me. For politeness, I took another sip of the bitter stuff.

'You will go through the door of rock,' said the old man. 'You will walk the path of cloud.'

His face was only an inch away, his eyes stared into mine. At the back of each eye burned a tiny spark, like the light of a cabin, far away on the black mountains. I was nearly asleep again; for a moment I thought I was on the mule's back, riding along through the cloudy night.

'You will see the grey mother; you will see the father of fire. You will tell him of our need. Tell him that we are hungry, and have no children to care for us.'

Now I felt as if I were floating in a boat, being carried smoothly down the flooded river. I felt the woman gently move my hands behind my back and tie them with a piece of leather. Then they each, the man and the woman, took one of my arms and helped me to my feet. I rose up and moved along glidingly, as one does in a dream; weary though I was, walking seemed to be no trouble at all. Somehow we passed through the low doorway – I do not remember stooping – and then we were outside, where all the rest of the people stood waiting, in a black knot against the grey of the bare mountain. I could see now that morning was not far off. The utter blackness of night was past, the sky had paled, and, from where we stood, many craggy ranges of mountains were visible, all around us, in varying shades of grey and darker grey, layered with cloud. The sky overhead was covered with a plum-dark shadow, but over in the direction where the sun must presently rise, one jagged skyline of peaks lay bared like broken teeth against a narrow band of silver light.

Nobody spoke, but we all began moving away from the stone huts, in a kind of straggling procession, I myself, still between the old man and the woman, walking somewhat ahead of the rest.

What we were doing seemed to me strange and mysterious, but also most natural. I thought, dreamily,

'Now they will show me the gate of rock, and the path of cloud.'

The old man, who walked on my left, was carrying, I noticed, an axe with a head made not of metal but of dark polished stone. That stone must indeed be hard, I thought vaguely, if it can be used for an axe-head. It was exceedingly heavy, too, I could see that: the old man, who was very bent, slow, and stooping in his walk, could lift it for short periods only, and was obliged to stop and rest it on the ground at every third or fourth step.

I thought of offering to carry it for him, but my hands were tied.

Then I observed that the woman on my right wept as she walked; I could not see her tears, but she kept wiping her eyes with the back of her hand. I could hear her sobs, a faint miserable sound in the stillness.

'What is the trouble?' I asked her. 'Why do you cry?' and she, unexpectedly, mumbled,

'*I* had a boy once, long ago, but he died.'

That brought Bernie into my mind, and her baby who had died, long ago; slowly I began to wonder, What am I, Felix, doing here on this mountainside? Where are we? Who are these people? What is happening?

We were making, I now saw, for the outcrop of rock under the jut of which the animals and the haystacks had their scanty shelter. The outcrop, which formed the summit of the hill on which the village stood, was sharp and craggy and big as a castle; a path, which I could dimly see, circled around it and climbed to the very top.

I heard one of the burros bray, and this roused me a little from my dreamy state.

'I want to give my mule some water,' I said to the woman, and she sobbed out,

'Yes, yes, it shall be done. Very soon!'

'No, but I would like to do it *now*. Untie my hands, please!'

'Hush!' said the old man angrily. 'No one should speak until the sun rises.'

Far away, I saw there was a great gap in the saw-toothed range of peaks that rose against the strip of eastern light. From the growing colour in the sky at that point, I guessed that when the sun did rise, it would show exactly in the gap, and its light would then strike the tip of the outcrop above us.

Suddenly three things happened. When I say *suddenly* I mean that they happened in the same moment, but it was a long, strange moment – as if time itself had stretched out so fine and thin that you could see right through it.

The parrot, tucked inside my belted jacket, began to mutter and scuffle, trying to flap her wings; and she suddenly poked her head through the opening at the front of the jacket, and shouted, 'Six o'clock!' Then, at a very rapid rate and in a loud, raucous voice, she began to recite a number of the Latin words I had been teaching her the day before:

'Amnis, axis, caulis, collis, clunis, crinis, fascis, follis – '

While I stood still, many of the villagers had caught up with us; now they stared at the parrot in stupefaction. There were cries of alarm.

A single eye-blink after that, the whole world around us was suddenly illuminated, not by the sun rising, but by a tremendous flash of lightning: not white light, but a great leaping reddish bronze-brown glare. Just for a second the scene reminded me of the fearsome picture of hell which hung in my grandfather's chapel: briefly this grim glare held over the landscape, and then there was an ear-splitting clap of thunder, directly overhead, and rain began to come down as if the sky had fallen.

I heard the woman beside me cry out in terror, and then – while its echoes were still dying away, muttering and grumbling farther and farther among the rocky peaks – I heard her whisper into my ear,

'I am going to untie your hands. Go now, run,

151

*run!* – otherwise they will kill you! They are going to kill you!'

As she said this she was fumbling with the strap that bound my hands; at last she had it undone – she gave me a push and said again,

'Go – run – run!'

And so I ran! I could hear the villagers behind me, crying out distractedly in their fear and amazement:

'He has two heads!' 'And one of them is a bird's!' 'The father of light must be angry!' 'What did we do that was wrong?'

Most of them fell flat on their faces, excepting the old leader, who still stood upright, with one hand clasping his stone axe, and the other covering his eyes from the dazzle of lightning-flashes which followed one after the other. There was something lost and piteous about his appearance. 'What is it?' he muttered.

But I did not wait to answer. During a brief period of glare I ran stumbling towards the overhang where the animals were tethered. Running with my head bowed against the rain I was helped by the bawling of the burros, who seemed as terrified as their owners by the sudden storm.

And indeed, it was one of the worst storms I had ever been in.

My mule, thanks to her morose and taciturn nature, did not seem greatly affected by the weather; she snorted and grumbled as I untied and led her out, as if to draw my attention to the fact that she had been given a very indifferent stable and no breakfast, but she paid little heed to the lightning flashes and the terrific peals of thunder overhead. Flinging myself on to her back I urged her past the great crag – as soon as we were out of its shelter the wind nearly blew us over – and away from the dome-shaped huts. In the next flash I perceived a rough track leading down between low, rising cliffs, and I turned the mule's head in that direction. I did not dare urge her into a gallop, for the light was still very dim, in between the flashes; day seemed to have turned back into night. But, glancing over my shoulder, I could see no sign of pursuit; perhaps the villagers had been so stricken with terror at the suddenness of the storm that they had lost interest in me, and given up their intentions.

As to what those were, I could only guess; and would rather not. I thought the woman was probably right when she said they meant to kill me. I hoped they did not kill *her*, instead, for letting me loose.

What use killing me would be for their bees or their goats, I could not fathom.

As the mule hurried grumbling down the narrow rocky pass, while the rain sluiced over my bare head, I slowly struggled out from the strange, dreamlike mood which had held me in its power for what, now, seemed a very long time; I could not remember when it had begun; only that when the old man had told me I would walk the path of cloud, it had seemed a perfectly sensible suggestion.

After a while I realised with dismay that I had left my hat and one of the saddle-bags in the hut; luckily it was the bag that held my two pistols and most of the food, not the more precious one which contained my father's papers and his book. I was sad about the pistols – but nothing in the world would have made me go back to that place, even if there had been no danger. I had conceived a mortal horror at the very thought of it; I could hardly bear to remember the hours passed in that disgusting fetid smell of that round hut, nor the food and drink I had been given; indeed, I have recalled those events only two or three times, with the greatest reluctance, up to this very day.

After an hour or so, we came to a mountain brook, where the mule and I both drank thirstily; then I was obliged to vomit, ridding myself of that evil liquor and disgusting food; then I drank again, washed my head, and felt a little better. Resolving to try and put the whole occurrence out of my mind, I climbed back into the saddle and rode on; and presently, as the clouds parted when we reached the top of a long, slow climb over a stony hillside, I was hugely relieved to discover again, far, far off, the thin silver line of the sea. By that I realised how very far I must have come out of my way in the fog; I would have almost a day's journey to regain the lost ground. This made me resolve, if caught in a mountain mist again, to stay still and wait patiently, no matter how long the mist took to shift, for there is no gain or sense in travelling on the wrong road.

Then I began to notice that the mule was walking lame, and, dismounting, I discovered with concern that she had cast a shoe, and had picked up a stone in her fore-hoof. The stone I was able to remove with my knife, but the shoe was a serious loss, for it might have been thrown off leagues back, there was no hope of coming by it once more. I therefore dismounted and walked by the mule, leading her, in hope mixed with dread: hope that we might find a village where a smith would provide another shoe; dread that if we found a village it would be another of the sort from which we had fled.

However no village of any kind did we discover until the day was well advanced, and we had descended from the high peaks and slowly made our way across a wide region of barren, desolate uplands. At last we did come within sight of one or two scattered hamlets. These, I was relieved to find, were composed of ordinary houses, a few barns, dovecots – not the round huts, thatched with turf, of *that place*; but these villages were poor and tiny, none of them boasting a smithy, or even the rudest kind of inn.

A farmer, whom I overtook, riding his burro loaded with so enormous a mound of hay that one could see only its legs and his hat, told me that I would find both a smith and a posada at Llanes, a village on the coast about three leagues farther on.

Those last three leagues seemed a weary way! Both I and the mule were limping by now, for one of my shoes had split, and chafed my foot at every step, though I tried to pad it with grass.

Llanes, when at length we reached it, proved to be a fair-sized little port, of prosperous-looking timbered houses set on either side of a rocky river which dashed through and then wound its way to a harbour between two claws of cliff, where small brightly-coloured fishing-vessels lay moored.

Now, however, I came up against a new difficulty, which was that all my stock of money – scanty enough, God knows – had been in the bag that was left behind. I and the mule were hungry, tired, thirsty, low-spirited, and footsore; I felt somewhat unwell; we both needed new shoes and a good dinner; and we had no money to pay for any of our needs.

Flogging my weary wits in vain to think of an escape from this predicament, I tethered the mule to a roadside tree, and sat down, dispiritedly, on the parapet of the bridge which crossed the river in the middle of the town. To add to my vexation, I could see a smithy on the quay, down below; I caught the glow of the smith's fire and could hear the roar of his bellows and the clang of his anvil. But he was a dour-looking, bracket-faced fellow, who worked at his task without a smile or a word to the passers-by; it did not seem to me at all likely that he would be prepared to shoe my mule in exchange for a spinning-top or a wooden flute.

(I was mistaken about the smith, as it turned out, but that I did not discover until later.)

There I sat on the bridge, so tired out and

dejected that I was quite unable to decide what would be best to do next. About the previous night I did not dare let myself think; that was just a blind patch, to be ignored; but I was somewhat concerned in case the alguacils from Oviedo might have come this way inquiring after me, or have sent word about me here; I glanced nervously at the passers-by, in case one should suddenly exclaim:

'That is the boy who escaped from the jail in Oviedo – seize him!'

But nobody spared me a look. The mule shook her head and snuffled as if to remind me of my duty to her. I supposed drearily that it would be a practical measure to sell her, for by now it was not too great a distance to Santander to be covered on foot; but, to tell the truth, I had not the heart; I could not bring myself to sell so staunch a comrade until the last possible minute. Likewise I could, I thought, have sold the parrot; but then the parrot had, in some measure, saved my life; it would have seemed too ungrateful to dispose of her for cash.

Lost in these unhelpful reflections I dawdled on the bridge, my stomach rumbling with hunger, my head weak with sickness, watching the customers enter a nearby posada, and sniffing the good smells that came out from it.

Then my notice was attracted by the sound of music, and a voice singing a very lively song. Looking to find the source of this heart-warming melody, I observed a man seated on the quay near the blacksmith's shop. He it was who sang, and at the same time played on a small kit, or traveller's fiddle.

The song he sang was one I knew very well, one that Bob had often sung me. It was in English: it was called 'The Faithful Farmer's Son'.

# 5

The words of the street-singer's ballad came
floating up in snatches to me, where I sat on the
bridge:

> Come all you pretty maidens
> And listen to my song . . .

I knew the music so well that it made my heart
swell inside with sorrow. It was a ballad that Bob
had sung to me many and many a time.

> I live on yonder river-side
> Where fishes they do swim
> And you may gather lilies there
> Beside the water's brim . . .

It was the tale of a girl refusing all her suitors,
because she loved a lad who had been dragged
away by the Press Gang to fight the French at sea.

> I have a sweetheart of my own
> And he my heart has won

> He lived in yonder village
> And was a farmer's son . . .

At last a stranger shows her the other half of a broken ring, and declares that he is her long-lost sweetheart.

> Though I was prest away to sea
> And many a battle won,
> From you my heart did ne'er depart –
> I'm your faithful farmer's son!

I used to think, though, when Bob sang me the ballad, that the girl must have been a great simpleton not to recognise her lover at the first; if she had really loved him, I thought, however long he had been gone, surely there would have been something so familiar in his step, his air, his voice, his whole bearing, that she *must* have known him? – Besides, what did the half of a broken ring prove? He might have received it from a dying shipmate, or taken it from an enemy. If I did not recognise the man himself, I used to think, I would need more proof than that!

While these familiar thoughts raced through my head, I had slipped off the bridge, and, without considering what I did, walked down on to the quayside, to get a closer glimpse of the singer. He had placed himself not far from the smithy, where the surly-looking smith was still clanging away with his hammer. The singer, seated on an upturned dinghy, was a lanky-looking fellow, clad in a velveteen jerkin and canvas pantaloons. His hair was brownish-fair, his eyes grey; his face was ugly, with a wide mouth, snub nose, and big ears that spread out so wide you could see the light through them, like those of burros. Despite all this, there was something very taking and likeable about his looks; he kept glancing up and smiling at the people passing by, as if this town had taken his fancy more than any other in the world; and he had such an honest, simple, hopeful air, as he sang his music, with his hat before him on the ground, that I could not help hoping with him that folk would be generous; so far, though, I saw, the hat held only a few copper coins, which very likely he had put there himself to encourage business.

Then he began to sing another song that I knew very well, 'Hodge told Sue'.

> Hodge told Sue that he loved her as
>     his life,
> And if she would be kind, he would
>     make her his wife . . .

This one was a catch, that is, the tune went round and round, so that different singers, could come in, one after another, all singing the same tune, like men who jump into a cart as it rolls along the road; and all the different bits of the tune would mix together into a pleasing harmony.

As the street singer was but *one*, he said the words, and played a second singer's part on his little fiddle, very cleverly I thought.

I could not resist moving nearer to him and joining in.

'Hodge – Hodge – Hodge told Sue – '

Between us, we made quite a rousing sound of it, and quite a few passers-by turned to look and listen. Several people laughed and clapped when we came, breathless, to a finishing-point, and a few more coins were tossed into the hat.

Then the singer, with a smiling glance at me, struck into another ballad. This had words I did not know –

> Come my dearest, come my fairest,
> Come my sweetest unto me
> Will you wed with a poor sailor-lad
> Who has just returned from sea?

but the tune was someway familiar to me, so I pulled out my pipe from my pocket, and began playing alongside of his singing. This, with the voice and the fiddle, went very well, and several people called out, 'Bravo!' Also many children gathered – evidently it was the hour when school ended, for most of them carried their books and slates – and stood staring with their fingers in their mouths.

His ballad finished, the singer broke into a lively Asturian country dance, and all the children began hopping and skipping about like so many grasshoppers. I knew this one too, for it was a tune the servants danced to at Villaverde, so I kept him company on my pipe, with a few extra flourishes, and presently not only the children but quite a few townsfolk as well were dancing gaily on the quay.

Now there nearly occurred a mishap which might have landed us in deep trouble.

The level of the water where the boats were moored was some twelve feet down below the quayside; this, as I discovered later, was due to the fact that the tide was low at that time. And the quay itself, as they mostly are, was littered with piles of nets, upturned boats, wicker pots for catching lobsters, iron mooring-posts, and the offal where the vendors who sold fish from their boats had gutted and boned the catch for buyers.

Close to where I stood was a big, foul-smelling heap of these fish-scraps, with gulls screaming down to it, and, as the crowd on the quay-side grew bigger and spread outwards, a little child, dancing past, trod on some pieces of fishy slime and slid, helpless, towards the edge of the dock.

Had she fallen over she must infallibly have done herself severe injury, perhaps broken her neck, for the drop here was as much as fifteen feet, and on to jagged rocks below.

By the mercy of providence I was close enough to save her; in spite of my sore foot I ran like a hare, grabbed her, and tossed her to safety on a pile of nets. But my own foot slipped in the offal and as my hands let go of her I fell headlong. My head crashed against something hard, and the world went black about me; I knew no more.

When I next regained consciousness, I was greatly surprised to find that I was not on the windy quayside, but lying in a bed.

I attempted to sit up, crying out anxiously, 'My mule, my mule! I left her tied to a tree – '

'Be easy about your mule, hijo,' a woman's voice said. 'She is cared for, don't fret. In front of her, at this very moment she has the biggest rack of hay in Llanes, and some barley good enough to make broth for the King of Portugal!'

Reassured by this statement – which was made in the most cheerful, cordial voice imaginable – I lay back again, for indeed my head felt hot and strange, as if it might split in half. I had struck it on one of those iron mooring pillars in falling, I afterwards learned, and was considered lucky not to have dashed my brains out.

Then followed nine or ten days of fever and sickness, in which I tossed about, very wretched and half out of my mind, with a tongue like a bolster, and hands and feet that seemed separated from my body and quite beyond my control. Sometimes I thought that Father Tomas was beating me, for my back ached cruelly; sometimes that I was still in the terrible round hut being forced to drink poison. Even when my eyes were open I could not see with any distinctness, nor could I eat; the very thought of food sickened me; the most I could do was swallow a little whey with wine in it, and the juice of lemons.

However, on the tenth day I began to mend, and felt very ashamed of my weakness. (Though it was later suggested by some that I had been given poison, up on the mountain, and that this had caused my illness.) Now, looking about me, I was able to see that I lay in a big, pleasant room with a great gabled window, outside of which gulls were flying and shrieking. I pushed myself up on one elbow so as to see better.

'Ola! Now you look more like the boy who saved our Conchita!' said the same cheerful voice that had reassured me about the mule. 'And that is good, for she wishes to come and thank you herself. A moment, till I prop you on a pillow.'

Abashed at not being able to help more, I suffered myself to be hoisted up, and found that I was wrapped in a fine linen shirt, much too big for me. The sheets, also, were very good cloth.

'Thank you, thank you, senora,' I muttered. 'I am sorry to be such a trouble.'

'Never mind about that,' she replied good-humouredly. 'Trouble? Think of the trouble you have saved us! To replace Conchita, Father would have had to marry again!'

Not at all understanding her, I looked towards the door, where, now, to my great surprise, who should enter but the gloomy-faced smith. He did not look so gloomy today, though; indeed his unshaven face wore a most friendly smile, as he came up to the bedside and gripped me by the hand, with a grip like that of his own tongs. On his other arm sat the little lass I had saved from falling, who could not have been more than three at the most; she stared at me with great wondering black eyes until her father set her down on the polished wood floor and urged her to thank the young Senorito.

Then she performed a little curtsey and exclaimed, 'Muchas gracias, senor! Muchas, muchas gracias!' after which, turning to her father, she exclaimed in a loud whisper,

'Papa! He is exactly like a canary!'

'Conchita!' said my nurse. 'That is not polite.'

'No, but it is true! Is it not, Papa?'

My nurse laughed at that – a beautiful bubbling laugh – and I turned my head to smile at her, seeing her clearly for the first time. She was a big handsome girl with curly black hair drawn up at the back in a knot, from which ringlets fell; she wore a brown stuff bodice, quite low-necked, after the Madrid fashion, and a red petticoat; she was so like the little Conchita that at first I took her for the child's mother, and then, when she too addressed the smith as 'Father' realised that they were sisters. Their mother had recently died, I learned later.

'I am sorry to have been such a burden to your household, senor,' I said feebly to the smith. 'It is very kind of you to have taken me in.'

'We would have done more than that for the one who saved our little wretch from tumbling off the dock,' he said. The scowling look returned to his long grizzled countenance. 'If I have told that Jose Galdos *once*, about leaving his refuse there, I have told him twenty times! Anybody might have fallen and broken their leg, or their neck. However

166

now he heeds me at last. After my child might have died! But how are you now, lad, on the mend, eh? We'll have you downstairs tomorrow, eating man's food again, if my daughter, Juana, allows it?'

I said I hoped so, and my smiling nurse exclaimed, 'We shall see!'

'And don't trouble your head about the mule,' added the smith. 'She is out in my yard, eating like a Bishop's secretary. A fine beast, eh? But you had come a weary way, you and she; she was as lame as my grandmother. I have given her a fine new shoe, tightened up the rest, and rubbed her cut leg with brandy.'

'Oh, how can I thank you, senor,' I said, angry at my own weakness. 'When I am better I will be glad to do any work that you ask.'

His smile flashed again – his big handsome teeth were yellow as amber – and he said,

'Don't trouble your head about that, hijo – your friend is down in my shop at this moment, making himself so useful that I don't know how I shall be able to part with him.'

'My friend – ?'

A flood of warm gladness passed through me. Although I had not realised it, as I lay in bed slowly regaining my wits, all the time a kind of troubled anxiety had lain below my fevered stupor; I had felt a pain of loss which I could not understand; this, I now perceived, was because I feared that the singer on the quay must long since have departed from Llanes and gone his way. Who he

167

was, what he was, what land he came from, I had no idea, not having exchanged two words with him; but the very instant I laid eyes on him he had aroused in me such a great warmth of liking that – strange and fanciful as it may seem – the belief that he had gone, that I would never see him again, had thrown me into the grip of a most sorrowful dismay, as if my own brother had left me without saying goodbye.

And yet I had never had a brother!

'Why yes – your friend the singer,' said the smith. 'He is as skilful with a hammer as if he had been bred up in a forge! And indeed he tells me that he learned blacksmith's work when he was a sailor in the British navy.'

'Is he English? What is his name?' I asked. I was becoming tired, now; my tongue seemed to thicken and clog; my words came slowly.

'English, yes; his name is Sam – Sam Pollard,' said the smith, giving it the Spanish l-sound, Pol-yard.

'Twelve o'clock!' proclaimed Assistenta from the canopy of my bed – which was a massive oaken fourposter – and little Conchita gave a shriek of laughter, dancing about the floor.

'Oh, that bird!' exclaimed Juana. 'She has frightened me out of my wits, times without number! Run along, Father, and take Conchita with you; it is time to give our guest a merienda.'

Suddenly I realised that I was hungry; after days when the very thought of food filled me with disgust, I longed for something savoury. Juana, as

168

if guessing this, brought me a basin brimming with the most appetising fish broth, the best I ever tasted, and a big crusty piece of fresh bread. After eating, I slept, and when I woke again, I discovered with great delight that the English singer, Sam Pollard, was sitting on a stool by my bed.

'Well, lad!' he said, and a smile broke out like a lighthouse ray from his ugly, cheerful face, 'Eh, lad, you surely did me a good turn there! I thought at first that we were like to be cast in jail for causing a disturbance on the quay – but Senor Colomas, our friend downstairs, is a great man in the town, it seems, and thanks to his gratitude for your saving his little Conchita, you and I are in clover. I'm treated like royalty wherever I go!' He chuckled comfortably. 'Which I little deserve! You'd best hurry up and get better so that you can come down and claim your own glory.'

'Senor Colomas – is that the smith's name? – said that you are working in his forge?'

'Why yes – seeing him so well-disposed – I made bold to ask if he needed help. And it turned out he did. I'd picked up a knowledge of smith's work – '

'And you are English?' I said in that language.

He burst into a roar of cheerful laughter. 'I might a' guessed, wi' that yaller crop, that you weren't a Dago!' he replied in the same tongue. 'I' fact I did think it, when you joined in my songs so nimble! But what's an English lad o' your age doing wandering about Asturias, speaking the lingo like a native?'

'My father was an English captain – he died in

169

General Moore's army. I myself have never been to England – but it is my wish to go there, to find his family.'

'Well, lord 'a mercy! Who'd 'a thought it? Where do your kinsfolk live, then?'

'I believe . . . in the town of Bath.'

'Bath – aye, aye,' he nodded. 'I know of it. A fine town, 'tis. That's in the West Country – not too far from my parts.'

'Where do you come from, then, Senor Pollard?'

'Sam, Sam, lad – or Sammy. No ceremony betwixt shipmates! I comes from Cornwall – Fowey town. 'Tis but a little place. Ye'll not have heard of it. 'Tis proper pretty, though.' he sighed.

'Why are *you* in Spain, Sam?'

He sighed again. 'Well, lad – that's a long tale.'

'I should greatly enjoy to hear it,' I said.

'Would 'ee truly? Well, if it 'ud pass the time for 'ee, while 'ee be obliged to lie abed – I'll tell it.'

So Sam told me his tale.

And as I lay in Senor Colomas's comfortable bed, listening to what had happened to Sam Pollard in the course of his twenty years, I discovered that my life, lonely and dreary as I had thought it, had been all sunshine, cakes, and kisses compared with what had befallen this cheerful, ugly fellow.

He had lived with his mother and father and elder brother on a little farm near the port of Fowey in Cornwall. But the brother when he was sixteen, had been taken off by the Press Gang, to go to sea and fight against the French.

170

(Bob had told me about the Press Gang, who went ashore from Navy ships and seized by force any strong, likely-looking man they saw, unless he was rich enough to buy himself off; I thought it sounded a most wicked practice.)

Then, when he was thirteen, Sam himself, who was a stout, well-grown boy, had been taken likewise.

'That were the trouble of living nigh to the port, ye see,' he explained. 'The lads as lived inland didn't fare so badly. O' course, by the time they took me, Boney was nigh beat, but still they wanted lads for the transport ships to Spain and to France... There warn't the danger to me, though, that there had been for my poor brother Jarge; he were killed at Trafalgar.'

'But wasn't it dreadful – being dragged away from your home like that?'

'We-ell,' he said slowly. 'Aye, I did cry for a night or two. But I learned a rare lot at sea – tales and songs beyond belief. And the chaplain, he learned me to read and scribe. And I had some good messmates. But my poor owd Mam and Dad, 'twas hard for them. They couldn't work the farm too well on their own, see, and then Dad stuck a pitchfork through his foot and lamed hisself. And the price o' food went cruel high. Ah, I reckon they both died of want. An', when the peace came, an' I got my discharge – that was two years later – I got home to find the reason why I hadn't had no news of 'em was acos they was both dead an' gone, an' the farm all to rack and ruin.'

171

'Oh, Sam – '

'Take heart, messmate, their troubles is all over now,' he said, smiling at me kindly, as if it had been *I* who had come home to that empty, ruined place.

'So what did you do then?'

'Ah, then,' he said, 'I got wed to my cousin Lily. She'd allus had an eye to me, an' I'd allus had an eye to her, ever since we was liddle 'uns. A proper pretty mawther she were – so white and tall as a white foxglove in a wood.'

He paused, and a clouded, thoughtful expression came over his face.

I was greatly surprised to learn that he had been married – he looked so young – and, from his silence, feared to ask what happened next. But he went on of his own accord, in a quiet voice,

'And we got us a smallholding near Falmouth – for my dad's place was more than I could tackle. And then we had a liddle 'un – our liddle Katie – and then she and her ma took sick of the croup in the winter three years agone – the place was so damp, ye see, not being in good shape – and things was gone amiss on the farm while I tried to tend them, the cow poorly wi' the colic and the hay were all rained away that year; and Lily had another babe an' the birth went contrary – an' I'd not enough money to buy food and doctor's medicine. My uncle Ebenezer Pinchplum – that was Lily's dad – had loaned me a bit o' money at a cruel high rate of interest – but when Lily and little Katie – died – he took the farm offa me to

172

pay the debt. And he took the liddle lad to rear him – liddle Mark – but then word came he'd died too. He'd had too bad a start, reckon. And when I was – when I went to see my uncle he said he'd have me flung in jail.'

'*What?*' I exclaimed. 'But why?'

'For debt.'

'But he'd taken the farm!'

''Twarn't but a small place, ye see,' said Sam apologetically. 'He said the debt were more than the place were worth – wi' the interest an' all. I reckoned to get a job as a smith in Falmouth, to pay it off, but they'd a smith there a'ready, no need for another. And, to tell truth, I hadn't much heart to stay nigh the place when my dearies was gone. So, to 'scape being thrown in jail for debt, I shipped to sea again.'

'I think your uncle sounds like the worst monster in the world!'

'Ah well, he were main grieved when Lily died. That soured him. He said I done wrong to a-marry her. But we had those happy years . . . I reckon we were as happy as any in the land. And the three of them are in Paradise now. I take comfort from that.'

He fell silent, gazing at his big bony hands stretched out on his long bony knees.

'What happened then?' said I. 'After you went back to sea?'

He smiled widely.

'A-well, you'll think I be the unluckiest chap in creation – or else the clumsiest. For a stay snapped under me when I were in the rigging – reefing for a blow in the Bay o' Biscay – and I got me a broken leg. That's why I weren't so quick, like you, to rescue the liddle maid when she took her tumble. A sailorman with a busted leg is no use, so they put me ashore at Santander, to find my own way home. Only I couldn't do that, ye see, I munna go back to England or they'd throw me into debtors' jail. So I tried to work as longshoreman in Santander, an' I did for a bit; but the takings weren't so good – the Basques along there are clannish, like, they stick by their own; so I reckoned to come along the coast playing my music and see how I fared. And I've fared none too badly.'

'But it's terrible that you cannot go home!' I burst out.

'Nay, nay,' he said, smiling his cheerful, easy smile. 'This land of Spain's none so bad. I like it well enow. They say every Cornishman has a drop of Spanish blood in his veins. And I can speak the lingo, for a Spanish shipmate learned it me when I were on board the *Thrush*. I play my bits o' songs and I get by right well – the Dagoes'll do anything in the world for a bit o' music. Soon's I begin playing, often enough, they're all around like wasps crying out 'Musica, musica!' – But still I'd be main glad to settle down and get a chance for some steady work. 'Tis not so chancy. And travelling on all the time do come hard on my leg. If Senor Colomas would keep me on, I'd stay here willingly.'

Sam then proposed that I tell him my history, in

174

return for his. Before launching into it, I said that I wished to get out of bed; I had lain there long enough; so he kindly helped me, and I saw for the first time that he did indeed have a bad limp, though he moved with it nimbly enough.

He established a seat for me in the big dormer window. All the houses in that region have these, I discovered later. The window was double – a roofed-in, glassed-in gallery ran across the front of the house, and inside this there was another separate window for each room, going down to the floor. Thus, in summer, both outer and inner windows could be thrown open, and in winter the glass gallery, with outer windows closed, made a promenade, protected from the wind, which blows very fierce along that Atlantic coast. In this gallery Sam now settled me.

I could look down on to the harbour, and beyond its stone arms I could see a yellow strand of sandy shore, and waves breaking in showers of white upon grey rocks. To my right were the red roofs of the town, and, behind them, green mountains. I thought the family of Senor Colomas were fortunate to live in such a beautiful spot, and that, if Sam Pollard went to work for the smith, he would be lucky too. And if anybody deserved luck, poor Sam did, after a lifetime of such wickedly undeserved misfortune, borne so uncomplainingly.

'Come, tell us your tale, then, young 'un,' said he, after he had settled me in a chair, with a cloak round my shoulders.

And so I told my story, beginning with the death of Bob. I told it as plainly and simply as I could.

Sam listened with the greatest interest. Sometimes he put questions; sometimes he laughed aloud, as I related some of my escapades; sometimes, when I told of some unjust punishment, he exclaimed, 'Nay, that were hard, then!' in a tone full of sympathy; but mostly he just sat with his chin on his fists, and his eyes upon my face.

Since I had grown old enough to reflect upon my lot, nobody in the world had ever paid such close attention to my affairs – not even for so much as ten minutes; and now here I was, uninterruptedly relating every chapter of my entire life! It gave me a strange feeling, as if the Felix I described were somehow a different person from the one I had become accustomed to thinking myself.

When I had finished – rather scurrying through the history of the fearsome happenings in the mountain village – Sam drew a long breath of wonder.

'Well, by gob! And here you are, right as a ram's horn, arter passing through all that! It do fair take the biscuit! You're a right plucked young 'un, law love you! I've heard tell o' places up i' the mountains where the folk is just about savages – *cannibals*, even, some say – I'll lay it was one o' those you struck on.

'And that duel, and the poor chap as died! And the flaysome chap wi' the pigs! Let alone the jail – that were a right bit o' luck you fared out o' there.'

He fell silent, reflecting for a few moments, and then said,

'Did you ever think o' scribing a note to your granddad, to say you was alive and bobbish, and farin' to seek for your other kin across the sea?'

'I – I suppose I could.' His question took me by surprise. 'I had not thought of it.' I pondered and then said, 'Do you think I should, Sam?'

'The way I see it – ' Sam looked at me rather shyly – 'but 'tis none o' my business, rightly – '

'Please say what you think, Sam?'

'A-well, some o' your kinsfolk, back where you come from, sound a right nasty crew. That old Dona Isadora for one – she'm a fair Tartar, by all accounts – and false-hearted too – telling all those untrue tales about you – '

'*That* she is!' I agreed with vigour.

'Do she have an interest in the place, by any chance?' Sam inquired reflectively.

'An interest? How do you mean?'

'She a spinster, or a married lady? Or a widder woman?'

'Oh, I see. She is a widow. She was married – not like the rest of them – to a Marques – but the French took his lands – and she has a daughter who's a widow too – and a grandson who goes to college in Madrid. My cousin Manuel.'

'Aha!' cried Sam with an expression of triumphant cunning which looked comically out of place on his open, simple countenance. 'That's it then, see? Acos you are the Heir! But if you was disgraced – or gone – then her grandson 'ud likely get the property – your granddad's estate – seeing as how you told me all your uncles was killed in the wars, and none on 'em had any children!'

'Yes ... I suppose that might be true,' I said, pondering. 'But then, no one at Villaverde believes that I really am the heir – because my parents were not married – only Bob did, and he's dead. I cannot think my great-aunt Isadora would be as cunning as that; I think she just dislikes me for myself.'

'Just the same, I'll lay Dona Isadora 'ull be main glad you've slipped your cable!'

'Yes, I daresay she'll be in high twig now I'm gone. Nobody to put crickets in her bed. And Father Tomas will not be sorry, either.'

'But your granfer, now,' Sam ruminated. 'I don't get the notion, from what you told, that he'm a maliceful one, like that? Stern, you said, but someway fair with it? Not spiteful? Not mean-minded?'

'No, that is true ...'

'And he've had a grievous time, poor soul, wi' all his boys a-killed in the wars – '

'Yes, it did make him very sad.'

'And,' said Sam, bursting out laughing, 'by all account *ye've* been a fair young limb of Satan, times without number, setting fire to hayricks – an' putting a toad in your grandma's *penella* – and hiding a rooster in the chapel – and setting the maize to pop in the brazier when the Cardinal came to visit – oh laws! – it fair makes my ribs crack, just to think on the life you must a' led those old folks!'

178

I laughed too. It was a great delight, at last, to have somebody who appreciated my jokes.

'But,' he said, the laughter still creasing his ugly face, 'maybe if you hadn't played all those pranks – maybe – ' He paused. 'My meaning is, maybe your granddad might love ye better than ye knew – if ye'd ever given him a chance to show it?'

'He is such a stern, silent man. I don't know – I think he dislikes all boys . . .'

I thought about my grandfather, Don Francisco: his heavy grey face, set in seams the colour of pewter; walking heavily with his stick; then confined to his wheelchair, carrying his sword beside him as if he could not bear to part with it . . . And yet when he was young, I knew, he had enjoyed riding; had a fiery Andalusian mare; had gone, every year, Bernie said, up into the mountains with the shepherds to fetch down the sheep at autumn time and had slept out with them on the mountainside. I had known him only when his life was near its end. What a great deal must have happened to him long before I was even born.

'I *will* write to him – if you think it would be a good thing to do,' I said slowly, at last. 'I will send the letter from Santander, just before I go on the boat. Then it will be too late for him to prevent me.'

'Aha, yon's a capital notion. Right sprack! See what the book-larning does for ye!'

I then bethought me to show Sam my father's belongings – the sad little plume and buttons, the book, and the written papers. He puzzled and pored over the letter for many minutes, but was obliged to acknowledge that he could make neither head nor tail of the writing.

'I came to the reading a bit late,' he said apologetically. 'Print I can master, but yon spiders' scrawls have me beat!'

But he said that The Rose and Ring-Dove was a very well-spoken-of inn, just outside Bath, and that if my kinsfolk lived there, if they owned it, I would be in luck's way.

I asked if he had ever been to Bath, but he said no, never; though he had heard it was a fine town. I read him a little from my father's book *Susan*, by an English Lady of Quality, but he found it foolish stuff, and, as I had done, wondered what a captain in Old Hookey's army should see in it, save that it reminded him of home.

Then he said that I had better rest again, or Juana would be a-scolding of him – 'And she has a tongue like a rope's end, when matters go amiss, I tell ye!' he said, laughing – and that he had best sheer off, for he had some tasks he had promised to do for Senor Colomas. So he left me sitting and gazing down at the harbour, where the fishing-boats were beginning to come in and unload their silvery catch.

I sat thinking about Sam Pollard. How simple he was, and yet how shrewd; until he had pointed it out to me, I had never considered that Dona Isadora might have a reason for her hostility, her sharp remarks and her tale-bearings. Perhaps she really did wish to get rid of me, wanted me out of the way of her grandson Manuel. Perhaps she had hoped that if she made my life dismal enough, I would go . . . Oddly enough, though, having Sam there to laugh and sympathise made me view the Felix who had lived at Villaverde in a different light. And although Sam had agreed with me about Dona Isadora's dealings, though he had said, 'Well, by gob, what a shame . . . Proper mean trick that were, the owd harridan! . . .' yet I had somehow been left with a much lower conceit of myself, and even, at this moment, thought that some of the pranks I had played were very childish . . .

While I had been setting fire to ricks, and letting snakes loose in the big saloon, Sam had been in the navy, or struggling to care for his wife and children. Still, he was quite a bit older than I, after all, six or seven years. – Then I wondered how *I* would have fared if I had been in Sam's place, and that thought made me so uneasy that I picked up my father's book and fell a-reading.

I had opened it at the place where Miss Susan, going to stay with her great friends in their abbey-residence, is terrified at night by a fearful storm and the discovery of a paper, hid in a closet in her bedroom, which she takes to be the confession of some wicked deed of blood – only to find, next day, that the mysterious paper is naught but a washing-bill! For the first time, this struck me as very comical; yet, reading it through again, I could see that the writer had represented the poor young lady's terrors very skilfully; just such a nightmarish terror had I felt myself among those unchancy

181

people in that heathen village – and yet, for all I knew, my fears were equally foolish and ill-founded! I began to see that this book was not such a simple tale as I had hitherto supposed, but must be attended to carefully; and I gave my father credit for better judgment than I had at first. This led me to wondering what kind of a man my father had been; and to hoping that some person in England would be able to tell me more about him.

How I wished that Sam were in a position to come with me to England. It seemed the most cruel bad luck that he was kept forever from his homeland.

As this wistful thought entered my head, I heard the voice of Sam himself, down below outside the forge entrance, uplifted in song as he scraped a horse's hoof before fitting the shoe to it.

He was singing a mountain song of Asturias, in which the shepherd asks a bird of the hills to take a message down to his sweetheart in the valley; it was a song Bernie had been used to sing, and I leaned from one of the windows in the gallery and joined in.

Little Conchita ran out on to the quay, laughing and clapping; in five minutes, half the people of the town were outside, all carolling away as if it were a fiesta day; and Juana, coming out with a tub of washing, laughingly shook her fist at me and called,

'If you can sing like that, my boy, I think it is time you left your sick chamber. No wonder my little sister calls you *el canario*!'

# 6

I stayed three weeks, in all, with the family of Don Enrique Colomas. During the daytime, in spite of Juana's objections, I soon began to help in the forge, blowing the bellows, fetching wood, taking a turn with the hammer when it was not something important that was being made; smith's work had always seemed a good trade to me, and I was glad to have a chance of learning more about it. I had sometimes stolen into the smithy at Villaverde and done small tasks there, but Father Tomas had always been angry if he found out; he said it was not becoming to my station.

I could see that Sam Pollard knew a considerable amount about the smith's trade, and that Don Enrique was pleased with his ability; indeed by the end of the second week he asked Sam if he would care to stay on there and work for him regularly. Sam was mightily taken with this offer; he told me that Llanes put him in mind of Fowey, the port near which he had grown up in Cornwall. He told Don Enrique that he would turn the matter over in his mind a while, before coming to a decision, but I thought he would probably accept, and I was glad for him. I thought his reason for not immediately saying yes was that he wanted to be certain that he would be welcomed by the rest of the family as well as by Don Enrique.

Meanwhile Sam and I, at odd times, after work was over, in the evenings, or at siesta time, down on the shore or out on the quay, sang and played our instruments together and discovered more songs that were known to us both. I was able to teach him some that he had not heard – and he knew many, many more that were new to me. When it came to music and songs, he seemed to have a memory like a granite vault; once the words and melody were stowed away – or merely the melody, no matter how short and simple, or how long and difficult – he could at any time recall the whole thing with ease and certainty. And then, too, he could do such things with the tunes he knew! – turn them upside down, inside out, stretch them, double them up, as it were decorate them with ribbons of sound, then bring them forth again plain and neat, as they had been at the start. He taught me a little of this skill – a skill which *he* had found out for himself – he said that no other person had ever taught him his music – and soon, besides collecting a crowd around us whenever we sang and played together, we were being invited by the people of Llanes to come and play our music at their houses – they were even *paying* us for doing so! And, to tell truth, I found this so pleasant that, even when I was quite healed from my sickness and knew that I should set out once more on my journey, I still lingered and delayed from day to day, and made excuses to myself. The Colomas family urged me to wait yet awhile – I was making myself useful in the forge – I wanted to learn all the smith's work I could, and all the tunes that Sammy could teach me – the mule would be the better for another day's rest . . .

One evening we were invited to sing at a feast that was being given to celebrate the betrothal of the Mayor's daughter to a wealthy farmer's son. The whole town was invited, the Colomas family among the rest. The party was held, not in the Mayor's house, but at the biggest posada, which was in the main street of the town, by the harbour. There was a large room downstairs which had at one time been used for a stable – now it was swept and clean but there were still racks and mangers round the walls, and although boards had been laid down over the brick floor, a dusty sweet smell of hay came up from between the cracks as the dancers stamped and twirled.

Between dances the young men kept to one side of the room, girls to the other, and the older people strolled in the middle. Sam and I perched on a platform that had been put up between two stalls to play our music, and we were assisted by the drums and tambourines and zambombas of a couple of travelling gipsies. At first while we played the betrothed girl (who was a cousin of Juana Colomas) walked round and round the room holding up an apple on the point of a knife, while all the guests tossed gifts to her, and her *novio*, following a step behind, caught the things and bowed polite thanks.

Then, presently, a trough of water was brought in and set down in the middle of the floor. All the girls were giggling and pushing, as they struggled to get close to it. I asked Juana what they were doing, since she happened to be standing near us just then, looking very handsome, I thought, in a red-and-gold bodice, embroidered all over so that it was quite stiff, and yellow ribbons in her black curls.

'Oh!' she said laughing. 'It is just a foolish game. There are pins in the water, you see; you dip your hand in and if, when you bring it out, there is a pin sticking to your skin, then that means that Saint Antony is going to send you a novio before the end of the year.'

Although she pretended to despise the game, I noticed that in a moment or two she strolled nearer to the group, looking carelessly about her – then contrived to slip in among the rest and worked her way through to the trough, where she plunged her arm into the water. Just then somebody moved between us and I lost sight of her, but later I observed her sticking a pin among the folds of her petticoat with a look of great satisfaction on her face. She thought she was unobserved, I daresay, but, glancing up, I saw that Sam, beside me, was watching her also; he looked grave, not precisely sad, but not too cheerful either.

Soon everybody was dancing again, and then there came the feast – smoked pork and peas, bream and anchovies, roast chestnuts and butter-cakes, a salad with sippets of bread in the oil, dried cherries, fried semolina balls in syrup, almonds and fritters and marzipan, *membrillo* – a conserve of quinces, very sweet and sticky – and wine and cider to drink. The girls, perched on boxes and barrels, were signalling to the boys in fan-language – a slow, disdainful movement meaning 'Go away, I don't care if I never set eyes on you again,' while a nervous lively quivering movement meant, 'Ola! I like your looks and would be pleased to talk to you if my parents would permit it.'

Juana, though, had laid aside her fan, and was talking to her cousin, the engaged girl; their heads were earnestly close together.

When the dancing began again, and Sam and I were back on our perch, playing away, Juana threaded her way round the sides of the room until she reached us, and said to Sam,

'Why do you not dance, sometimes, Senor Polyard? You surely do not have to play *all* the time? The gipsies can make music on their own for a while.'

'Thank you, senorita,' he said, 'but I am too lame to dance. My limping leg prevents me. I am happier playing for your cousin's guests. And I am very happy watching *you*! You dance so beautifully.'

'Oh!' she said, blushing, half-disappointed, half-pleased with his praise. 'Well – but dancing is really very stupid. I am tired – I think I will sit down for a while.'

'No, you should not do that at your cousin's party,' said Sam. 'Besides, that would deprive me of the pleasure of watching you. Why don't you dance with Felix, here?'

'No, no!' I began to protest, feeling very foolish – for Juana was a good head taller than I – but she said,

'Yes! I will dance with Felix,' and, seizing me by the hand, obliged me to drop my pipe and follow her into the centre of the room.

I had danced sometimes at Villaverde when the servants had a feast – danced with the maids in the kitchens, so I knew how to do it – but that was another thing forbidden by my grandfather; he said that it was vulgar to share in the amusements of servants, and also that, considering the sad state of the country and our family in particular, there was no occasion for merrymaking. I had done it sometimes, nonetheless – just to defy him – but I never really cared for the pastime, being so short, and therefore feeling that I looked ridiculous.

But this evening, since there was no escape from it, and feeling that, in a way, I was dancing in place of my friend Sam – dancing *for* him, as it were – I resolved to do my very best. Juana was a fine dancer: moving with tremendous spirit and assurance, her arms and head drawn up, her neck as straight as a pillar, she stamped and swung and swirled, clicked her heels together and flicked her fan, with wrists like running water and eyes that flashed, daring me not to equal her her vigour. So

I, too, danced as if my life depended on it, thumping my feet on the dusty boards, spinning around her, bending my knees, bounding off the floor, snapping my fingers together, and wondering how long I could manage to keep going like this! The speed made my head whirl. By degrees all the other dancers dropped out to watch us, people began clapping their hands in time to Sam's music and shouting *Ole!* And Sam's music went faster and faster, until the room around us was nothing but a dizzy blur.

At last Juana consented to stop – only just in time, for I was ready to fall to the floor from exhaustion – and, laughing, she said to me, 'Bravo, Don Felix! If your friend could dance as well as that – if he danced as well as he plays – he would be very nearly perfect!'

'He is perfect without the dancing!' I panted. 'I think he is the best person I have ever met.'

Her eyes brightened at that, and she gave me a very friendly look.

'What do you know of him?' she asked, handing me a cup of cider. 'Tell me his story, if you please.'

So I told her Sam's story, repeating just what he had told to me. At the sorrowful part her eyes misted over as if she were suffering his trouble herself, and when I told her about the uncle who had taken Sam's farm away, she could hardly contain her indignation.

'What a wretch. He ought to be hung up by his thumbs! He ought to have all *his* goods taken away.'

'Perhaps,' I said, for I had been thinking much about it, 'if, when I reach England I can find my family – and if they are people of substance, as Sammy thinks they might be, if they keep a big posada at Bath – they might be able to bring the uncle to justice, or pay off the debt, and then Sam could go back to his own home.'

But with this Juana did not agree.

'No, no, he is much better off in Spain! England sounds to me a hateful country. I wonder that you wish to go there!

'But still,' she added thoughtfully, 'if the uncle could be made to give back what he has stolen from your friend, that would be good, too.'

And she gave Sam another very thoughtful look.

At last the party came to an end and we all went home to bed.

Next day I announced that I must be off. I hated to leave Llanes, which was one of the handsomest towns I ever was in, with its rocky river, and harbour full of brightly coloured boats, its timbered houses and sandy shore, and the mountains rising behind – but still I had the urge to go on and search for my father's family. The things that Sammy had told me about England increased my wish to go – he said that Bath was a famous town, with grand streets and handsome houses and many stores; that famous people, including the king of England himself, came there to take the waters, for there was a hot spring with minerals in it which cured many ailments; and that it was a wonderful place for music too, he had heard, where you could listen to the finest singers and players in the country.

The Colomas family seemed truly sorry when I announced my intention – little Conchita, for whom I had carved many potato-dolls, clung to my leg, and wailed,

'No, no! Don't go, don't go!'

But they looked even graver when Sam announced that he would go with me. Their faces brightened, however, when he added,

'I will travel with Felix as far as Santander. I have many friends on the waterfront there; I daresay I shall be able to discover some ship on which he can sail to England without having to lay out all his savings.'

(For, from the profits of our music, I had been able to amass almost as much as from the sale of the Andalusian horse.)

'And then you will come back here?' said Juana to Sam, while little Conchita, clapping her hands, cried,

'Yes, come back, come back, Senor Sam!'

'If Don Enrique will have me,' said Sam, laughing, and Don Enrique, with his grave smile, said,

'I have already told you that I shall be glad to have you, my friend.'

So, that settled, everybody was happy: the Colomas family rejoiced that Sam had decided to remain in Llanes, and I was glad that I did not have to say goodbye to my friend quite so soon.

Don Enrique offered to let us have a burro for the journey.

'Really, senor, you are too trusting,' Sam reproved him. 'Suppose we sold your burro with the mule in Santander and never came back?'

'My boy,' said the smith, 'when you reach my age you learn how to distinguish between honest men and thieves.'

However we said we did not need the burro. We would take turns riding the mule (privately I resolved that Sam should have all the turns); then Sam would bring her back to Llanes and the Colomas family would keep her. Indeed, this was another part of the plan that made me glad, for I was greatly attached to my hardy and untiring, if bad-tempered companion, and had hated the notion of selling her to a stranger. Don Enrique wanted to give me money for her, but I said that I would prefer him to take her in requital for three weeks' lodging and Juana's kind nursing while I was sick; when he protested that anybody would have done as much, I pointed out how much it would comfort my heart, when in England, to know she had such a good home. At this he agreed, but said they would continue to think of her as mine, so that I could always come back and claim her; thus the matter was left, and later, as events turned out, how glad I was that I had not taken his money.

Our parting, therefore, was not so sorrowful as it might have been, though I was melancholy enough at leaving yet another set of kind friends and such a pleasant place.

As I travelled farther and farther out into the world, it amazed me to discover how many friendly people it contained – which had not been at all my expectation when I left Villaverde.

We left at first light on the second day after the Mayor's party. The journey to Santander would take us two or three days, depending on the weather, and our adventures along the way. Juana gave us a bag of food to take with us, and Don Enrique recommended us to a cousin of his who owned a posada at Santillana, which was one of the towns we must pass through. The whole family (indeed, half the town) turned out to say goodbye to us; and so we went on our way, Sam taking first turn at riding the mule, who seemed quite pleased to be on the road again; she snuffed the air and went loping along at a good speed, while I ran with a hand on the stirrup.

Our path now lay along the coast, with a mighty range of mountains rising to the south of us; since the day was clear and brisk, every crack and seam of their rocky slopes appeared as close as if they were but a stone's throw from us, though in truth they were some three or four leagues distant.

At first we passed by orchards and vineyards; then we reached a bare and dismal region of rock and stone, with no tree and hardly a blade of grass on the hard bare ground.

This was one of the most melancholy sections of my journey – as regards the aspect of the country –

and yet, looking back, I cannot recollect any happier time in my whole life than those hours, as we travelled along, with the sea on our left and the great rampart of mountains on our right, singing ballads, inventing new melodies for old words, trying different harmonies for old tunes, reminding each other of our favourite airs. Even the mule seemed quite pleased with our music; she put back first one ear, then the other, arched her neck, and picked up her feet as if she had been trained by the Mamelukes.

Sam, who had travelled this way before, told me that the mountains hereabouts are all seamed with caves, many of huge size and going for miles underground. The local people put them to all manner of uses, from storing hay to holding religious services. This recalled to me my adventure at the round-hutted village and, with a shudder, I changed the subject, asking Sam how long he thought he would remain in Llanes.

'All my life, if God permits it,' he said gravely.

I inquired if there was any person in England to whom I should give news of him – was there nobody who might be gladdened by the knowledge that he was alive and well, and prospering in foreign parts? But he said no, his parents being dead, while his uncle would only be displeased by the news; and all his friends were sailors and no doubt scattered about the sea.

By dusk of that day we reached the town of San Vincente, which is approached by a great grey bridge of thirty-two arches, across a deep, wide inlet; the bridge was very ancient and crumbling; in some parts the footway was only just wide enough to cross, and at that, with considerable danger. The town, though larger than Llanes, proved very poverty-stricken and miserable: the port was almost silent, with green, barnacled, rotting timbers on the wharfs, and very few boats. We found the largest posada, and played our music there, but it was a dark and dismal place; the main room had an earth floor where travellers slept on sacks of straw in among the goats and poultry of the household; a fire burned in one corner where we might cook our own food; none was provided. We got but little money from our music; it seemed that in San Vincente nobody had any money to spare; however that did not trouble us, since we had sufficient for our needs, and plenty of food provided by Juana – ham, eggs, olives, cheese, and bread. We therefore played for our own pleasure.

People retired to bed early in that town, and we did too, but slept badly, tormented by fleas. We were later roused entirely by a terrific raging thunderstorm which broke out over the mountains to the south of us; flashes of blue-white lightning followed one after another, with a glare hardly to be described, accompanied by such deafening peals of thunder that many of the guests at the posada stuffed their ears with hay lest their eardrums should crack. The rain rattled down with such violence that soon the streets of the town were awash with water, which began to flow under the door of the posada, and soon, since the level of the floor was lower than the street, we found ourselves lying in a pool.

Since nobody could sleep in such conditions, presently Sam proposed that we should rise up and continue on our way. By now the storm had died down, and the moon shone out, clear as if it had been washed by the rain; travelling on by its light seemed greatly preferable to lying in half an inch of dirty water and sodden straw. So we paid our small bill and went on our way, leaving the town of San Vincente without regret.

Now for some leagues we travelled along the seashore, with the moon above us and the waves thundering in white majesty on our left hand. From time to time a shallow river ran down across the beach, which we must ford, but none of these gave too much difficulty. After an hour or so the sky began to lighten, and at last the sun rose, dazzling our eyes with its brilliance, for since we travelled eastwards it lay directly ahead of us and spread a flashing path across the wet sand of the shore. Indeed so blinding was the light in our eyes that we resolved to turn inland for a space, and so left the beach and made our way into a thick wood of wild fig and cork trees and tangled vines; among the trees there were also rocks and gorges and the dark clefts of caverns. Sam told me that this forest had a bad name, which was why the path ran along the shore; robbers were supposed to lurk here, and evil deeds to be committed in its dark depths; but the hour of sunrise seemed an unlikely one for robbers to be abroad, and indeed we saw no persons of that sort, and passed on our way undisturbed.

Towards the eastern edge of the wood (which was very large) we did, however, come across a surly-looking fellow driving a large ox before him into a gully which led to a cave-entrance.

The man gave us an unfriendly look as we approached him, and did not seem best pleased when Sammy – who would fall into chat with the devil himself – gave him a cheerful greeting.

'Good day, friend! Are you intending to plough the floor of that cave?' For the man carried a ploughshare over his shoulder.

'No!' replied the man shortly, and gave the ox a thump with the wooden plough, to hurry it on its way.

'Then,' said Sam teasingly, 'I can only suppose that you are taking the ox to shelter. Perhaps you have not noticed that the storm is over and the sun is drying the ground?'

'I am not taking the ox to shelter,' replied the exasperated man. 'I do not know why you are prying into what is none of your business! However, as you are strangers, I will tell you that I am hiding the ox in the cave because the priest is anxious to borrow it to plough his land; he has no beast of his own, and the miserable cadge never loses a chance to sponge on somebody else; he has had a day's labour from every beast in the village except mine, and I'm determined he shan't get his hands on it. Get on, you!' And he gave his ox another tremendous whack on its bony quarters which made it start hurriedly forward and disappear into the dark cave, where he followed it.

We went on our own way, and Sammy remarked,

'Lord 'a mercy, if that isn't a prime case of cutting off his nose to spite his face!'

'How do you mean, Sammy?' said I.

'Why, that surly fellow will very likely spend the day in the cave with his ox – losing its labour as well as his own – he might just as well have lent it to the priest and done something useful at least.'

'That's true,' I said, 'but' (thinking of Father Tomas), 'if the priest is really a scoundrelly sponging sort of a fellow I don't know that I blame him.'

'Maybe,' agreed Sammy, 'though most of the priests I have dealt with have been good enough men.'

In fact we were soon to encounter that same priest, and were much surprised at our first sight of him.

We had now come within sight of the little town of Santillana, which lies about a league inland from the sea, among green hills, and fertile farmland, all planted with walnut trees, apple trees, palms, and patches of maize and blue-flowering flax. Santillana is a small, pretty place, of cobbled streets and thick-beamed stone houses.

As we walked up the main street the cows were being milked in the stables under the houses. We bought a cup of milk from a pretty girl and asked her the way to Don Enrique's cousin's house. She directed us to the seaward end of the village. Here we saw the church, at the top of a sloping open square. In front of the church grew a huge ash tree, and as we approached this, we saw the priest come out of the church door, carrying what looked like a bundle of sticks. He was followed by a boy in a white acolyte's robe who carried a lighted taper. Priest and boy passed out of sight behind the thick bushy trunk of the ash tree, and apparently came to a stop there; we heard the priest say:

'Thank you, my child; very good; now pass me the taper; excellent; now step well back and cover your eyes!'

To our great astonishment we then heard a series of loud reports as several rockets shot up into the air and exploded, one after another, with sharp claps of sound; a huge cloud of starlings, who had been roosting in the ash tree, left it and circled frenziedly about the sky above the church tower, screaming and complaining, while down below the mule snorted with fright, and Sam and I stared at one another in wonder.

'Do you think he did it to scare away the starlings?' said I in a low voice. ' – For if so, I do not think he is going to be successful.' (Indeed the birds were already beginning to return to their perches.) 'And why should he wish to do so?'

'Fair has *me* in a puzzle,' agreed Sammy, grinning and scratching his head.

At this moment the priest came round the thicket tree and, seeing us stand so amazed, burst out laughing. He was a merry-looking little dumpling of a man, round and brown as a chestnut, very different from tall pale Father Tomas.

'Are you wondering at my fusillade?' he said. 'I will explain it to you later – for I see you are strangers. But first come in to mass.'

The bell was now being rung lustily in the tower, doubtless by the boy who had carried the taper. A number of townspeople began to appear, coming rather slowly down the street and across the square. We followed them into the church and heard mass. It was the first time I had done so since leaving San Antonio, and I was glad to be in a church again; I felt that I had a great deal to tell God about my adventures and about the world I was discovering outside Villaverde which was so very different from what Father Tomas had led me to expect. I wondered what this priest would say about that. God Himself had nothing to say at that time, but it seemed to me that He listened to me in a silence that was full of interest and sympathy. I felt much more comfortable with Him in that bare church than I had ever done in the richly furnished chapel of my grandfather's house.

After mass, the priest invited Sam and me to come and have coffee with him; he seemed delighted to entertain visitors. We found that he lived in a wretched little house on the edge of the village, where a thin old lady in a black shawl brought us dry bread-biscuits and some very good coffee.

'Coffee is my one luxury,' said the priest (he told us he was called Father Ignacio). 'I came here from

Pamplona where the French (when they were there), taught me to enjoy it more than chocolate.'

He told us about his life in Pamplona, where he had been for ten years. He had lived there during the French wars and through a great battle when the British attacked the town and finally won it from the retreating French. He had many interesting tales of this terrible time, of eating rats and dandelion roots; and he told us about the spring festival which they celebrate in Pamplona with bulls running wild through the streets.

'It must seem rather dull to you in Santillana,' said I. 'This seems a very quiet place.'

'A little too quiet,' Father Ignacio agreed. 'The priest who was here before me, Father Jose, died at the age of a hundred and two. He had become so old that he was unable to perform most of his duties, and so the people in the village did as they liked; nobody bothered to dig Father Jose's land, which was all grown over by bushes; and very few people ever came to mass, because they said that, when the wind blew from the west (which it generally does here) they could not hear the sound of the church bell.'

'Oh I see,' said Sammy laughing. 'So that is why you let off the rockets and scare the starlings.'

'Just so! Even if they are away in the fields, they cannot say they do not hear my rockets. And even if they were deaf they would see the puffs of smoke and see the birds whirling about in the sky, and know that it was time to come and pay their respects to God.'

We took a great liking to Father Ignacio, and I felt certain that the farmer whom we had seen hiding his ox in the cave had done so entirely because of his own grudging, spiteful nature, and not due to any fault on the priest's part.

Father Ignacio told us that he made the gunpowder for his rockets out of pigeon dung (another thing he had learned from the French) and that he was gradually persuading the people of the town into better ways.

'The children enjoy my fireworks,' he explained, 'so they come to visit me, and by degrees I make friends with their parents also.'

Then he asked us about ourselves, and we told him our histories. Since I had told my full tale to Sam I could hardly do less to this good man. He asked me if I would like him to write a letter to my grandfather, just to say that he had seen me and that I was alive and well. I thanked him and said I would be grateful, especially if he would be so kind as to wait a few days, until I should have found a ship at Santander, and be safely embarked for England.

At that he laughed, very kindly, and said,

'So be it! I have run away from home myself – I suppose every boy has to do it once – I will not hinder you! But mind you write to your grandfather from England.'

'Oh yes, of *course* I shall do that.'

Father Ignacio was interested to hear that Sam was going to work for Don Enrique whom he said he had often heard spoken of as a worthy and honest man.

Then the priest's housekeeper came to say that a sick woman was asking for him, so, walking out on his errand, he accompanied us as far as the posada of Don Enrique's cousin. This man, Don Manuel Colomas, was a big brawny fellow; he greeted us civilly but gave rather a gruff good-day to the priest, who bade us goodbye and went on his way.

Don Manuel led us into his house, received a note we had for him, and asked how he could serve us – Don Enrique's friends were his friends also, and everything in his house was ours to command. Had we breakfasted? We said yes, at the priest's house.

'That one!' he muttered. 'Father Interference! I'll wager you got scanty enough pickings under *his* roof.'

But we said no, we had done well and that Father Ignacio had been very kind. However since, after travelling most of the night, we were now decidedly fatigued, we asked if we might lie down and sleep in some corner for an hour or two.

Don Manuel hospitably provided us with a large bedroom overlooking the front courtyard of his posada, as well as a stall for the mule. We flung ourselves down on well-stuffed flock mattresses and were soon fast asleep.

When I awoke I was amazed to find that the sun lay low in the west; almost the whole day had gone by, wasted in sleeping. Sam was already awake, leaning on the windowsill and watching the people and dogs in the courtyard.

Very vexed at having slept so long, I asked him why he had not awakened me sooner. He said,

'Eh, lad, ye needed the rest; why should I rouse ye? 'Tis not long yet since ye lay sick abed. And all life lies ahead; there's time a-plenty! Besides, I've been well amused, looking out here.'

I joined him and saw a group of village men who were watching with laughter and applause while a lively little hunchbacked fellow poured wine from a bottle which he held at a great height above his head, first into his mouth, and then into a whole trayful of cups without spilling a single drop. Then he handed the cups to all in the crowd.

'Hollo!' said Sammy. 'Here comes our friend from this morning?'

'You mean the priest?'

'No, no – t'other fellow – the farmer who was so nice of his ox. He looks fair bewattled about something.'

And indeed the man from the cave-mouth, who rushed through the yard gate just then, appeared to be in a perfect passion. We observed him with great interest as he launched into what seemed a furious tirade, waving his arms up and down, holding them out wide, bawling until he was red in the face, and stamping his feet. We were too far away to hear his words, but after a few moments Sammy said, laughing,

'I tell ye what! 'Tis all Lombard Street to a china

orange that his ox has got itself stuck fast in the cave – look at the way he holds his arms!'

'I believe you are right,' said I. 'Let us go down and find out.'

We went down to the courtyard. Don Manuel was there too, now; he received us politely but absently – he was listening to the farmer's indignant tale.

The latter was shouting,

'And it is all the fault of that meddling prosing aggravating officious busybody of a priest! – if it weren't for him, I'd never even have *thought* of taking the beast into the cave. I say, damn the day he came to this town!'

Some of the bystanders laughed unkindly, and one called out,

'The priest has had the use of everybody else's ox, Pepe! Fair play, now! Why should yours be the only one to escape? This must be the judgment of heaven – you might as well resign yourself!'

'Ah, have a heart, neighbours!' said Pepe indignantly. 'I don't come here to be laughed at – I need help! Who'll come and help me drag the wretched animal out? For pity's sake – it will die of cold and hunger in there!'

Half-mocking, half-sympathetic, a crowd of them went along with him, over the fields, back to the wooded hillside where we had met him in the morning. Sam and I followed, curious to see what kind of fix the ox had got itself into, and how they would rescue it.

Some of the men had brought ropes with them,

and torches made from tarred bundles of rushes, and these last were needed, for the ox had gone quite a long way into the cavern. Pepe, foolishly, had not tethered it, but had simply tied a hurdle across the mouth of the cave so the animal could not get out. Consequently it had wandered farther and farther back, along a narrow passage, until its horns had jammed against the rock walls on either side. Then, struggling, pushing, terrified no doubt, the poor beast had become even more tightly wedged, and now stood rigid like a prisoner in the stocks, bawling and bellowing lamentably; in that rocky enclosed place its frantic noise, doubled in volume, sounded like the Trump of Doom.

Since the ox had become fixed while going inwards along the passage, the men could not get at its horns to put a rope round them, for its massive body occupied the whole space. They tried roping its hinder legs and dragging backwards, but the passage took a turn not far from where the ox had stuck, and became very narrow, so that they could not get sufficient purchase to pull it out. The men hauled and struggled and cursed, the poor ox groaned and trumpeted, but no progress was made; if anything, during the struggle, the wretched animal thrust itself farther in.

'The cursed beast will die here, in the cave,' said Pepe, raging and weeping.

I had a thought, and said to Sammy. 'I shall fetch the priest.'

He burst out laughing and said, 'Do 'ee know, I

had that very same notion! But go ye, lad – ye can run faster than old dot-and-go-one.'

So I ran back across the fields to the priest's house, where, by luck, I found him at home. When I explained the problem he laughed too, and said,

'Well, well, we do not know that it will work, but it is certainly worth trying. Ah, that Pepe! He is the stingiest rogue in the village. He would burn down his own barn, rather than let anyone else have a day's use of it. Perhaps this may be a lesson to him. Let us hope so.'

As we approached the cave, it was plain from a good distance away that nothing had changed. We could still hear the ox bellowing mournfully inside, as if it thought its last moment had come. Sam, outside the cave mouth greeted us cheerfully and said,

'You will be welcome here, Father. I think they are at their wits' end!'

Indeed the group of men had run clean out of strength and patience.

In spite of Pepe's protests, they seemed inclined to return to the posada and leave the ox to its fate.

'It got itself in there, let it get itself out,' one said, and another, 'Maybe it will find its own way out during the night,' and a third, 'You will just have to bring a saw tomorrow, Pepe, and saw off its horns.'

'Saw the horns off my beautiful Zea, who has the widest pair in the village? Never! Besides, how would I get at them. Neighbours, neighbours, don't desert me!'

'Well, well, Pepe, what's this?' blandly inquired Father Ignacio. 'In trouble, are you?'

Pepe looked very foolish when he saw the priest, but as he had no other source of help, he swallowed his pride and said, 'Oh, Father, if you have any notion how to get this obstinate animal out of there, I wish you would tell me. I would be greatly obliged!'

'So it's the ox that is obstinate, is it?' said Father Ignacio, laughing. 'I wonder if animals reflect the natures of their masters? However, let us see what we can do. This boy here, who fetched me, has an idea which may perhaps help to shift your poor Zea out of the awkward spot where it has wedged itself.'

'Oh, Father, if only you can budge it, I will plough your land every day for a month.'

'Easy, friend, easy! You had better not make any rash promises. Besides,' added the priest, smiling, 'the last corner of my little bit of land would only take that great beast of yours half a day. But now, let us study the situation. Are there other passages in this cave? Is it possible to get round to the front of the ox?'

Unfortunately there were no other passages. The cave consisted of a single tunnel, threading deep into the hillside. And the ox was plugged well along it, like the cork in the neck of a bottle.

Father Ignacio made his way to the ox's hind-quarters – the villagers politely standing aside for him. The passage, quite wide at the mouth, became narrower and narrower, to the point where the ox had become fixed.

'Humph,' said Father Ignacio, turning to me (I had followed behind him, carrying his equipment), 'this is not going to be so simple.'

'What is the plan, Father?' asked Don Manuel, who must have arrived while I was fetching the priest.

'I want to give the ox a fright from the other side, so as to startle it into going backwards,' explained Father Ignacio, and he said to me, 'Do you think you could climb through underneath the ox, my boy? I believe you are the only person here who is small enough to do so. It will not be very pleasant,' he added calmly.

I was of the same opinion. There might be just room to squeeze past the animal's legs, but there was considerable risk of being trampled. Also the floor of the passage was slimy and disgusting where the ox had stamped and struggled and slipped all day long and voided its dung in terror and exhaustion.

However I was not going to show myself a coward in front of these strangers, or Sam, so I said,

'I will try, Father.'

After all, it was I who had had the idea in the first place, so I supposed it was up to me to carry it out.

'Don Pepe,' said Father Ignacio, 'have you any means of soothing your beast while the boy crawls under his legs? Can you talk to him? Calm him down? We do not wish the boy to be trampled to death.'

'Anything Pepe says to the animal is more likely to put it in fear of its life!' somebody shouted teasingly. But others called out,

'Sing to the ox, Pepe! Sing the song you sing while you plough! Perhaps the ox will go to sleep!'

They all began to sing a slow, rhythmic chant which, it seems the men of these parts used when they are ploughing:

> Walk, buey, walk,
> Bite, plough, bite,
> Carve up my field; turn it into bread!
> Walk, buey, walk,
> As the knife cuts the loaf,
> Carve my red earth into white bread.

Among all the voices I could hear that of Sammy, cheerfully upraised, and then he began to invent new twirls and flourishes to vary the tune – and perhaps to let me know that he hoped I was managing my part of the business without too much fear or difficulty.

Crawling between the legs of that ox was certainly one of the strangest and most disagreeable tasks I have ever undertaken. I would sooner spend twenty hours learning Latin or reading about the martyrdoms of the saints with Father Tomas than go through that again. Although the calm regular sound of the men singing *did* seem to soothe the ox in some degree, I could tell that it was still very nervous and ready to panic at any new occurrence. I had to creep and squirm, thrusting my way past its bony hocks, expecting every minute that it would pick up a huge cloven hoof and plant it on some part of my body.

Having wriggled my way past the hind legs, I crouched underneath it and found that the worst part of the task still lay ahead of me, for the front legs were much thicker, and seemed immovably planted in the narrow passage-way. When I tried to push and squeeze between them the ox became frightened and bellowed; the sound coming from directly above me was like a tremendous clap of thunder.

'Are you making good progress, my son?' called Father Ignacio calmly. He was holding a torch, but its light did not penetrate past the bulk of the ox.

'I am having a little trouble with the front legs, Father,' I called back. I had one elbow in a patch of mud, and was trying to lever myself past a massive hairy leg with the other elbow, pulling myself sideways over the rocky, slimy ground like a crippled lizard, and expecting at every moment that the ox, with some hasty fretful movement, would crush me like a slug against the cave wall.

At last, after what seemed like hours of pushing and squeezing, but was, in reality, I suppose, about ten minutes, I managed to struggle past its knees, and took a few moments to get back my breath. Beyond the ox, the passage was about four feet wide; it felt like a huge hall, and I stood up, enjoying the sensation of being able to straighten my shoulders and stretch my arms. Then I found the muzzle of the ox in the dark, and gave it a pat, to show that I bore no sense of grievance for all the trouble it had given me.

The poor ox started and snorted at my touch. I passed my hand up its great horns and found that one of the tips appeared to be caught in a narrowing crack.

'You will have to go backwards, brother,' I told it. 'And I'm afraid you don't seem to have the sense to do that.'

'Do you have the rope?' called Father Ignacio.

'Yes; it is still tied round my leg,' I called back.

'Pull then!'

I pulled, and presently, with some trouble, managed to drag a leather sack through between the legs of the ox. From this I drew out Father Ignacio's steel and yesca, and was able to light a torch.

'Very good – well done!' called the priest, seeing my light. 'Now; go a good way back if you can – we do not want to hurt the ox! Is the passage quite high?'

'Yes. It is very high,' I called, holding the light above my head and looking upwards. The roof was almost out of sight. Above me on the sloping walls I was surprised to notice many great pictures of animals – deer and oxen and dogs, and some men carrying bows and arrows – but I was too much occupied with the task in hand to pay any heed to these. I walked back thirty paces or so along the tunnel and then turned to look at the ox

212

– it was now a black bulk at the end of the gallery but I could catch the flash of its great wild eyes in the torchlight.

Jamming the torch into a cranny, I pulled some of Father Ignacio's rockets from the leather bag and lit their fuses. Then I retreated a few more paces and covered my head with my arms. It was as well I did so, for the rockets flew screeching up to the rocky vault above (sounding like demons of the cave) and there burst with the most ear-splitting series of bangs that it is possible to imagine – echoes crashed and rattled from end to end of the gallery. Fragments of rock came thundering down, and I was peppered all over with dust and splinters and some larger-sized pieces of stone, and began to wonder if the whole cave would come down on me.

Amid all this thunderous noise I could hear the ox bellowing, also, but could see nothing, for my candle had been extinguished by dust, and my eyes were full of dust also.

After a few moments I heard the priest call,

'Well done, my boy! Are you there? Are you unharmed?'

'Yes, thank you, Father. I am here!' I called back, fumbling to find the sack and the torch. I struck a light and discovered with great satisfaction that the ox had gone from where it had been fixed; our plan had worked exactly as we had hoped.

Making my way gingerly through the fallen fragments I returned to the mouth of the cave. There, just outside, I saw the whole group of men surrounding the ox – they were patting it and inspecting it, looking for wounds or damage.

At my arrival they fell on me, as they had on the animal, patted me and praised me and asked if it had been very disagreeable crawling under the ox's belly.

'Oh, phooh!' said I. 'It was nothing! I could do it three times a day! – But still, I should be glad of a bath.'

Indeed I was covered with mud and filth, and stank most disgustingly.

So we all returned to the village in a triumphant procession, the men congratulating Pepe, not without a certain amount of mockery.

'Well, Pepe, if your ox should ever chance to wander in there again, you know what to do – just send for Father Ignacio and his rockets.'

But Pepe did not even answer; he had his arm over the ox's neck, as if it were a child he had thought lost for ever.

Back at the posada I was led into a downstairs room where they washed the linen, and there I stripped off my clothes and climbed into a great earthenware tub full of hot water sweetened with bunches of rosemary. How I revelled in that bath! There had been several moments, under the belly of the ox, when I thought I would never be able to get out of the cave with all my arms and legs still attached to my body, so it was a great pleasure to rinse and soak them in the hot and fragrant water. Two of the maid-servants took away my soiled clothes to wash them, and while they were drying I was supplied with a velveteen jerkin and a pair of leather breeches belonging to one of Don Manuel's sons, which were so large that I had to tie the breeches on with a cord.

Then Sam and I were treated to a handsome dinner (for which nobody would allow us to pay a single peseta): meat cooked with tomatoes, and chicory salad, bread sprinkled with salt, and a tart of apples, which grow very plentifully in this region.

All the men of the village appeared to be in the posada, drinking the health of Pepe's ox, and teasing him that he was now bound by his promise to plough Father Ignacio's land every day for a month, whether or not it needed ploughing. Don Manuel and his little hunchbacked assistant were kept busy pouring wine for all the customers, and there was a great deal of gaiety.

Pepe, however, once he was assured that his ox was well and had suffered no hurt, soon returned to his original complaint, that the ox would never have been imprisoned in the first place had it not been for Father Ignacio's inconvenient request, and that the whole affair was the priest's fault.

'What an ungrateful scoundrel!' I whispered to Sam.

He shrugged. 'Ye can't make a silk purse out of a sow's ear, lad!'

Father Ignacio had returned to his own house, after inviting Sam and me to breakfast again the following morning before we departed. (We could not go on to Santander that night, for my clothes

215

were still wet.) The temper of the village was now on the priest's side, rather than on that of Pepe, who presently took himself off, grumbling that nobody sympathised with his troubles.

The rest of the men remained in the posada until nearly sunrise, laughing and drinking. Sam and I sang some of the songs, to a most welcoming reception, and then retired, I to dream that I was suffocating inside a jar made of rock and filled with mud.

# 7

On the following morning, my clothes being dried and returned to me (cleaner, indeed, than they had been since I was given them), we made ready to depart and asked Don Miguel what was to pay. He said, nothing at all, and, when we protested, told us that we had brought more custom to his inn last night than he could normally expect in four or five days. Besides, we were friends of his cousin Enrique.

'Come again whenever you wish!' he invited us. Sam therefore agreed to spend a night there on his way back to Llanes from Santander.

This talk of Sam's return made my heart heavy, for it reminded me that our parting was now not far distant. However there was no profit in dwelling on this sad thought, and so we walked along to the church, where, we were entertained to observe, what must have been every soul in the village had now assembled to watch Father Ignacio setting off his morning rockets for mass.

'Pepe's ox has won me a larger congregation than any of my preachings,' he said to us cheerfully, after mass had been celebrated. 'But all is corn that comes to God's mill! I hope you are none the worse for your adventure, my boy?'

I said that I was a little stiff, but the ride to Santander would soon put that right.

At breakfast, Father Ignacio asked where we would lodge in Santander, supposing that I could not immediately find a ship that was about to embark for England. This thought cheered me. Perhaps I might have to wait some days, even a week!

We said we had given the matter of accommodation no thought, but would probably find some sailors' lodginghouse; Sam knew of several. Father Ignacio suggested instead that we stay at a monastery on the outskirts of the town, and he wrote us a note of recommendation to the prior. This reminded me of my promise to the duellist on the mountains above Oviedo. I still had the note he had given me for his stepdaughter in the Convent of the Esclavitud, and I asked Father Ignacio if he knew of its whereabouts.

'To be sure I do, my son; it is not a stone's throw from the monastery.'

Having given us instructions how to find them both, he bade us a cordial farewell, saying to Sam, 'I shall hope to see you again very soon,' and to me, 'God watch over you during all your adventures, my son, and give you always as stout a spirit as you showed yesterday.'

With which blessing we departed.

Santillana is no great distance from Santander – six leagues at the outside – and we reached the port before noon. What a different scene we found here from the small places we had hitherto visited! Santander seemed greater by far even than Santiago de Compostela, which was the largest town I had seen up to now, and indeed Sam told me that he believed thirty or forty thousand persons dwelt there. The town lies on the edge of the Basque provinces, and the Spanish they speak there is often hard to comprehend, but indeed there is such a mixture of races in the place that you may hear a different language spoken every minute of the day – French, Dutch, Italian, Greek, English, Portuguese, or German. Ships tie up at this port from all over the world, and the buildings along the quayside were more splendid than any I had ever seen. The bay, between hilly headlands, was full of shipping, and I thought that among such a tangle of masts and rigging there must lie a barque that would take me to England. Though sorrowful at the prospect of parting from Sam, I could not help but tingle with excitement at the thought of crossing the sea.

Sam pointed out to me various naval vessels, some large merchant ships, doubtless on their way to the Indies, fishing boats, and small coastal craft, and many more kinds of ship than I could count or name. Sam was easily able to distinguish one from another.

Within our first five minutes on the dock-side, moreover, he had encountered several acquaintances from his former life at sea, or as a longshoreman, and exchanged greetings with them in English, French, and Spanish. He talked to them, imparting and receiving news of other messmates, while I stood apart, feeling somewhat excluded.

Now I come to a sad part of my tale. I will not attempt to excuse my conduct, but will simply relate what happened, though it is painful to do so.

After we had met nine or ten of Sam's friends or old shipmates, and I was becoming somewhat restless at all the talk in which I had no part, Sam said to me,

'Felix, lad, this 'ud be a rare good time for ye to go on yon errand o' yours to the convent. Then I can have a crack here 'an yon wi' my old shipmates, and, come suppertime, 'tis a herring to a half-guinea but I'll ha' nosed out some barque that's about to set sail for Old England. I'll come out to the monastery and meet ye there, ye'll ha' done your business, and that way there's no time wasted.'

Of course what he said made sound sense. But I, feeling that this might be our last short space of time together, was terribly reluctant to leave him. Also, I am ashamed to confess it, I was jealous of all these friends of his, these other sailors whom he seemed to know so well, who had been known to him before he even met me or the Colomas family. True, he made me known to them, he said, 'This is my friend Felix, with whom I have travelled from Llanes,' but just the same I felt that with these others, these old mates of his, he had shared a life to which I would never belong; and this made me dejected and sore at heart.

I felt younger than all of them – ignorant – out of place – and unwanted.

Standing still, clutching the mule's bridle, I said, stubbornly,

'Why should I? I don't wish to go to the convent just yet. Why can I not stay with you, so as to see the ships? And then later we can both go to the monastery and I can leave my letter at the convent, for did not Father Ignacio say they were close together?'

My voice was surly and ungracious. I blush to admit that I was dangerously near breaking down, at the thought of the parting that might be so close.

Sam looked at me gravely. He had been unusually silent on the road from Santillana, wrapped in his own thoughts; to my surprise, and slight hurt, he had not once today referred to the rescue of Pepe's ox, nor commended my part in it. I felt this more keenly because in general none could be quicker than he to mark out the smallest merit and commend it.

Now it struck me that he looked very troubled; almost angry. But he said, mildly enough,

'Nay, lad, think. There might be a ship ready to sail on this evening's tide – 'twould be a shame if ye were obliged to miss it acos you'd not yet run your errand. I think it best ye go to the convent now.'

'There will be enough time! Let us find the ship

first – *then* I will go to the convent. I would rather stay with you, Sammy.'

'And I,' he said; he paused, then went on calmly, 'I had rather ye went, lad.'

At that I burst out in anger.

'You don't *wish* me to remain with you. Why?'

His friendly ugly face broke into its familiar smile, though his eyes were still grave.

'Why – for a start – ye cannot drag the poor mule along a lot o' catwalks an' gangplanks all around Santander harbour while we hunt for a likely vessel. Might as well stable her out at the monastery and give the poor beast a rest.'

This, though reasonable in its way, sounded like a mere pretext to me. I said obstinately,

'That is not your real reason for wishing to get rid of me, and you know it! Why don't you tell me the truth?'

Sam gave me a thoughtful look. Then he said,

'See here, Felix lad. You and I ha' been rare good messmates, ha'n't we?'

'Yes.'

'We've had some handsome times together – making music an' talking – times I've felt like a brother to you, and you to me I daresay?'

'Yes,' I said, swallowing.

'Ye've been gently reared, wi' a mort o' book-larning I never had – ye've learned me a power o' things, I never knew, nor was like to. But just the same, Felix,' Sammy said, and his voice suddenly gripped me, like a rope that is drawn tight, 'just the same, I *am* seven years older than ye be, I've that much start of 'ee, and there's things *I've* learned that ye have not, that ye must take on trust. And if I *was* your older brother, ye'd have to mind what I say. I think it best ye go to the convent now, Felix, and that's all there is to it. Leave your note for the man's stepdaughter, then stable the mule at the monastery, and bide in the guest-chamber there till I come. I *wish* ye to do that Felix, I'll not be longer than I can help, I promise ye that.'

And he turned sharp on his heel and limped away.

I stood on one spot with my knuckles clenched, staring like a fool, for some few minutes after he went off. My heart was beating rat-a-tat, my throat was tightened up with anger, as it had not been since I left Villaverde. If there had been a stone at hand, I believe I could have hurled it after him! But there was not, for there I was on the wide, paved quayside with not a soul about, and the mule tugging impatiently against the rein over my arm, as if to say, 'What *is* all this?'

In the end her tugging reminded me that – as Sam had pointed out – I could not lead her through the network of mooring ropes and bollards to find a ship for myself – as had been my first angry intention.

But I thought, 'I am not a child! Why should he treat me like one? I have made my own way as far as this – I can very well find my own ship! I will take the letter to the convent directly; then leave the mule in the monastery stable; then I will come back here and arrange for my own passage to England. I will show Sam that I don't need him to see after my affairs.'

Accordingly I was turning away from the quay-side to take the eastward road to Bilbao, beside which, Father Ignacio had said, the convent was situated, when I heard myself accosted by a soft voice that said,

'The young Senor wishes to travel to England?'

I was somewhat startled, for I had thought that no one was at hand.

Then I saw a small man rise up from behind a great coil of rope, where he had been seated. He was a skinny, weatherbeaten, and shrivelled-looking little monkey of a fellow, who wore a red handkerchief rolled round his head, a long cloak, much torn and patched, sandals on his bare dirty feet, and a kind of tattered tinsel waistcoat under the cloak.

He did not speak in Spanish, but in a mixture of the Basque language and French. Since Bernie had some Basque blood (all the best cooks come from the Basque country) I had learned some of the language and could just make out what he meant.

I said,

'Why yes, I do, senor. Do you know of a ship that is sailing to England? I cannot pay a large fare, however – I have very little money.'

This I said out of a sense of caution, not wishing to sound too eager.

'*Errequina*! That matters little. If a ship sails,

224

she sails. Some friends of mine may be putting out for England and Ireland tonight. On a fine ship, a grand ship, a splendid ship! The young gentleman would glide across the Gulf of Gascony like a feather on a gull's wing! It would cost him no more than twenty dollars.'

I had saved more than that, from the profits of our music-making at Llanes. However I haggled and said,

'I can pay no more than twelve.'

'Fifteen! For fifteen we carry the young lordship in as much comfort as the King of the Indies!'

'Very well. What is the name of your friends' ship?'

'May it please your honour, she is called the *Guipuzcoa*.'

'And where can I find her?'

'My young master, she is not in port yet. She will dock this afternoon, if it please God, will take on water and provisions, and will leave on the night tide.'

'And where will she berth, while she is here?'

The small man looked around him warily. There was something about his tattered and furtive appearance – and also about the exceedingly swift arrival and departure of the ship – which led me to believe that his friends must be smugglers; a considerable wine- and brandy-smuggling trade went on, I knew, between the Basque ports and England. I guessed that was why the passenger fee was so low, since there might be some hazard to the crossing, if the ship was pursued by Revenue boats. But the fee suited my purse, and the risk certainly troubled me not at all; it would be an added adventure, in fact.

The small man's answer to my question confirmed my certainty that his friends were engaged in running contraband goods.

'The *Guipuzcoa* will berth where she can, my young senor. Probably, since she remains at Santander so short a time, she will not come in to the harbour at all, but will anchor out yonder by the island.'

He pointed to a rocky height of land by the western arm of the bay; I had taken it for a headland.

'How could I get myself out there? And how shall I know if your friends' ship has arrived?'

'Why, as to that, if the young lordship would condescend to meet me here later today, I would be able to take him out to the island, if the *Guipuzcoa* has docked.'

'Very well. At what time?'

He scanned the sky, and then the harbour-mouth, with his narrow, creased black eyes.

'Just at the hour of dusk. When a black thread can no longer be distinguished from a white one.'

'Bueno! I will see you here at dusk.'

He nodded, and slipped rapidly away, scurrying like a lizard into the crack between two tall warehouses.

Feeling highly delighted with myself, in that I had successfully negotiated something that Sam had seemed to believe might prove so troublesome,

I looked about, hoping that I might see his distant figure. But of course he was long gone out of sight.

Accordingly I scrambled on to the mule's back and kicked my heels into her sides, turning her head towards Bilbao. Only fifteen dollars! Sam had expected that I might have to pay quite twice as much.

I chuckled, imagining his face of astonishment when I told him that the matter was all arranged, and so easily.

After five minutes' ride along the Bilbao road, the town was mostly behind me; I had a rocky hill on my right and some marshes on my left, with great banks of feather-headed rushes on either side of the road, pale gold like the fur on old Gato's under-belly.

A heavy sadness came over me, as I remembered my old cat – how very far away he seemed! Over the mountains and the valleys, past the towns and the estuaries. And would soon be farther still.

Suddenly I felt ashamed and angry with myself that I had parted from Sam in such a mood of resentment. He meant well, I was now sure of that. Very probably – it now struck me – he had wanted me out of the way while he bargained for a lower passage-fee, which, doubtless, knowing the ways of the sea, he believed he would be able to secure more easily than I should.

Well – I decided – the moment I see him I will tell him that I am sorry for my anger. But still, he should have told me that was his intention! It is partly his fault for treating me as a child.

Now, beyond the bowing golden heads of the rushes, I perceived two clusters of grey buildings, on either side of the road, which I guessed must be the monastery and the convent, each surrounded by a high stone wall, each with an arched gateway and a barred gate.

The monastery was somewhat bigger, and had a tower on its chapel. Looking through the gate, I could see two brown-robed Brothers talking inside. So I knocked, and presented Father Ignacio's note to the porter, who told me that the prior was at present in the town on business, but that I might in the meantime take my mule to the stable, and would be given supper and a bed in the guesthouse at any hour after eight in the evening.

I thought of explaining that I might not need their supper and bed, if the *Guipuzcoa* arrived as expected – but since I was not certain of that yet, I resolved not to mention the possibility.

Meanwhile I saw to the stabling of the mule, gave her a feed and a drink, then walked back around the cloister and out through the front gate to visit the convent.

This, I saw at once, was much smaller and shabbier, and had fewer inmates that the monastery. Indeed there was no portress at all, so, after my knock had gone unanswered, I made bold to walk through the open gate and past the empty lodge into a panelled parlour, which had a tiled floor and smelt freshly of beeswax, but was also empty. In one wall there was a barred grille, but no one behind it.

I called out, 'Is anybody there?' but received no reply.

Walking out again, into a small herb garden with apple trees, which occupied the central square, I hesitated outside another doorway, encouraged to do so by a warm smell of baking which came from it.

'Is that you, Sister Dolores?' called a voice. 'Fetch me a straw from the broom, will you?'

This request instantly transported me back to Bernie's cosy red kitchen, full of the smell of baking cakes. How many times had I heard Bernie call to me, or Pedro, or whoever happened to be at hand, 'Quick, bring me a straw from the broom, I want to try this cake.'

Without thinking, I plucked a dry grass from the herb border and walked inside holding it.

'Ay, Dios mio, who are *you*?' exclaimed the same voice in astonishment.

I saw a short, stout nun, with a friendly wrinkled face and a white apron tied over her black robes, who was just lifting what looked like a large butter-cake from the oven. At sight of me, she nearly dropped it, but recovered, and placed it on a table. I offered her the straw, and, without a word, she took it from me, wiped it on her apron, and carefully slid its end deep into the middle of the cake. Taking it out again she peered at it short-sightedly, sniffed it, and then, nodding her head, said with satisfaction,

'Very good! Done to a turn! Now tell me, who are *you*, my young sparrow, and how do you come to hop into my kitchen? I suppose you would like a crumb, hmn?'

When she smiled, her face wrinkled up even more, like a tortilla. She handed me a little pastry-cake, sprinkled over with nuts, at the sight and smell of which Assistenta poked her head forth from my jacket and exclaimed,

'Amo, amare, amavi, amatum!'

'Ay de mi!' exclaimed the old nun. 'Here's another of them! And I suppose that one wants something too?'

She handed Assistenta a crust of bread, which the parrot took gravely, stepping out on to the table and holding it with her claw.

I ate my cake, which proved to have marzipan in the middle, and was one of the best I have ever tasted.

'Thank you, Sister,' I said, licking my fingers. 'You make wonderful cakes! But I didn't come for crumbs – I came with a letter for Sister Annunciata. May I give it to her?'

'Ah – ay – no, that you can't!' the old nun exclaimed. 'Sister Annunciata has left us.'

'*Left* you?' I said in a fright, wondering if she had died – but the old nun explained,

'She has gone, two days ago, to our House in Madrid, for she had some family business to settle. Now I daresay she will stay on in Madrid, but it is a pity. There was not enough for her to do here, it was too quiet. There are not many of us left, and we are all too old.'

'I am sorry she is not here,' I said, disconcerted

by this news. 'If I leave the note, can it be sent to her in Madrid? It is from her stepfather.'

'Oho?' exclaimed the Sister, looking at me curiously. 'You have a note for Annunciata from her stepfather?'

'Yes, senora.'

'Just a moment, my boy.'

She went to an inner doorway and shouted,

'Sister Angeles!'

A distant voice replied,

'What is it, Sister Benedicta?'

'Could you leave polishing and come here a moment if you please?'

After a few moments another black-robed Sister appeared, even more elderly. She carried a beeswax-smelling cloth, and limped heavily with a stick.

The cook-Sister said to her,

'Sister Angeles, here is a boy who looks like a day-old chicken. He bears a letter to Sister Annunciata from her stepfather.'

'Ave Maria! He certainly does look like a day-old chick,' said the second old lady, after inspecting me critically. 'He *must* be the one!'

'Should we call Sister Superior?'

'No, why wake her? She is sleeping, and she has so much pain and gets so little sleep, poor thing. This must be the right boy!'

'What are you speaking about, senoras?' I asked, greatly mystified.

'Do you have the letter there, child? The letter for Annunciata?'

'Certainly I do,' said I, and passed it to Sister Angeles, who inspected it carefully, nodded her head, and said,

'Very good! This shall be sent to Madrid. Now, my child, we have a letter for you, if you will tell me your name?'

'Of course,' said I, even more puzzled. 'My name is Felix Brooke. But from whom can you possibly have a letter for me?'

'Why, from the stepfather of Annunciata, to be sure! Wait here, a moment, and Sister Benedicta will fetch it.'

I waited, in a ferment of curiosity, while stout Sister Benedicta bustled out of the room with a swish of robes and a slap of rope-soled shoes. While she was away, Assistenta, thoughtfully regarding the butter-cake remarked,

'Two o'clock!'

A moment later we heard the chime of the monastery clock.

'Madre de Dios!' exclaimed Sister Angeles. 'Your bird keeps good time! We could use her here! It is a long time since the convent clock slowed down and stopped.'

I hardly paid heed to her. I was thinking of that strange, calm, grizzle-bearded man whom I had met in the mountains up above Oviedo, who had invited me to accompany him on his treasure-hunt. What had befallen him, I wondered. And why should he write to me? Had I even told him my name? After some thought, I believed that I remembered doing so, while explaining my intention to go to England and search for my father's family.

Perhaps – I thought suddenly, and my heart beat faster – perhaps he had come across, or had recalled, some clue, relating to my father, which he had taken this means of transmitting to me! And I thought, what a fortunate thing that I had kept my promise to bring his letter to the convent!

Sister Benedicta returned with a dirty folded square of paper which she handed to me.

'Shall you object if I read it here, senoras?' I asked.

'Not in the least, my child. Sit and read at your case,' said Sister Benedicta, pushing a stool towards me, and she began chopping herbs on a board.

So I sat on the stool and read:

'To Felix Brooke: From Astorga. It will be a marvel if this reaches you, for I have no money to pay the carriers, a pair of the most surly-looking Maragatos I have ever encountered, and therefore must trust to their good-nature. Also, it has been written in snatches, on the way to my trial at Oviedo, from which, almost certainly I shall be sent to the galleys.'

Alas, poor man, thought I – what has become of him? Did he not find his treasure, after all? I wondered how he had persuaded the Maragatos to carry his letter. They are a strange people, who dress like Moors, shave their heads, on which they

233

wear wide-brimmed hats, and they carry goods and mail all over Spain, preferring this trade to the hardship of tilling the stone fields around Astorga. Though surly, they have the reputation of being very faithful to a trust – and, it seemed, had proved so in this case.

I read on:

'As you may guess, I did not succeed in removing the treasure. There it still lies, under ten feet of snow – enough gold to have saved General Moore's army. The thought of the waste enrages me – but in any case, the treasure is no use to *me*, for my nights out in the mountain snows have brought on a lung-rot which, in all likelihood, will carry me off before the convict-chain even reaches Oviedo.

'Listen, Felix Brooke! I am writing to warn you. If this letter comes to your hands, I owe you a good turn, for it will mean that you faithfully delivered my note to my step-daughter.

'While taking measures to remove the treasure, I had the ill-luck to be caught by a band of highway robbers, and, while with them, was arrested by carabineers, and removed to the town of Villaverde where your grandfather is Governor and Corregidor (as you know). Your grandfather, questioning me, discovered that I was not a member of the band, but told me he had instructions to keep me in confinement. A message had been circulated from the alcalde at Oviedo, giving my description, and a warrant had been issued for my arrest, on suspicion of having murdered my comrade. I, of course, denied having murdered him, and said that it had been a fair duel, of which you had been the witness.

'Your grandfather seemed greatly shaken at receiving this news of you, and asked many questions regarding your destination and intentions.'

A singular feeling of sorrow and regret stirred in my heart at this unexpected mention of my grandfather. How very strange it was, thought I, that he had encountered the grizzle-bearded man, and that they had spoken together of me.

I read again:

'I was not treated harshly while in your grandfather's charge,' the letter went on, 'but was imprisoned in a stable-loft. During my confinement there I was visited secretly by an elderly lady called Dona Isadora de los Campinos de la Fuenta la Higuera, who informed me that she wished to make further inquiries about you. She told me – which your grandfather had not – that news had come from the authorities at Oviedo regarding your incarceration there under suspicion of having killed my comrade – for which I am most heartily sorry. I told her that this was a false accusation and that I was prepared to testify to your innocence. But then she informed me that you had escaped from the jail at Oviedo – for which, accept my congratulations, my boy! – and she told me therefore that my testimony on your behalf was not needed, since you were already at liberty. I said in any case, since I had killed my comrade in fair fight, and was prepared to say so, there could be no more question of your being accused of the crime.

'What was my horror, then, when this evil woman invited me to lay the crime on *you*, and thus free myself! She wishes your death, I soon discovered – and indeed she promised me my liberty as well as a handsome sum of money, if I would bear false witness against you – or even follow you to Santander and assassinate you!

'Therefore I write this letter to warn you, my boy, that this woman is your bitter enemy, and will stop at nothing to make away with you. Since I refused her blood-money, she may find other agents. Alas, because I had told your grandfather of your intentions, she knows of your plan to take ship from Santander. My advice to you, therefore, is to be continually upon your guard, especially in Santander, and to take ship without delay and leave Spain as soon as you may.

Your friend, George Smith.'

Having read this letter once, I read it again, for I was so dazed and amazed that I could hardly take in its meaning – or believe it when I had done so.

That my great-aunt Isadora was a mean, malicious, sanctimonious, tale-bearing, prying, ill-natured old hag, I had long known, but that she was actually plotting my *death*, I still found hard to credit. And yet I remembered Sam's comment when I had told him my story: 'If *you* warn't there, her grandson 'ud get the property.' Sam had been right, it seemed. 'I'll lay she be main glad you've slipped your cable,' he had said. But she had not even been content with that! I still found it difficult to believe that thin, grey, pale-eyed woman had harboured such a devilish plan.

No wonder, I reflected, taking a survey of my life at Villaverde during the past two or three years, no wonder my grandfather had been less and less friendly to me, no wonder he had become so sad and stern and withdrawn from me. Doubtless the old she-vulture was croaking away in his ear the whole time, telling her poisonous tales, blackening my name.

And no wonder, too, I recollected, that she had been so startled, and even alarmed, when she saw that I had the papers of my father's that Bernie had given me. She must have feared they might prove that my parents were truly married and that I was their legitimate son. No wonder she had seemed so relieved when she saw that the writing was impossible to read!

Thinking of the papers made me wish to look at them again, and I pulled them out of the little oiled-skin pouch that Juana Colomas had kindly made me, in which to carry my book and papers, so as to protect them from the weather.

I said to Sister Benedicta, who was still placidly chopping away at her thyme and lemon – to this day I cannot smell herbs without thinking of Dona Isadora and her wickedness –

'May I ask, of your kindness, Sister, if you could read the words on this paper?'

'I will try, my child,' she said, 'and gladly,' laying down her two-handled chopping blade. She took the papers and pored over them short-sightedly, but was obliged to confess after a while that she could not make out a single word. Nor could Sister Angeles, nor a couple of the other old religious, whom they presently summoned for a consultation.

Greatly disappointed, I thanked them and put the papers carefully away again, then wondered what I had best do. All of a sudden my situation seemed so perilous that I hardly dared set foot outside the convent gate, in case great-aunt Isadora's hired bravos darted out from some alley-way and stabbed me to the heart!

Then I felt a great coward, and tried to laugh at such foolish fears. Had I not come all this way, through more perils and adventures than great-aunt Isadora could possibly dream of? Had I seen any signs of assassins prowling after me through the streets of Santander?

I had not – but how, I wondered, would I know an assassin if I saw him? – except by his knife in my ribs. Whereas *he* would know *me*, I reflected glumly, without the least difficulty, as the holy Sisters had done: 'a boy resembling a day-old-chick'. Not for the first time I regretted my conspicuous yellow hair and short stature. Then something else occurred to me.

I said to Sister Benedicta,

'Sister, you seemed to be expecting me? How could that have been?'

'Why, my child,' she said comfortably, 'you must have been some little time, have you not, on the road to Santander from wherever it was that you met Sister Annunciata's stepfather?'

'Yes – yes, that is true.' I thought of the day lost fording the flooded river, my wanderings in the mountains, and the three weeks passed at Llanes.

'Four days ago,' Sister Benedicta went on, 'the news reached our Sister Annunciata of her stepfather's death from lung disease. He wrote her a few last lines on his deathbed, bequeathed her some property in Madrid, and recommended her to look out for a boy like a day-old-chick who might come bearing an earlier letter – if he had not already arrived – asked her to give him the letter which you have just read, and to urge him – you – to leave the country, for safety's sake. Which we would have done, my child, before you quitted this place.'

All the old nuns gazed at me benevolently, and I remarked with some heat,

'Sister Annunciata's stepfather wrote to warn me that my great-aunt is plotting my death – and the best advice is that I should escape from the country? Am I not to have justice against that evil woman?'

'God will look after that part of the business in His own way, my child,' said the oldest of the group, a frail, white-faced old shred of a woman like a withered leaf, who was called Sister Maria. 'It is not for you to concern yourself in the matter – indeed your best course is to save her from further wrong-doing by putting yourself out of her reach. God will punish the sinner in His own time, never fear.'

This seemed to me very annoying advice, but since no other course appeared open to me at present, I felt myself obliged to take it.

I thought of writing to my grandfather – but what could I say? 'Dear Grandfather, Dona Isadora is a liar and a would-be murderer. She tried to persuade Senor Smith to assassinate me.' He would never believe such stuff! And besides, my doing such a thing seemed disagreeably like Isadora's own methods.

However, these thoughts put me in mind of my promise to write to my grandfather from Santander, and I asked the old Sisters if I might have the use of a pen and ink and a scrap of paper. These were hospitably provided and I was led to the parlour, where, sitting at a small, highly-polished table, I wrote:

'Dear Grandfather: I am now in Santander, about to take ship for England and seek my father's family. I earned the money for the passage by my own work and have not begged or stolen or disgraced you in any way.

'I am sorry now for some of the tricks that I played on you and Grandmother.' I added, 'But not for those on Dona Isadora,' then decided to scratch it out again. I ended, 'Please give my best greetings to my grandmother and to yourself – your respectful Grandson.'

When I had folded and sealed this letter, the Sisters very kindly promised to see that it was sent to Villaverde. I offered to give them money, but they refused, saying that they had few needs, whereas I, going over the sea, might have many. So then, visited by a sudden notion, I said,

'Sisters, would you like this parrot? She is very good at telling the time, and knows many things about healing herbs and the planets. To tell truth, I would be glad to find a good home for her; I should be anxious, taking her across the sea, in case she was overtaken by some mischance.'

In fact I had thought of giving her to Sam, but decided she would be of more use to the Sisters, who were delighted to receive her, and promised to look after her carefully. I thanked them for their help and hospitality, then returned across the road to the monastery, where, to my rage, the porter called me as I passed through the gate, and said,

'Your friend with the lame leg was here while you were gone. He left this note for you.'

'Where is he now? When did he leave?'

241

'How should I know?' The porter shrugged. 'He left eight or nine minutes ago. He didn't tell *me* where he was going.'

Hastily I read the note, which was only a few lines.

> 'Arranged passage for you on English ship, the *Beauty of Bristol*, sailing two days from now to Bristol which is right close to Bath so will be handy for you. Passage fee will be thirty dollars. *On no account* leave the monastery till I see you. I will be back by nine. S.P.'

Now I was in a most awkward predicament and could have gnashed my teeth at my slowness in returning from the convent. If only I had returned a few minutes earlier! Indeed I ran back to the gate and looked along the road to the town, but Sam was not to be seen. Could he have heard, somehow, of Dona Isadora's schemes – was that why he wanted me not to leave the monastery? Why could he not have waited?

'Why did you not say I was just across the road?' I demanded of the porter, a big, stupid ox of a fellow, who replied, raising his brows,

'I didn't know that, did I? I wasn't looking where you went. Your mate asked where you were – I said, likely you'd gone back to town.'

No wonder Sam had left again so quickly; now he was probably scouring the town for me.

I was terribly tempted to go after him – but then I thought how slender a chance there would be of coming up with him in that maze of ships and docks.

Trying to curb my impatience, I sat down and wrote him a note.

'Dear Sam, I have had a warning to leave Santander without delay, as my great-aunt Isadora is trying to have me murdered. You were right about her, you see! It is kind of you to arrange my berth on the English ship, but I have already found one for myself on a Basque ship, the *Guipuzcoa*, which leaves tonight (I hope) & the fare is only fifteen dollars, so I had best take it and get clear away, though I do not like to run away, and hope the old Fiend burns in Hell. I shall write to my grandfather about her from England. Dear Sam, I hate to part from you, especially without a Goodbye, after all the fine songs we have sung together. When I find my English folk, I shall ask them to have the Law on your wicked uncle and then you, too, can come home.

Your affec. Friend, Felix.'

The writing of this took me some little time – in fact I had to re-write it three times, for at first it sounded too gloatingly triumphant over my success in finding a ship for myself, and then too babyishly sad at parting from Sam – in fact I had much ado to prevent my pen from begging him to come to England also, although I knew he must not.

At last it was done, and I left it with the porter, and a few coins for his trouble. I had a little time, still, so I sat reading my father's book in the cloister, longing for Sam to appear before it was too late. But he did not.

Then I went to the stable and said goodbye to my bad-tempered friend, rubbing her nose and giving her a couple of maize-cakes which Sister Benedicta had tucked into my pocket.

'Take care of Sam,' I said to her softly. 'Don't play any of your tricks on him, but carry him safely back to Llanes – ' at which her only response was a snort – as if *she* knew very well what the future held in store for Sam, and for her, and for me too!

Then, since dusk was now beginning to fall, and in a very short time it would not be possible to distinguish a black thread from a white one, I walked away along the road back to the city, looking out vigilantly on all sides, and behind me too, as I went quickly and quietly towards the harbour.

# 8

Despite my anxieties I reached the port without hazard or hindrance, and sought again the spot where I had encountered the small red-kerchiefed man. I found the place at once, and easily, for he was there ahead of me, jigging impatiently from foot to foot, and looking all round him with his quick, darting black eyes.

'Very good, very good, it is the young senor, follow me if you please, for the ship has already arrived and the captain wishes to make passage again without delay!' he exclaimed in a rush of words the moment he saw me; and, snatching at my hand in his impatience to be off, he began leading me, almost at a run, along the sides of wharves, over narrow catwalks, in between great piles of timber, among casks and bales and crates, until I was thoroughly confused and had no notion whether we were going east or west or north or south, but could only follow him in blind trust. I was slower than he liked, though, first because I was burdened with one of my two saddle-bags (I had left the other, the one with the food in it, for Sam), and also because I was still hoping to get a glimpse of Sam and longingly craned my neck this way and that, as we came out from behind ships and crossed bridges. Nowhere did I see him, though, and the little man crying, 'Hasten, hasten!' urged me at a faster pace.

At last we descended a flight of weed-encrusted steps, and stepped into a small boat which lay moored at the bottom. I was hardly in the boat before the man had untied the mooring-rope, pushed off, and begun rowing away across the tossing green water.

Now, through gathering dusk, I saw that we must have made our way to the western side of the harbour, for the town with all its lights lay behind us and to our right. Ahead of us a dark bulk of land began to loom up which must, I guessed, be the island off which the *Guipuzcoa* lay at anchor.

After ten minutes' rowing our boat bumped on a sandy bottom, and my guide jumped over the gunwale and pulled the boat up on to a shelving beach. Then he assisted me to disembark and bade me follow again. This I did, across the beach, along a twisting path through bushes, up, up, and then down again on to a small, slippery jetty and thus to where, I suddenly realised, a ship lay moored, so low in the water that, behind the spit of land we had just crossed, she must be almost invisible from the main harbour.

My first impression of the *Guipuzcoa* was her smallness. Could a ship of that size – she looked scarcely larger than a farm waggon – really be capable of braving the wild Gulf of Gascony and the treacherous English Channel?

As we threaded our way along by the shadowy creek where she lay hidden, all I could see of the ship was a mast, a complicated tangle of rigging, a carved figurehead with dim indications of gilding on it, and more traces of carving and gilding along the deck-rail. A few dark figures were flitting to and fro along a gangplank, carrying stores or cargo – sacks, casks, bottles, boxes, a ball of tow, a coil of rope.

My guide, approaching the gangplank, said in a low voice,

'I have brought him.'

This message, it seemed, passed rapidly through the ship, and in a moment, from among the dusky confusion of stores and tackle on the deck, a cloaked figure somewhat taller than the rest detached itself and crossed the gangplank.

A deep voice said,

'This is the young senor who wishes to cross to England? Be pleased to step on board, your worship! We shall make sail in a few moments.'

I turned, and would have rewarded my guide, but to my surprise he was nowhere to be seen.

'The young lordship had best come into the caboose,' remarked the deep voice. A hand grasped mine and led me over the gangplank and into a kind of deck-house, where I saw that the deep-voiced man was tall, with hair like tar under a kerchief, and that he was shrouded in a brown serge boat-cloak.

I was glad to get into the deck-house, for the small deckspace outside seemed completely occupied by all the things that were being carried on board, and while the hasty stowage continued, I seemed in danger every minute either of tripping over something or being knocked flying.

The caboose was a small windowless place, smelling of hot oil and garlic, where an old man was blowing up a turf fire in a clay box. Over the fire dangled an iron pot. A talc-lined lantern swung on a hook from the ceiling and gave dim illumination to the scene.

'Sit there, young master,' said the tall man who had led me in, and after giving some rapid instructions to the other, in the Basque language, he went out again, shutting the door behind him.

I perched myself on a wicker hamper and watched the old man cutting up bacon, pimentos, fish, and onions, which he tossed into the pot, together with herbs and chick peas. The broth he was making smelt very savoury and reminded me that I had not eaten – except for Sister Benedicta's cake – since our scanty breakfast with Father Ignacio, which now seemed a very long time ago.

Outside, the bumping of stores being dropped on the deck seemed to have lessened.

'Now we shan't be long, your honour,' mumbled the old man in my direction – it was the first notice he had taken of my presence. Since he was quite toothless, and spoke the Basque language – addressing me as 'Khauna', 'lord' – it was not too easy to understand him.

He went back to stirring his soup, mumbling out the verse of a song, tunefully enough, in spite of his great age and lack of teeth. I knew the song, for it was one that Sammy had picked up in Bilbao, and which he had taught me:

> I chasca urac aundi
> Estu ondoric agueri –

'The waters of the sea are boundless, and their bottom cannot be seen.'

I joined in with the old man, mainly to cheer myself, for, to tell truth, such a reminder of Sam, from whom I had just parted, very likely for ever, made me feel so stricken with sorrow that I could have howled like a dog.

At the sound of my voice the old man gave me a great glance of wonder. Besides excelling at cookery, the Basques have a high esteem for music. Father Agustin once told me that the Roman name for the Basques, *Cantabri*, meant 'sweet singers'. At all events, after I had sung with him, the old man seemed to accord me much more respect than he had done previously.

Presently, becoming impatient of my confinement in this small place, I would have opened the door, but the old man mumbled,

'Wait a little, let the young lordship wait! Later he shall see all that is to be seen!' and he waved his hands about to suggest that just now the crew were so busy on deck that I should only be in the way.

Rather reluctantly I sat down again on the uncomfortable wicker basket and stared round at the caboose. Overhead, beside the lantern, swung a dead kingfisher, suspended by its beak. Sam, I remembered, had told me how some ignorant sailors believe that a kingfisher hung up in this way will always turn its breast to leeward.

'How many are there in the crew of this ship, old Grandfather?' I asked the cook politely.

'Four, my young lordship – the Captain, whom you have seen, and three others – all brave, skilful sailors, thank the saints. And two other passengers.'

'For what port in England is the ship bound?'

'We go to Falmouth, lordship, and then on to Black Harbour in Ireland.'

'And your cargo?'

At this question the old man smiled his toothless grin, and drew a finger across his throat, as if to convey that answering me would be more than his life was worth. From which I guessed that my first conjecture, as to their being smugglers, was a correct one.

Now it suddenly occurred to me that since I had come on board the *Guipuzcoa* nobody had asked me for any passage money, although I had it ready, wrapped in a small piece of rag (while the rest of my savings were hidden in the false lining of a belt that Juana had made for me).

This fact – that no one had asked me for any money – seemed to me both strange and disturbing. The more I thought about it, the less I liked it. These were wild lawless men, the brigands of the sea; their ship was so small that there scarcely seemed room for extra passengers, besides the cargo they carried; was it likely that they would take any person on board without making perfectly certain that he had the money to pay for his trip?

'What kind of a ship is this, old Grandfather?' I asked the cook, to conceal from him, and perhaps from myself, my growing uneasiness.

'It is an *urca*, my young master – a Biscayan felucca,' he replied.

This also went to confirm my guess about the men's calling; Sam had told me that the felucca, or Biscay hooker, was the craft most commonly used by smugglers, for it is equally at home in the open ocean or in creeks and hidden, enclosed waters – a lateen-rigged ship that manoeuvres very easily on account of its long helm, and can be rowed as readily as it can be sailed.

'And what course shall we take to England?'

'We cross the Gulf of Gascony, lord, steer west of the Isle of Ushant, and then, bearing northwards, steering for the pole, we cross the English Channel and come to Falmouth.'

'How long will that take us?'

'That is as God wills and the winds blow. Perhaps four days, perhaps eight – we shall see.'

At least, I thought, the old man seemed friendly enough, and did not display any threatening attitude. Perhaps – having me secure on board – my smuggler-hosts were biding their time to ask me for more money, confident that I must give them all I had. Perhaps, I began to think, it would have been wiser to wait for two days, lying concealed in the monastery, and then embark on Sam's *Beauty of Bristol.* Had I been a fool? Was it plain obstinacy that led me to entrust myself to this questionable little ship?

To distract my mind from these uncomfortable thoughts, and the possibility that I might arrive in my father's land without a penny to my name and be obliged to beg my way – I opened my bundle and pulled out the second volume of *Susan.* During my re-reading of this work I had now reached the highly dramatic moment when poor young Miss Susan, paying a visit to her grand friends, is suddenly turned out-of-doors by their angry father, who has hitherto shown her nothing but favour and civility. She is utterly at a loss to know how she can have earned his displeasure and, penniless and wretched, has to make the best of her way home across England. I read all this with deep interest. Still, I could not help contrasting her lot with mine. She, at least, had a friend to lend her the coach fare home; she also had a loving family waiting to welcome her at the end of her journey; whereas, what did I have? Privately I considered that Miss Susan was none too badly off; though I did think it unkind of the old General to turn her out so abruptly.

Musing in this way I glanced up from the page to find the cook's eyes fixed on me with as wild a look in them as if I had flames coming out of my ears.

'Ay, ave Maria!' he muttered, crossing himself three times. 'Is the young lord a sorcerer? Do not cast a spell on poor old Luc or his broth, your lordship, I beg!'

It seemed that he had never seen any person reading a book before, and therefore took it to be some manual of witchcraft. As he stirred his broth he kept taking terrified peeps at me, then fortifying himself with gulps from a flask he wore attached to his belt. And all the time he muttered to himself about the spirits of drowned sailors, who may be seen flying through the mist, carrying lighted candles in their hands, and who bewitch living sailors with their evil arts, so that they too jump into the waves and perish. He seemed to think that I might be in league with these spirits, or even be one of them in disguise.

It struck me that his superstitious fear might be turned to good account, so I said calmly,

'Do not distress yourself, old Luc. I have a little power over the *Estadea* – ' (this was a Gallegan name for these spirits which I had learned from Pedro) ' – and I will do my best to see that they do not hurt you while I am aboard the *Guipuzcoa*.'

Later I was to remember these idle words.

The old man's terrors were somewhat pacified by this, though he still eyed my little book as if it had been a viper that might shoot a long neck across the room and bite him.

Now the tall captain reappeared in the doorway and said,

'Luc! Give the young lord a bit of bread and a mouthful of spirit.' He indicated with a jerk of his head a wicker-covered flask that hung from a nail on the wall, and said to me,

'It will be rough when we are out at sea. An east wind is blowing up. The young senor is not used to a sea passage? I have sailed the Cantabrian Gulf for thirty years, but even I still become queasy if I do not settle my stomach with a drop of *aguardiente* beforehand.'

Then somebody called to him from the forward end of the ship, and he left again, shutting the door.

'Thirty years?' the old man muttered. 'Chacurra! I have been at sea *seventy years*, and the Mar Cantabrico still makes my heart lodge between my shoulder-blades! But that liquor in the flask is not good for the young lordship. Here – have a dram of my *ardoa* – it is better – it is better – ' and he detached the flask from his belt and passed it to me. I took a small gulp of the fiery liquor it contained, and ate the piece of maize bread he handed me.

Now a voice outside cried, '*Andamos!*' The ship gave one violent heave, and then began a regular dipping motion – I guessed that our mooring ropes had been cast off, and that we were being towed out to the creek mouth by a smaller boat.

Soon the *Guipuzcoa* started to pitch and roll with an increasingly lively motion. Old Luc bustled

254

about securing his utensils and stuffing loose odds and ends inside baskets. From the wind blowing against the caboose I concluded that we must be nearly beyond the mouth of the bay.

Then, all of a sudden, we heard loud shouts, several men's voices together, some hailing from a distance, some from the deck of the ship.

'*Hein?*' muttered old Luc. 'What is to do now?'

There was a jarring bump – I guessed that it was a boat, hitting the side of the ship. My heart began to bang against my ribs, for I thought, suppose the authorities from Oviedo, having had word of my arrival in Santander, have sent alguacils to arrest me for the death of the man on the mountain? Now that poor Senor Smith is dead, there is nobody to give evidence that I am innocent! Or perhaps this is some agent of great-aunt Isadora, sent after me to secure me?

All these wild thoughts tumbled through my head as I felt the *Guipuzcoa* check her progress, and then there was a thud and a lurch as somebody jumped on board, and a fresh outburst of angry discussion just outside the door of the caboose.

I could hardly contain my curiosity, and old Luc stood with his head cocked sideways and his spoon in mid air. Prudence withheld me from opening the door and looking out. Suppose an alguacil had come on board?

Then, to my astonishment, I heard a thoroughly familiar voice exclaim,

'Well, you have got me now – having cast off my friends so rudely – so you will just have to make the best of my presence – unless you wish to put back to Santander and lose the tide? Where is my friend? I wish to join him.'

'Sammy!' I gasped out, dropping *Susan* in my amazement. I ran to the door, just as it opened, and Sammy limped in, his hair and face all wet with spray. When he saw me, a smile of relief spread over his ugly face.

'Eh, there you are then, lad! I'll be bound you thought I'd missed the boat – an' so I should a' done, had not a good-hearted pair o' shipmates rowed me out as fast as if Old Scratch were swimming arter us!'

'But – ' I began, utterly bewildered, 'But you were not – ' Then I saw Sam's finger on his lips, and his eyes glance past me in warning, as he saw old Luc. The tall captain followed him in, and began haranguing us both in loud angry Basque. It was very inconvenient of Sam to have come on board – he had not the space for more than three passengers, he had not expected a fourth, nothing had been said to him of Sam's coming, and so on.

To all of which Sammy calmly replied,

'Very good, Capitano! If you do not want me and my friend, put us ashore! We shall be sorry to miss a passage on such a beautiful ship as yours, but there are other ships, after all.'

Grumbling, the captain withdrew, beckoning Luc to follow him, and a long, muttered confabulation broke out, farther along the deck.

'They are wondering whether to put back,' Sammy whispered. 'I dinna think they will dare, though – the Revenue chaps are after 'em, see. I reckon they'd be glad enough to make eastwards an' drop you and me on the French coast, but the wind ain't favourable for that.'

'But Sammy – ' I whispered, '*Why did you come? You* don't want to go to England!'

I would have liked to believe it was because he found he did not care to part from me – but I knew Sam too well to think he would act in such a feckless manner. His face was very pale, despite the smile, and the look in his eyes told me that his reason was a graver one than that.

'Ye've run yourself into a real nest of adders, here, lad,' he whispered.

'I know they are smugglers,' I began protesting. 'That was why the fee was low. But I could take care of my – '

'They are worse than smugglers, lad – they are Comprachicos,' he breathed into my ear.

'Compra – c-comprachicos?'

At first I thought I could not have heard him aright. Then I could not believe him. Then I *did* believe him – Sam would not make up such a tale – and, despite myself, my teeth began to chatter.

From Bernie, and others in the kitchen at Villaverde, I had heard tales of the Comprachicos – tales whispered in horror, under the breath, to frighten Pedro and me into good behaviour.

The Comprachicos were a secret people, wandering in groups over the face of Europe, sometimes seeming to vanish for fifty or sixty years together, then, apparently, coming to life once more. In the wake of wars and civil disturbances, plagues or bad seasons, when food was scarce and times were hard, then they would appear, plying their evil trade. What did they do? They supplied the raw material for fairs and peep-shows. And to do this they bought children from hungry parents – or they took orphans whom nobody claimed – they never stole, they drove hard but honest bargains – and they re-made these children, by terrible arts of their own, turning straight bodies into hunchbacks, dislocating joints, manufacturing dwarfs by stopping their growth – sometimes by constructing jars around them, it was said – grafting tails on to human bodies, making normal children into monstrosities. By their skilful surgery they could alter a child's face so that its own mother would not recognise it. At the end of Napoleon's wars, when Europe was full of starving families and homeless children, there were the Comprachicos again, like refuse collectors, picking up human rags and turning them into profitable goods.

I had only half-believed Bernie's awful tales about them. Compra-pequenos, some people called them: child buyers. They were part-Spanish, part-Basque, part-Arab, part who-knows-what? They had, it was whispered in Villaverde, taken away the unwanted five-year-old stepson of Esteban Lopez when he married the widow Arriguerra, turned the child into a monster with the body of a boy and the head of a dog, and sold him to a travelling circus. Could this really have happened? Certainly little Pepe Arriguerra had disappeared. Once I asked Father Agustin about the Comprachicos – were there really such people? He said it was all a great deal of exaggerated nonsense – but he crossed himself and muttered a prayer. While practising their dreadful surgery, Bernie said, they used a stupefying drug, invented by the Chinese many hundreds of years ago, which sent the victim into a deep sleep. When he awoke he remembered nothing of what had happened, or who he had been before.

'Dear Father in heaven,' I whispered, 'don't let this happen to me . . .'

Then I looked at Sammy, pale and grim.

'Oh, Sam! And you came on board to warn me – but what will they do to *you*?'

'Eh, lad! I'm a man grown! There's little they can do to me. And now I'm aboard – and my friends will witness that I came – I doubt they'll not dare touch ye.'

'How did you hear about them?' I whispered shamefacedly.

'One o' my mates that we met this morning had seen ye colloguing wi' the little fellow who brought ye aboard. My mate knew him for the assistant of a man they call the Doctor – my mate's a bit in the smuggling line, that was how he came to hear about them – '

'Oh, they smuggle then as well?'

'Ay, they practise many trades and carry many cargoes.'

'But why – ' Why, I wanted to ask, had Sam

259

come on board, why had he not simply bidden
me come back to Santander with him? But I did
not know how to frame the question, and besides,
I feared I knew the answer. He had been afraid
that I would refuse, out of obstinacy and ignor-
ance, and then he would have had to force me. He
wanted to spare my pride. He thought I could not
endure to be dragged back to safety like a child.
And it was all through my childish stubbornness
and refusal to accept his help that I had landed us
both in this trouble.

Sam guessed what was going through my mind.
He said in explanation, ''Tis mighty choppy in the
bay now, ye see, an' the ship was under a fair bit
of way a'ready. We only just caught her, an' while
I was scrambling aboard, the crew was fending off
my mates' boat – they reckoned we was Customs
men, likely – so by the time I was over the rail,
my mates was a fair way astern – they'd never
catch up. They'll go back to harbour.'

'Is this ship really bound for England, then,
Sammy? What will you do? You must not land
there?'

I felt so full of shame and rage with myself that
I would gladly have thrust my hands into old Luc's
turf fire, if that would have made any difference.
Here was Sam, who had had a secure future and
a comfortable home waiting for him in Llanes, by
my stupid fault aboard this horrible little ship,
threatened with perils both at sea and on land.

'Ah, they'll run to Falmouth a'right,' he whispered. 'My mate told me he'd heard as they've a

cargo of brandy they are carrying for a lord in those parts.'

'But what will they do – '

'Hush!'

The door flew open, and the tall captain strode into the caboose again, followed by old Luc, who returned to stirring his pot, muttering anxiously to himself. The captain approached us, and in the most peremptory manner now demanded our passage money.

'How much, senor?' demanded Sammy politely. I pulled out my bit of rag. But the captain said,

'Thirty dollars apiece!'

'Why, the man who brought me on board said it was but fifteen,' I objected.

'That was for *one*. For two, we demand a higher price. It is not convenient to carry so many!'

He was evidently very angry. I was about to try and haggle the price down, but Sam said,

'At that rate, we pay the money *on arrival*, not before! And I do not wish to go to Falmouth. You can take me on to Achill Head in Ireland, where the lighthouse keeper is my uncle.'

I wondered if this were true, but could not tell from Sam's countenance. He was looking calmly at the captain, who seemed taken aback by this announcement and glared at us both. – I have not described the captain. His long tanned face had something Eastern about it – the one eye visible tilted up at the corner. The other eye was covered by a black patch. Under his boat-cloak he wore a belted canvas blouse over sailor's breeches, and a long knife tucked into his belt. He looked a stern and formidable man. Strangely enough, he reminded me of my grandfather – I could not have said why.

Sam remarked to me softly, in English, 'I do not have enough money on me to pay the fee. But my uncle will pay it. His name is Fergus O'Faolin, and he is the richest miser in Achill.'

Now I was sure the tale was invented, but I saw the captain give him a careful look; it seemed he understood English, or enough to make out the meaning of what Sam had said. He growled at us.

'The fare to Ireland is thirty-five dollars. And if you wish to eat, you must pay for your own victuals.'

Then he quitted the caboose abruptly, slamming the door.

Sam watched the old cook blowing on the broth and tasting it, then said to me in a low voice, still in English,

'Don't touch any food that you have not seen somebody else taste first.'

I shuddered, thinking of the Chinese drug. And I wondered if Aunt Isadora had paid these men to dispose of me in their own dreadful way. What would have happened to me, had Sam not come on board? In what state would I have arrived at Falmouth?

By now the ship was pitching more and more wildly, and old Luc, going to the door and putting his head out, called,

'Anyone who wants a bowl of *potaje* had best come and get it now, before it is all over the floor!'

Three men then took it in turns to come and drink a bowl of soup, eat a crust of bread, and leave again. Sam greeted them all politely, and they gave him a brief word in return. One was an Arab, one a Gael from the isle of Inishturk, who spoke partly in a strange language of his own, which the cook seemed to understand. The third was a Basque, like the cook and the captain. He, before eating, took bowls of broth outside: apparently the other two passengers preferred to remain on deck.

Sam and I paid the cook some pennies and received bowls of broth, which, since they were ladled from the common pot, must be harmless enough. Indeed, the soup was very good.

Now that we were at sea, we were allowed to step outside the caboose. Darkness lay all around; there were very few stars to be seen in the cloudy night; the lights of Santander gleamed very faint in the distance behind us.

I saw the other two passengers, shrouded in boat-cloaks, seated at the foot of the mast. Passing near them I saw one was a small, pale, grave man, with soft white hair and round, colourless eyes like those of an owl. He gave me a strange, measuring look as I passed, and I trembled, imagining his knife carving my flesh and bones into new shapes, but he said nothing, only sat thinking his own thoughts. The crew all addressed him as 'Doctor' and he was treated with great respect, I noticed. During the voyage I heard the captain once or twice ask his advice on points of navigation. Beside him, cross-legged and silent, sat the small man who had guided me on board. He had now lost all his vivacity and sat mute; when I passed he looked at me as if he had never laid eyes on me in his life.

I heard the Doctor say quietly to one of the sailors:

'I can see the Three Magi – that is a bad sign.'

Sam told me that by this he referred to the three stars in the constellation of Orion which are known as Orion's belt.

It was very cold on deck. A bitter wind came scouring from the right hand, or starboard, side; it sang in the hemp rigging and caused the little *Guipuzcoa* to bounce over the waves, which were already as large as whales. A light at the end of the bowsprit faintly illuminated the sea, and showed the ship's boat, suspended below.

Even now that the cargo and stores had all been stowed in the hold, there was very little deck-space. We had to pick our way carefully between coils of rope and various pieces of gear. Sam tried to explain the sails to me – there were two mainsails as well as topsails – but his explanation was so complicated that I could not follow. The rigging seemed all a mysterious tangle. I began to feel a fool in every possible way – a self-willed, unthinking dolt, to have cast Sam into this dangerous predicament – and besides that, a thick-skulled dunderhead who could not even grasp the principles of seamanship. Sammy patiently went on to point out other features of the ship: the helm, at present being manned by the tall captain, who gave us a cold glance as we came near him, but said nothing; and the compass, set in a square case and balanced on two copper frames.

Two of the sailors were busy making fast the sheets and seeing that all the rigging was in good trim; they, likewise, spoke to each other but not to us.

'Reckon they wish we wasn't on board,' Sammy murmured to me.

They could not have wished it any more heartily than I did myself.

If only there were somewhere on board where we could be private! But on such a small ship there did not seem to be a single space where we would not be overheard. Sam suggested that we ask the captain if we might go down to the hold to sleep among the stores, but by this time the ship was rolling and pitching with such a violent motion, as it breasted the waves, that my stomach felt likely to heave its way through my teeth at any moment. I could not bear even the smoky, fishy atmosphere of the caboose, let alone the idea of some dark, cramped enclosed den, where we might perhaps be shut in if we fell asleep.

'No,' I said urgently, gulping, partly from nausea, partly from dejection at our plight and my stupidity in bringing it about. 'Let us not go below. I'd sooner stay in the open.'

'Cheer up, lad!' said Sammy, laughing at me, but not unkindly; he never was that. 'By tomorrow you'll ha' got your sea-legs an' be ready to give the cap'n a hand wi' the steering. Maybe there's sense in your choice though; 'sides, a night on deck is as good to me as a month's wages; takes me back to old times. We'll make us a nest up for'ard.'

Which he did, with his cloak, and a piece of canvas which he found in a sail-locker, first asking the captain's permission to use it (which was granted by one surly, silent nod).

Here, huddled together, we were somewhat protected from the icy wind by a part of the ship which Sam, with a yawn, told me was the cutwater. He then fell peacefully asleep, his head pillowed on a coil of rope, and soon began snoring as if he had not a care in the world. I marvelled that he could take his plight with such calm. Suppose the crew, who seemed so hostile to us, knew that Sam had an enemy in England who would be glad to have him thrown into jail? Might they not, out of sheer revengefulness, hand him over to the authorities when we reached Falmouth? True, it seemed unlikely they would know about Sam's history – unless they were acquainted with any of his previous shipmates.

Then, my thoughts switching in another direction, I thought: Perhaps, after all, these men have no wicked designs on me. Perhaps it is merely chance that I was offered a berth on their boat. Perhaps Sam need not have risked his liberty to come and warn me.

But this hope was short-lived. Not long after, as I lay wakeful, listening to Sam's snores, I was alerted by the sound of voices.

It was those of the captain and the Doctor.

'Where are they?' said the captain. He spoke in French.

'Yonder, asleep, as you may hear,' replied the Doctor in the same language.

Thinking, I suppose, that even if we were awake we would not understand them, they did not particularly trouble themselves to whisper, but spoke in low tones which I could hear clearly enough.

'What shall we do about the Englishman?' the captain asked. 'We dare not kill him – he has too many friends in Santander, and it is known that he is aboard the *Guipuzcoa*. We should be putting our necks in a noose. Besides, I do not like to kill.'

'*Eh bien* – do as he asks, then,' said the Doctor indifferently. 'Deliver him to Ireland. Make your passage to Ireland *first*, before you go to Falmouth. Then, after he has landed at Achill, I can do my work, on the boy.'

At his words, my skin crept, and my blood ran like ice.

'Suppose he wishes the boy to land with him?'

'My good friend! You are paid to use your head as well as your ship! Some accident may be contrived – a swinging boom, a dropped block – or a drop of my liquor in his *podrida*; then the young man may be carried ashore, unharmed but senseless, and handed over to his friends; after that we may anchor in some quiet creek and deal with the boy. And if the man later makes inquiries, what is our tale? We landed the boy at Falmouth, as he asked us, and know nothing more.'

My breath seemed caught in my chest, cold as snow-flakes.

'Oh; very well,' the captain said at last in a surly tone. 'I shall be losing money though; I had planned to drop my cargo at Falmouth first and take on elixir of honey there to carry to Black Harbour; this way I lose trade; also my customer in Falmouth will be angry, for I shall be a week later than I promised.'

'Do not disturb yourself,' said the Doctor calmly. 'I am sure our patron will see that you are reimbursed if necessary.'

He used the French word *patronne* in the female gender, and I thought, Saints save me! That must be Dona Isadora. For what other woman in the world wishes evil to me?

The two men moved away, and I lay shivering, remembering the various pranks I had played on Dona Isadora: sprinkling snuff in the folds of her fan, or grit in the toes of her slippers, hiding her missal, slipping a pinch of salt into her chocolate before Bernie took it in. These tricks seemed very childish now, and I could hardly blame her for being angry at the time – but still! For such stupid pranks, what a dark and terrible revenge she seemed to have planned! Ay de mi, thought I, if ever I live in a civilised household again, I vow that I will never put salt in any old lady's chocolate – not so much as a single grain!

Then I bethought me to have a discussion with God on the subject.

'Please listen to me, Father in heaven, for this is important!

'I know it was very bad of me to play jokes on Aunt Isadora – and it was stupid and headstrong not to take Sam's advice in Santander. And, if you think this danger I am in is a just punishment for these faults, bueno!' (I always talked to God in Spanish) ' – Though I, for my part, consider it decidedly harsh of You, and it is more than I would do to someone who had behaved in such a way. Besides which, You have involved Sam in my punishment, and that is *wholly* unfair, for I don't believe he ever committed a wrong action in his life.'

Then I felt I was wandering from the point. I said,

'All this, Father, is beginning to upset the better notion of You that I have had since leaving Villaverde. Can Father Tomas have been right about you after all?

'Now listen, Father. I don't *want* to think worse of you again. For it had seemed to me that You must be better than anybody – better than the best person I know – which is Sammy – and *he* certainly would not do such a thing to You.

'So I do hope and pray that You will graciously suggest some means to get us – or at least Sammy – out of this pickle.'

Then I considered for a while and wondered if I was being unfair to God – in a way, almost obliging Him to help us; so I added,

'Nevertheless, not my will, but Thine be done,'

to show Him that all the teachings of Father Tomas had not been entirely thrown away upon me. And then I lay in the dark waiting for His answer.

It took a long time coming. Meanwhile the *Guipuzcoa* rushed onwards like a thing pursued – up the huge sides of waves, up, up, and up, until we seemed about to topple off the edge of the world; then down, down, even deeper down, boring, as it seemed, to the utter depths of the ocean, until I was holding my breath for terror, since it looked as if some great curving weight of water from over our heads would crash upon us, and we should never be able to climb out of the trough.

Also, with the wind battering her starboard quarter as it came hissing out of France, the ship leaned so far to port as she fled away that sometimes it seemed as if her mast must dip right into the waves and she turn upside down. But this did not happen, and we sped on, on, through the darkness, while Sammy slept peacefully beside me on the slanting deck.

And then God put a notion into my head.

Wriggling out from under the coverings, without disturbing Sam, I quietly made my way back to the caboose, clinging to every rope and stay on my perilous course. The Doctor and his assistant were still murmuring together at the foot of the mast; I went softly by on the other side without their observing me; indeed, this was not difficult for the sound of the wind in the shrouds drowned all other noise. The captain was once more at the helm, and he was directing two sailors to trim the ship by reefing some of the sails; he did not appear to notice me.

I slipped into the caboose, where the turf fire was all but out, damped down to a smouldering glow. The third sailor and the old cook both lay asleep, huddled between some of the stores and the angle of the wall. The iron soup-pot, covered with a heavy lid, had been set aside, slung in a wooden cradle so that the motion of the ship should not cause it to spill.

The lantern-flame burned dimly behind its talc screen.

And there, just as I had remembered it in my mind's eye, hung the wicker-covered flask, from a nail in the wall.

'Give the young gentleman a bit of bread and a mouthful of spirit,' the captain had said, nodding at it.

And old Luc had said – what had he said? – '*That* liquor is not good for the young lordship,' and had given me some from his own flask. Because he was afraid of me and thought I might be related to the spirits of drowned sailors.

Moving slowly and deliberately, as if I had a perfect right to do it, I took the wicker-covered flask, uncorked it, lifted the lid from the soup-pot, and poured in most of the contents of the flask, which I then recorked and hung up on its nail again.

The two sleepers did not stir, and I left the caboose without being noticed. Then, even more carefully than I had come – for the ship was now pitching with a motion like that of my bad-tempered mule – I edged along to where Sam lay and settled down once more.

I felt quite calm.

Perhaps the liquor in the flask was no more than brandy – in which case it would have little effect on those who drank the soup. There was nothing to do now but wait; and with this resolved in my mind, I soon fell asleep.

# 9

I was awakened by the sound of a wild yell. As I lifted myself confusedly on my elbow – having come abruptly out of a heavy, dream-filled slumber, in which Dona Isadora was chasing me with one of Bernie's frying-pans, and I was dodging to avoid the drops of boiling fat and hissing fishes from it – I saw that some considerable time must have passed, for the sky was much lighter – a pale, leaden grey – and could readily be distinguished from the sea, which now looked as if it were covered by a dark, oily skin, seamed by a thousand wrinkles.

Beside me, Sam shot upright, his keen sailor's nose having detected an odour that I, unaccustomed to the sea, had not yet taken for a menace. Smoke!

'Hey! Are we afire?' Sam was on his feet in a second, tottering as his weight came on to his weak leg. I sprang up and took his arm to balance him. We both looked aft along the cluttered deck. My first thought was the caboose – the fire in its clay box – could my interference with the soup have somehow caused the fire to burn up – ? But neither flame nor smoke came from the doorway.

Then we heard more yells, and beheld the most amazing sight.

A man appeared from behind the mainsail; he was dancing on the caboose roof. He seemed to be waving a banner of live flame. – Then I saw that he held a great fragment of tarred canvas, which was alight; it burned furiously, with tongues of fire leaping away from it, breaking off and taking flight on the wind. And he danced up and down, singing some mad song, in Basque and French and his own language. It was the bearded Irishman, and so far as I could make out, he sang that he was Coullain, the Hound of the North, and that he would slit the gullets of all Queen Maeve's enemies.

'I learned my swordsmanship in the Land of Shadows!' he bawled, 'I received my weapons from Scath, Queen of the Witches, and I can hurl a spear farther than any man in the West. Where is Queen Maeve's champion, where is Ferdia? Let him come hither, for Coullain is waiting to give battle!'

'What has got into that lunatic?' yelled the captain furiously. He was at the tiller, but could not leave go of it, for the ship was careering along, even faster than last evening, it seemed, between the piled and evil-looking criss-cross waves.

'Matthieu!' called the captain. 'Luc! Abdullah! Catch hold of the idiot and knock him senseless with a marlinspike, before he sets fire to the ship!'

'Eh, eh, he'm in a proper frenzy,' muttered

Sammy, watching the dancing madman. 'If he were a Malay – I had one as a shipmate once – I'd say he'd gone amok. I've seen him wild like that when the fit took him. – We'd best try to head him off at this end, lad – if he burns the ship, we'll all go to the bottom together.'

And he took a length of rope from a coil beside us and formed it into a noose, then said to me,

'Do you move that way, lad, and I'll go this side, and we'll see if we can edge him towards the stern.'

The other three men were now at the after end of the caboose, and the captain, beads of sweat rolling down his face, was steering so as to try and keep the mainsail away from the dancing madman, who continued his wild capering, waving the burning banner, and roaring that he was King Conor's trusty watch-dog who would rend any man that touched a hair of his head.

Sam crept closer and closer, keeping the sail between himself and the maniac. I was on the other side of the ship, and the wind blew from the madman to me. Every now and then I had to duck as a piece of flame whirled past me. The man saw me and his eyes seemed to bulge; they were reddened in frenzy and the veins of his neck and forehead stood out like writhing snakes; he was a truly frightening apparition. He made as if to jump down on me, then suddenly turned in the other direction, and with a great shout:

'*Wait for me, Ferdia!* I will fight you at the Bridge of the Leaps!' he bounded off the roof with a spring that took him right into the ship's well.

Sammy, at that same moment, very adroitly hurled his rope, noosing the man's arms to his body and stopped him in mid-leap, so that he fell helpless to the deck and lay stunned. Matthieu and Abdullah instantly flung themselves on him, snatched away the burning canvas, and tossed it overboard.

'God be thanked!' said Abdullah. 'Another minute, and he would have set fire to the sail.'

'Tie him up!' said the captain grimly.

'No need, Capitano. He has knocked himself unconscious. He will be sane when he recovers, doubtless.'

'Tie him up just the same. – That was well done,' said the captain, curtly, to Sam, as if he regretted having to be under an obligation; and, turning back at once to Abdullah, he asked,

'What got into Shaemus? – Had he been drinking – or taken hasheesh?'

'No, captain, not to our knowledge,' said Abdullah, removing Sam's noose in order to re-tie the man's hands in front of him.

By now daylight was near, and a faint band of light appeared eastwards over the lead-coloured sea. I looked around the ship, wondering where the Doctor and his assistant had passed the night; and, as if summoned by my thought, they made their appearance at that moment, emerging from the hold and climbing the ladder. The small swarthy man led the way, and, seeing his face, recollecting how I had been brought aboard the *Guipuzcoa*, I thought what a stupid gull I had been. I felt older now by twenty-four years, not hours.

The Doctor and his assistant were paying me no heed just then.

'What is to do?' said the Doctor, looking at the body on the deck.

'The Irishman has run mad,' growled the captain, 'and burned our spare *vela menora*; we shall have to pray that God does not see fit to damage the one we are using. You had best give the idiot an opiate, Doctor, to prevent his doing any further mischief.'

'Let me have a look at him,' said the Doctor.

But as the Doctor and his assistant bent over Shaemus, the latter recovered from his brief spell of unconsciousness. Dragging his wrists from the hold of the startled Abdullah, he roared out,

'*Ferdia! Well met! Now* we shall see who is master!' and, showing all his teeth, he flung himself on the Doctor's assistant. Wholly unprepared for this onslaught, the small man staggered backwards; Shaemus seized him by both arms and shook him as a bird shakes a worm. The smaller man, however, was quick to recover, and, spitting out some furious Basque oath, he whipped a knife from his stocking and jabbed it at the Irishman's ribs. This served only to inflame the latter's fury and, yelling with pain and rage, he too pulled out a knife and with a flickering upward motion drove its blade at the other man's throat.

'*Stop them!*' shouted the captain furiously. 'Here – Matthieu – take the helm, damn you – *I'll* soon stop them – ' for the two men, now engrossed in their fight, had jumped up on to the deck and were ducking, feinting, and stabbing at each other as if they were lifelong enemies, all the time drawing towards the forward end of the ship.

Matthieu took the helm and the captain, drawing out a knife of his own and snatching up a heavy wooden spike, went after the two men and circled round them, watching for a chance to stun the Irishman. 'Hey – you! You seem to have some sense!' he bawled at Sam. 'Help me put an end to this madness!' – for the Doctor, shrugging as if he saw no recourse but to let the men kill each other, had returned to his original position and sat down at the foot of the mast.

Sam picked up his noose again. I was afraid of what might happen if he came too close to the fighting pair. With his lame leg he could not move quickly. And already the captain, aiming a blow at the Irishman's head with his spike, had received a savage slash on his arm which made him retire a step, cursing, and tie his kerchief over the cut, which was pouring blood. The deck was already spattered and slippery from the blood of the two combatants, who had given each other various wounds, which they treated with as much disregard as the utter lack of reason for their battle.

Having tied up his arm the captain came on again – I had to admire his courage – and landed a vigorous blow on the head of Shaemus, who, shaking his head as if a bee had stung it, growling with fury, now picked up the smaller man bodily, and, bellowing,

'We shall see *now*, Ferdia, who can leap the farthest!' he bounded like a stag into the air.

The ship, under the handling of Matthieu who, it was plain, was by no means so skilful a helmsman as the captain, had been slewing nervously from side to side like a balky horse, and at this moment she chanced to give a particularly violent, shuddering heave to starboard, as she staggered between two fierce gusts of wind. The result was that both combatants, still grappled together, were hurled headlong over the rail into the crisscross waves, and both disappeared from view without a sound or a cry.

'*Diablo*!' said the captain, and flung a rope towards the spot where the men had sunk. But no hand came up to seize it. No sign of a living form could be seen.

Now the Doctor, for the first time since the start of this strange duel, showed signs of concern.

'Put the helm about!' he called sharply to Matthieu, and, to the captain, 'Lower the boat!'

'In this wind? In this sea? Impossible,' said the captain shortly, leaping back to take the helm, for the ship was falling away from the wind, and seemed in near danger of capsizing. 'We'd lose the vessel and *all* of us would drown, not just those two fools.'

'How shall I do my work without Jaca?'

'Train another helper,' growled the captain. 'I'll

miss that mad Shaemus too – he was a handy sailor. But I rate the ship above men's lives.'

'Jaca was no common sailor; he had many skills!'

'He was also a murderer and dangerous hothead. Why did he have to fight that drunken Irishman? Now we are two men short and shall be in a bad way if the weather worsens. Go back to your slumbers, Doctor, and leave the management of the ship to me.'

Muttering angrily to himself, to the effect that the Irishman had blood on his head and was no loss but that Jaca was irreplaceable, the Doctor went below. The captain, in an equally bad humour, summoned old Luc to bind up his arm more firmly, and then shouted to Matthieu and Abdullah to reef the top-sails.

By now day had come, but the light brought little cheer, for the skies were low and thick, the sea evil and creased-looking, while the wind came in wilder and wilder gusts, causing the mast to bend like a blade of grass. Although, as Sam had prophesied, my queasiness had diminished, and I no longer had the urge to vomit after every lurch of the ship, I was not at all happy in my mind at the captain's curt words, 'If the weather should worsen.' How much worse than this could it grow? I wondered to myself.

By now, too, there seemed a sense of brooding depression about the *Guipuzcoa* which was understandable enough. Two men had been lost in an outbreak of stupid, wasteful violence: what did this portend?

We went into the caboose, for a little shelter from the incessant tugging of the wind, and found old Luc muttering to himself,

'The Estadea are angry with us; yes, they are angry!'

'Good morning, Old Father,' Sam said to Luc. 'Can you give us a mouthful of breakfast?'

'All I can give you is dry bread,' grumbled the cook. 'That mad pig of an Irishman came and finished off the potaje while I was asleep in the early watch. Much good it has done him! What a waste of good soup! Now he has taken it to the bottom of the sea. – You are a friend of the Estadea, young lord, and I think they are looking after you,' he said to me, breaking off a piece from a great round loaf.

'Can't you please tell them to leave *me* alone, at least? I am a poor old man who only does what he is told and means no harm to anybody.'

The captain at that moment bellowing that he was hungry, and where was his breakfast? Luc picked up the rest of the loaf and went out.

'What did he mean?' Sammy asked me in a low voice. 'Why does he think you are a friend of the spirits?'

'Because I was reading my book in here, and he thought it must be some book of wizardry.'

I did not tell Sam the rest of the dark and frightening thought that had possessed my mind. I had poured most of the contents of that flask into the soup. Shaemus had drunk it, thus getting the draught that was meant for me. He was a grown man, of large stature; perhaps the draught that would have stupefied me had merely made him wild. By my deed I might have saved myself, but I had robbed two men of their lives. One of them was a murderer, true, and the other had decoyed me to this ill-omened vessel – but still I feared that the results of what I had done would haunt me for years, if not to my dying day. I decided, however, that I would not burden Sam by telling him about it, for he was saying, cheerfully enough,

'At all events, we're rid now of two possible enemies – an' that's no bad thing! Now the cap'n's short-handed, he'll likely value our company higher!'

And indeed, during the day, as the weather steadily worsened, the captain approached Sam and, in a more friendly tone than he had used yet, said,

'I have heard that you are a sailor, *Ingles*. If you are a better helmsman than those two idiots who are left to me, I will remit your passage-money and give you a free berth to Ireland, for my best steersman was the maniac who went overboard; he had a feeling for the ship which those two have not.'

Sam, always obliging, said he would show what he could do, and gave me a nod to follow him – 'In case,' he muttered in English, 'these raskills might do 'ee a mischief while I'm fixed at the tiller. So keep by me, lad.'

I did so, but it seemed at present the captain had no other thought but to supplement his reduced crew, for after watching Sam's handling of the tiller for a while, apparently satisfied with his skill, he went off to survey the damage that Shaemus had done before his sudden and violent end. There was a charred patch on one of the two mainsails that gave the captain much anxiety. – 'If the wind would but drop, we should exchange that sail for the spare, but I dare not try that in this gale,' he muttered, scanning the burnt spot uneasily.

Worse still it seemed that Shaemus, in his madness, had dragged the spare sails out of the lockers and slashed up one of them to provide himself with his flaming flag, while others of them had been hacked and one at least was lost entirely, probably fallen overboard before his crazy activities were detected.

Grinding his teeth with rage at this discovery, the captain set everybody to work, stitching rents and sewing on patches – everybody except the Doctor. I and old Luc spent most of our day stitching with sailmakers' needles, and the two remaining sailors helped whenever it was possible for them to do so.

I thought that the captain should remit my passage-money, too, in return for my services, but did not dare suggest this, for, as the day drew on, and the wind blew harder and the sky darkened, his brow, too, grew blacker as if it reflected the murky bank of cloud to the east of us. The cloud was like a huge, slow-growing pyramid, lying over the invisible coast of France: lurid white round the edges, then grey, then a deeper grey, almost steel-blue, in the centre. Even Sammy's ugly cheerful countenance became puckered with worry as he glanced over his right shoulder at the ominous pile, and at the hurrying scud behind us.

'Yon's a snow-cloud if I'm not mistook,' said he. 'And I'd as lief not meet a snowstorm in mid-Channel in this little bucket of a hooker; even in one o' His Majesty's men o' war I'd as lief not face it, if the truth be told! Still, there's this to be said, the wind is helping us on our way; I've ne'er crossed the Gulf of Gascony in quicker time! We oughta pass Le Conquet and the Ile de Ouessant during the night, at this rate; and though the English Channel is no friendlier than the Gulf in bad weather, there's more chance o' meeting other shipping.'

He did not explain these ominous words, nor did I ask for an explanation. Up to now, we had seen no other shipping at all, but the low-flying clouds and high-whirling spume kept the view from the *Guipuzcoa* down to a cable's length around us. It was a wonder to me that the captain could grope his way through this cauldron of cloud-wrapped seething water without a sight of the sun; but Sam seemed confident in him and said that he was a good navigator. As the day drew on the captain seemed more and more absorbed in his battle with wind and water and his care of the ship; he paid little attention to the rest of us.

By now the motion of the ship was far too

violent to permit a fire, or cookery – all we had to eat that day was more bread, wet with salt spray, and some dried figs and goat's cheese. Sam and I agreed there could be little risk in eating our share of this, for the food was divided among all, though we had to pay for our portion.

Night came early, with an increase of the bitter cold; the captain, relieving Sam after a long spell at the helm, advised him to go to rest at once and take what sleep he might as soon as possible – 'For,' said he, 'I don't care for the feel of the wind; I may have to call on you during the night.'

Sam and I therefore settled in the caboose. Water was now continuously bursting through the hawse-holes and over the gunwale, so that our previous perch up in the prow would have been too wet for comfort – quite apart from the hazard of being thrown off into the sea as the ship bounded up and down.

I had intended to ask God whether it was His purpose that those two men should be drowned, or whether I had erred in supposing it His will that I should pour the contents of the flask into the soup. All day, sewing patches on the sails, I had been very distressed in my mind about this. But when it came to the point, so wearied was I from the long, frightening day, and the unremitting howl of the wind, that as soon as I laid my head on the deck, I fell instantly asleep. Perhaps God intended me to do so.

I was awakened, not by any sound, but by a

bright, knifelike glare, which blazed through my closed eyelids as if they were made of tissue.

At first, in terror, I believed that some spark from the Irishman's wild fire-dance must have remained hidden, and that the ship was now ablaze. Confusedly crying out, 'Where's the fire? Quick, we must put it out!' I stared up and sprang to my feet.

'Easy, lad!' said Sam's voice – and what a comfort it was to hear him, for the light had died again, I could see nothing at all in the black dark – 'Be easy, there's no fire! Or at least,' he added in a thoughtful tone, 'only in heaven.'

Next moment the cabin was illuminated again, down to the last breadcrumb, cobweb, and curl of onion peel, by a wild red pulsing light.

'What is it?' I gasped out. 'Where are we?' wondering if we might be near some lighthouse with its flashing beam, or if a savage sea-battle was raging close at hand.

But Sam said, 'It is lighting.'

'Then why is there no thunder?'

'Because of the snow,' he said gravely.

I was not then aware of the fact, but electrical storms at sea, if there be snow also, are seldom accompanied by thunder.

We went out into the well, where the captain was calling out loudly for Sam.

'Here! You, Ingles! Come and take the tiller. We must reef the mainsail.'

Once out of the cabin I felt as if I were being stung all over by giant bees. Snow, mixed with hail, was hurling itself at the ship, pouring down so fast that it lay like a white quilt on the surface of the sea. I could hear its hiss and crackle, as it struck the water, mixed with the whine of the wind, while overhead, against the repeated red-brown glare of the lightning, the snow-flakes appeared black like a cloud of grasshoppers, a million sooty whirling dots. The ship was all coated with snow, and slippery with ice; the ropes wore a silvery coating and whenever the lightning glared out, the whole ship sparkled as if made from crimson glass. It was most beautiful but frightening.

Sam, looking calmly about him at all this turmoil – the white, curdled, snow-covered sea and the massive piled mountain of cloud in the sky, copper-coloured in the glow of the lightning – said to the captain,

'Senor, I think you had best make straight for Falmouth. It should not take you too long to get there, with this wind behind us, even after you have reefed the mainsails. I am a Cornishman, and I do not think it advisable to sail round Land's End in weather like this.'

'Of course I shall make for Falmouth!' snarled the captain. 'Do you take me for a fool?'

'But – ' I began. Sam shook his head at me and laid a finger on his lips. When the captain went to see to the reefing, I said to Sam,

'But *you* must not go to Falmouth – you might be sent to prison!'

'Felix,' he said gravely, 'the way things are, I'd think myself as snug in Falmouth jail as in the

287

King's palace! We *must* put in to Falmouth; in the state they are, his sails would never take him across the Irish Sea. Ah – look – '

For, as the sailors shook the mainsail, trying to wrestle its frozen breadth into the folds necessary for furling, the wind put black claws into the burnt patch and tore the sail into shreds, which whirled away into the darkness like the shredded petals of a poppy. The shrouds blew out, and were dragged away from their fastenings; one of the sailors, Matthieu, was carried away likewise; I had a moment's terrible view of him, spreadeagled in the sky like an angel, dyed red by lightning, his mouth a round black O of horror – then he was gone, God knew where.

With a fearful curse, the captain called to the Doctor to come and take Matthieu's place.

Now I noticed the Doctor for the first time since I had been awakened. He still, with immovable gravity, maintained his position at the foot of the mast; but I saw that he had passed a rope through his leather belt, and taken several turns of it around the mast behind him, so that he was fastened there. He shook his head calmly in response to the captain's summons, and replied,

'No. It is my duty to preserve myself as long as possible, for my brain contains secrets unknown to any other in the world. I must not hazard my life in such a manner. Yours is the responsibility of the ship; it is not my concern.'

'You fool!' screamed the captain in a passion. 'If it were not for your persuading me to this insane trip we should now be safely berthed in the Ria de Laredo; look what you have done to us! And now you will not even stir yourself to help, though I have lost my two best men; you will be drowned through your own obstinacy, and we shall too!'

'I shall drown if it is the will of Fate,' replied the Doctor. 'You will receive no help from me. I am a man of science not a sailor.'

Cursing him again, the captain called me. In response to Sam's nod, I went to help him and, mastering my terror as best I could, received instructions from the captain and Abdullah on how to brail up, furl the sails, secure the clew-lines, and put preventer-shrouds on the block-straps, so that they might serve as back-stays. Like a sardine in a net, I dangled and struggled among the black, frozen ropes; again and again I thought my last moment had come. We battened down the ports and the hatch to the hold; we removed every needless bit of gear from the deck, so that the ship might offer the least possible resistance to the wind; we hurried as if the devil were after us, we sweated and struggled like slaves, while the captain cursed us and urged us to work faster, and toiled alongside of us.

That night seemed to last for a lifetime. My fingers, wrists, and arms were numb and black with bruising, my nails torn; my feet were frozen, and every inch of my clothing was soaked by spray and snow; the snow lay in folds of my collar and under my hair, it poured into my mouth, nose, and eyes, so that at times I could hardly see;

yet I was not cold; we were kept too busy for that; and, strangely, in all this frenzy, and facing the imminent risk of death, I did not find myself afraid, but rather filled with a wild cheerfulness and gaiety, as I battled to carry out the captain's instructions, and even felt that I was doing not too badly, earning from time to time his brief commending nod.

Oh, I thought, if Bob, if Grandfather, if Aunt Isadora could see me now!

And when I remembered my great-aunt Isadora, by whose contrivance I was here, in this danger, I could almost have thanked the old vulture; and I thought that probably never in the whole of her miserable envious spite-filled life had she known anything like the joy of this crazy struggle to keep the ship watertight and battened against the gale, trimmed to take advantage of the pursuing wind and not be overwhelmed by it. We secured the compass and binnacle; we lashed the ship's boat more tightly to the bowsprit, where it hung, Basque-fashion, like a cocoon dangling from a twig; we pumped, by turns, to reduce the water in the well; and we bailed with leather buckets when the pump jammed.

Sammy, at the helm, said once, laughing,

'Eh, lad, 'ee'll make a sailor yet! If your kinsfolk are not to be found, 'tis best ye go back to sea!' and I felt pride rise in me as high as the towering waves.

Morning brought no relief from the gale; indeed, the wind blew harder still; but we could see more easily what had to be done. The wrack of cloud grew thicker as the day advanced; and the snow fell faster. Hailstones like pebbles rattled about the deck and caused us to slide and stumble.

Then I heard Sam say quietly to the captain, between two gusts,

'Look: there are the two light-houses on the Lizard Head.'

'You have good eyes,' the captain answered, in a tone of disbelief, screwing up his own eyes against the whirl of snow. 'I see nothing.'

'I could not be mistaken,' Sam said. 'I know this coast like the palm of my hand.'

A few minutes later I thought that I, too, could perceive a low, wrinkled coast-line, white as the sea, but separated from it by a thread of black cliffs.

And then, when hope had us suddenly quivering, our hearts beating faster than they had all through the terrors of the night – suddenly there came a terrible crash. In one instant the top-sails were blown clear off the ship, the shrouds were carried away, and the mast flew off on the back of the wind, like a piece of straw, carrying the Doctor with it. Dismasted, the ship at once became wholly helpless. She would not answer to the helm.

Sam was steering at that moment, but the captain leaped to take his place.

'Lash me here!' he shouted. We tied him to the tiller, but even he, with all his skill, could not keep the *Guipuzcoa* under way. A wave carried away part of the rail, as the ship wallowed, aslant to the wind. Another, following, took off the figurehead.

'The ship is lost,' Sam said to me quietly. 'We had better free the boat.'

Old Luc came forward to help us with this task, no easy one, as the bowsprit swung up and down, now pointing at the sky, now buried in the waves, like a giant's pencil writing a letter across the storm. Behind us we heard a yell, and turned to see a huge wave, larger than the whole of my grandfather's house, fall shatteringly upon the poop of the ship. We felt the *Guipuzcoa* lurch and stagger, as if she had been mortally wounded; when the spray cleared away and the stern rose, we saw that the captain and the helm had both disappeared. Next moment another wave had broken off the bowsprit, and had taken us with it into the waves.

I was not much frightened, although I could not swim. I thought only of maintaining my fierce grip on the rope which secured the boat to the bowsprit.

For a moment I was under dark green water, my mouth, eyes, and ears were full of it; then my head came out of a wave, and I saw Sam not far off, clutching the gunwale of the boat, which, by good fortune, was the right side up. The broken bowsprit drifted alongside, with old Luc clinging to it.

'Quick: pull yourself on board!' Sam shouted to me. 'Now!' – as a wave bore me up; and, with a wild, scrambling heave, I managed to throw myself into the boat and then, on my knees, grasping at his arms, struggled to drag Sam in over the side.

'Hold on to me, old Father,' said Sam to Luc, and reached out a hand to the old man, who still clung to the bowsprit. 'Leave go of the spar and give me your hand – bueno! I have got you.'

But at that moment a short steep wave lifted up the end of the bowsprit and brought it down like a club on the old man's white head; without a word, without a sign, he sank under the water and did not reappear.

I have remembered that moment, at different times, ever since.

Meanwhile the *Guipuzcoa*, broken, breached, and dismasted, had turned over in the water like a dead herring. A few casks, a chest, and a basket bobbed away from the hull. We peered, rubbing our eyes against the snow, for any sign of Abdullah or the captain, but the heavy carcass of the ship was settling fast, and our boat, much lighter, was drifting away from it, borne shorewards by the wind. We were helpless, for we had no oars; they must have been thrown out when the bowsprit broke off.

'There is nothing we can do for those poor fellows,' said Sam. 'And *we* are not out of the wood yet! Our boat may capsize – or the wind may carry us on to the Lizard point, in which case we shall be cracked as a thrush cracks a snail. So don't get your hopes up too high, lad,' he said to me with a wry grin. ' – Though if we do make Falmouth Haven, 'twill be one o' the fastest passages on record, and should be set down in the annals of navigation.'

Now the coastline was closer; I could see the black cliffs more clearly, and a spatter of white waves breaking at the foot, and small white fields rising above the clifftop.

Sam said thoughtfully,

'To think how I used to long and pray for a sight o' the coast o' Cornwall again. Little did I reckon 'twould be in such a way as this!'

'Those poor men!' said I. 'Matthieu – Luc – Abdullah – the Irishman – what had they done to deserve such a death?'

'Oh, 'tis odds but they had plenty on their consciences,' Sammy consoled me. And he added gravely, 'Every sailor knows full well, the first time he puts to sea, Felix, what his end may be. Say a prayer for them if you wish, lad, but don't waste yourself wi' grieving; those men knew what they were about when they shipped i' the *Guipuzcoa*. An' as for the captain and the one they called the Doctor, I reckon that pair were dipped deep i' wickedness as a rope in tar; I heard tales o' them from my mates as 'ud turn your hair white to hear!'

'I believe you,' I said, 'for the night before last, while you were sleeping, I myself heard the captain and the Doctor – '

Then I stopped short in horror, for, as if our words had conjured him out of the depths of the sea, we saw the Doctor himself floating towards us, still bound by a rope to the main-mast. Even drifting thus, helpless in the water, his aspect was very frightening, with his bony pale face like that of a corpse, and his streaming white hair. For a moment I thought he *was* a corpse, and then the silvery eyes opened and looked at us without expression.

'Quick, throw him a rope,' said Sam, for there was one on board. I flung it, as we drifted closer to the Doctor, but he ignored it, only fixed his colourless eyes on me.

'Lay hold of the rope, senor!' called Sammy urgently. 'Make haste, or it will be too late. We have no oars!'

Gravely the Doctor swayed his head in refusal.

'It would be of no use,' he said. 'My legs and body were crushed when the mast broke away. I have not an hour to live: no help could save me. I regret it,' he said to me, 'for your great-aunt Isadora had paid me much money to arrange for your disappearance; and, the minute I laid eyes on you, I knew that I should be able to transform you into something uncommon and remarkable; who knows with my scientific art, what would have . . .'

All of a sudden his jaw dropped, his mouth opened wide, and the sea bubbled into it; then the mast bobbed away carrying him with it, still calm and dignified, even in the act of dying.

Greatly distressed at this horrible encounter, I had much ado not to weep, and for a moment I hid my face in my hands.

'Easy, easy, lad!' said Sam, in a kind, encouraging voice, 'Pipe your eye if you must! But, to my

way of thinking, the world is well rid o' that one
– he mid just as well use his scientific art in hell,
where for sure he belongs.'

I knew Sam was right; still, I could not shake
that strange white face from my thoughts, as it
floated past, fixing its solemn eyes upon me.

Sammy went on thoughtfully, to distract me, I
daresay, 'That aunt Isadora of yourn must be a
rare 'un! What a pair she and uncle Ebenezer 'ud
make. I'd dearly like to see 'em together on some
desert isle!'

And he went on to imagine how the two villains
would deal together, in such a ludicrous fashion
that presently I could not help laughing a little and
forgot some of my horror.

'Come, that's better!' said Sam. 'Why don't us
sing a catch or two, to draw the notice of our
saints to the pickle we're in, and to show 'em we
bain't afeared?'

And so we sang some of our favourite airs,
wishing that we had Sammy's kit and my pipe,
which had been left behind with our bundles in
the caboose. But I was glad that I had my father's
book and papers, in Juana's oilskin wrapping,
tucked inside my shirt, next to my skin. I hoped
that perhaps, since my immersion in the water had
not lasted very long, the water had not penetrated
the package and the writing might have been pre-
served.

Every now and then, breaking off from our
songs, Sam would say, 'Now I can see the Lizard
light-house plain. Now I can see Coverack church;

now I see St Mawes, all in the snow. Lucky for us the tide is a-making and the wind has set to the south-west; 'tis carrying us right toward Falmouth creek. Look at yon snow on the cliffs; it be rare, I can tell 'ee, for snow to lie long in Cornwall.'

But there was a false cheer in his voice and I could guess why; because the current was carrying us faster than the wind, and instead of drifting in the direction of St Mawes church which, he had told me, lay on the east side of Falmouth creek, we were drawing all the time steadily to our left, towards the great cliffs and crashing white waves that ran along the foot of the Lizard Point.

We sang together until we were hoarse, and then, in a pause, I said haltingly,

'Sam, I would just like you to know how very glad I am to have known you – '

His ugly face broke into a smile. 'Lad, I don't mean to die yet!' he said. 'For one thing, just afore we left Llanes, I plucked up my courage an' put the question to Juana – an' she said Yes!'

'Oh, Sam!' I had thought my guilt could bite no deeper, but now I felt the keenest pang of all. 'She will curse the day I met you – '

'Hold it, lad!' Sam said cheerfully. 'Let's not be scribing our epitaphs yet awhile! For I can see a boat this minute as ever is, a-pulling out o' Falmouth Bay!'

Turning to strain my eyes, I saw that he was right: what looked like a many-legged water-beetle was pulling steadily towards us over the white surface of the sea.

'Reckon they mun ha' spotted the wreck from up top o' the lighthouse, and sent word to the life-boatmen,' Sam said. And he added in a wondering tone, 'Now, bean't that a 'mazing thing that from a whole shipload o' raskills, you an' I, Felix, should be the ones to be saved. It do make one think that Him above mid have some task for us to do!'

I had been thinking the same thought.

Soon loud, cheerful voices called, 'Keep your hearts up, lads! Here we be!' and the rounded, stubby life-boat tumbled alongside of us, pulled by ten red-faced, black-eyed rowers, who exclaimed, as they pulled us aboard,

'Why, if 'ee bain't a couple o' true-blue English lads! Fancy that now! Word come as 'twas one o' they Biscay hookers as had foundered.'

'Ay, an' so it was,' said Sam. 'But English lads can ship aboard o' Biscay hookers.'

One of the oarsmen turned his head.

'I should know *that* voice!' he said. 'Bean't you Sammy Pollard, as come from the liddle owd farm up to Tregarrion?'

'That I be – an' glad to get a sight o' Cornwall again, I can tell 'ee!' said Sam. He spoke cheerfully, and they all exclaimed in a welcoming chorus, but my heart sank. All Cornishmen know one another, it seemed; how long would it be before news of Sam's rescue reached his uncle?

After about forty minutes' rowing we reached Falmouth harbour. The snow was still pouring down, and I could see little of the small grey stone town as we clambered up steep steps on to a granite pier.

From there we were led to a custom-house, close by, where we had to go through brief formalities (in consequence, it seemed, of a law passed during the French wars) declaring our names, and information regarding the ship that had sunk, its name, owners, port of embarkation, cargo, and so forth. These questions we answered as best we could. I thought that, if only Sam had not already been recognised, he could have given a false name. Mine I gave as Felix Brooke, and said that I was travelling from Spain to my father's family in Bath.

The Customs Officer, a most kindly, well-meaning man, asked what was the direction of my father's family in Bath, so that he might inform them by a message on the mailcoach that I was here cast up on the shore in Falmouth, penniless and wet as a herring. For fear that he might have me apprehended as a vagrant, I gave the address as In care of the Rose and Ring-Dove Inn. He promised that a note should be despatched forthwith. Who would read it? I wondered.

Meanwhile, since we were soaked and half-starving, we were now permitted to take ourselves off to the nearest inn, one on the quayside.

Falmouth consists of one long narrow street leading up a hill to a castle which Sam told me was called Pendennis Castle. I was all eyes for everything English – but felt obliged to admit to myself that the narrow street, full of snow and sailors, and the little white-washed inn, did not either of them display the grandeur I had expected in England.

However we were led to a blazing fire, which was most welcome, and I awaited the food we had ordered with curiosity. This too, when it came, was something of a disappointment: the meat was half-raw and the vegetables tasted like sea-weed; the bread was bitter and the cider was horrible: sharp enough to tie your stomach in a knot. The best part of the meal was a dish of large savoury pastries, made with a thick crust, and filled, I think, with mutton and turnip. Cornish Pasties, Sam said they were called.

While we ate, sitting beside the fire, all manner of persons entered the inn parlour, to look at us with wonder and congratulate us on our escape; for it seemed that the storm had been so fierce, along the Cornish coast, that no fishing boats had put to sea for three days, and the packet from France had been long overdue; so the sight of our boat from the cliff-top had been a cause for general amazement.

In the midst of all this cheerful commotion, a little black-clad fellow sidled into the parlour where we sat. His appearance reminded me, all in a moment, of the mercado at Oviedo, and my heart jumped up into my mouth.

Next moment he was tapping Sammy on the shoulder.

'Is your name Sam Pollard?' says he.

'Yes, it is!'

'Then I would have you know,' says the little fellow, 'that you are under arrest for debt!'

# 10

Sam's arrest was a piece of the most arrant ill-luck. Had the weather been different – had our ship not been wrecked – had we not been washed ashore near Falmouth, where he was well-known – or had we landed a day later, after the storm had abated, when Sam could have put off again directly on one of several packets that were in port, waiting to leave – matters would have fallen out otherwise.

But it so happened that his uncle's bailiff, or agent, a man of a mean contriving nature named Jonas Brewer, had been in Falmouth for three days, impatiently awaiting the arrival of a load of silk expected from the port of Le Havre, which was overdue because of the storm. It seemed that Sam's uncle Ebenezer had sold his farms, gone into the cloth business, and prospered amazingly; he was now Mayor of Truro. But his spite against the nephew who had married his daughter was still bitter, and the bailiff, knowing this and chancing to hear the tale of our lucky rescue noised about the town of Falmouth, made haste to earn his master's favour by informing the constables and instructing them to arrest Sam.

I asked the bailiff how much the debt was, for which Sam had been apprehended, since I still had thirty-five Spanish dollars tucked in my belt, which amounted, I learned to about a hundred and sixty shillings or eight pounds in English money.* I offered this sum, but the man smiled scornfully and said that Sam owed his uncle more than eighty pounds.

'Eighty?' said Sam. 'Why, it was but fifty!'

'Arr, but you be reckoning without the interest, my young jack-dandy,' said the bailiff – who was a most evil weaselly-looking little fellow – 'interest have been a-mounting, while 'ee've been galli-vanting in furrin parts.'

And he smiled in a satisfied way, no doubt at the thought of his master's delight in having caught his enemy at last.

Despite all my protestations and prayers, two constables and this horrible man took Sam off in a coach to Truro. I was not even allowed to accompany them! I begged and beseeched, but was pushed rudely out of the way. All I could do was press my money into Sam's hand to pay for necessaries in jail, keeping only a couple of coins. Oh, so long as I live, I hope never to suffer another parting like that one! Sam, it is true, bore his arrest stoically enough; 'Mayhap 'twas fated to fall out like this,' he said calmly. 'Don't grieve, lad!' But I was nearly mad with rage and sorrow and self-blame.

* One Spanish dollar was worth about 4s.6d. or 22½p.

'What can I do that's best for you?' I asked, in the brief moments before the coach came to the door and he was taken away.

His face broke into its usual grin.

'Why, lad, the very best is that you should find your great kinsfolk, and have them recognise you and take you in! Naught would ease my heart so much as to know that you were in safety and comfort; it frets me sore to be obliged to leave you thus, wi'out a single friend in a land that's strange to you.'

'Oh, *that* is no matter,' said I. 'I shall do well enough. And I *will* find my great kin, Sammy, and I shall ask them to pay off your debt.'

'Nay, lad,' he said laughing. 'Eighty pound English is more than you reckon! A man could hardly earn such a sum in three years. Never fret about me – I mun abide my fortune as best I may.'

And then they led him off to the coach.

I stood there in the snowy street, watching the horses pull the coach away up the hill, and my heart felt like a stone inside my chest. I thought of poor Juana in Llanes, waiting for Sam to return. I wished the earth would open up and swallow me. I wished that I had been drowned when the *Guipuzcoa* went down. I wished that Sam had never had the ill-luck to meet me: I cannot say what else I wished. And I felt more miserably alone than ever before in my travels, and looked about this English town with hatred. The little stone white-washed houses appeared utterly dingy and poverty-stricken, the sky was grey and gloomy, the street was foul with snow and beasts' droppings, and the people's voices sounded harsh and strident.

However, as I stood shivering in the roadway, without a notion in my head what to do next, a kindly voice broke into my sad thoughts.

'Hey-day, my lad! Do 'ee wish to travel to Bath? Eli Button, up to Customs House, did say as 'ee had folks a-living there? My son-in-law Ned, 'e be a carter, an' 'e be setting off for Bath town, directly, wi' a load of salt pilchards; Ned'll take 'ee along and welcome! A waggon bain't so fast as a stage-coach, mind; 'twill take 'ee the best part o' three days, but 'ee'll get there in the end, sartin sure.'

It was the landlord of the inn who addressed me, and suddenly, looking round, I realised that, instead of being friendless as I had thought, I had many people on my side; there was general sympathy for poor Sam and indignation at the heartless way in which he had been snatched off while his clothes were hardly dried yet after the shipwreck.

''Tis a proper shame,' the landlord's wife said. 'But everyone do say that Ebenezer Pinchplum be the meanest curmudgeonly old maw-worm this side o' Tamar. Arr! someone'll inform on *him* one o' these days and then he'll laugh on t'other side o' his face!'

A whole group of people commiserated with me on my friend's misfortune and said that one of these days old Pinchplum would choke on his own meanness, and I began to feel more kindly disposed towards the English.

Then Ned, the landlord's son-in-law appeared –
a big, smiling simple fellow, dressed in a coarse
linen tunic; he pulled his forelock shyly and said
he'd be main glad of my company on the road to
Bath, for he had to travel it once a week and had
driven it back and forth so many times that he was
fair wearied by it, and had much ado to keep
awake along the way.

So, as I had no reason to linger in Falmouth,
and no wish to, I paid our reckoning at the inn,
said goodbye to the friendly innkeeper, and
climbed on to the waggon, which was drawn by
four massive grey horses – I had never before seen
such beasts, they seemed more like elephants than
our slender horses and mules in Spain. I soon discovered that they were necessary, however, for the
hills in Cornwall are steep – not high, but very
sharp – and the roads very bad, muddy and slippery with snow.

It seemed late in the day to set out, but Ned
explained that we would spend a night with his
aunt, who lived in a village the other side of Truro;
that would give us a good start on the morrow,
and then, by the night of that day we would be
able to reach Exeter, where he had a cousin who
would give us a bed. Then, if all went well, we
should arrive in Bath by the evening of the second
day. I asked how far it was to Bath and he said
about a hundred and forty miles; the English
reckon in miles rather than leagues.

Dusk soon fell as we rumbled along, and I, being
weary and heartsick from all our adventures, and

the loss of Sam, fell into a kind of doze, curled up in the waggon among the barrels of fish, under a piece of sack which Ned kindly provided. Indeed, so tired was I that I was sleeping when we passed through Truro, and so missed seeing the town where Sam lay confined. This filled me with shame when I discovered what I had done.

I remember little of that night. We halted at a small place, called, I think, St Morion, only two or three houses, which seemed to be situated in a wilderness. I helped Ned feed and stable his horses in a stone barn; then we went into his aunt's house, which was very tiny, with stone walls and stone floors, and a fire of earth-coal burning in an iron grate; we were given some broth of mutton and turnips by the aunt, an old, white-haired woman who was bent double by rheumatism; and then I asked if I might lie down to sleep since I could hardly keep my eyes from closing, and was led up a little narrow flight of wooden stairs to a room no bigger than a dog kennel, where I flung myself down on a mattress so damp that it reminded me of my bed in Villaverde.

I had meant to expostulate with God on Sam's fate and beg for His help, but sleep carried me instantly into forgetfulness, and I knew nothing more until next morning when I found Ned snoring beside me as I woke to a hollow feeling of loneliness, sorrow and guilt.

The aunt gave us breakfast long before dawn, of eggs and hot yellow bread spiced with saffron; I offered to pay from the three small coins I had remaining, but both the old lady and Ned said no to that; and he added that he brought her so many goods free of cartage on his journeys back and forth that she was glad to give a free room and board to him and his companions.

That day the weather was better, the snow beginning to melt away, and, by noon, a pale sun shone forth. Oh, the land across which we travelled was most strange – in all my journey across Spain I had seen nothing like it! A pale brown moorland stretched on all sides of us, with hardly a house to be seen, but only small sharp hillocks, each rising to a point of rock, and many fords, where little brown brawling streams ran across the road. There were no men or beasts abroad, and Ned told me that the people of these parts make their living by working underground, in the tin-mines.

I did my best to divert Ned with songs and tales of Spain as payment for my ride, but, though kindly, he was a slow-witted fellow, and required to have everything repeated to him two or three times over before he could understand it, so that I found the day long, and most tiring and tedious; many and many a time my heart was pierced with longing for poor Sam, laid by the leg in Truro jail, and I wondered what was happening to him.

We travelled on until long after dark, and came to Exeter around midnight, so I saw little of the town, which seemed to be large, but very dirty and evil-smelling, with numerous narrow lanes and much mud. Ned told me though, that Exeter's chief trade is with Spain and there are many Spaniards living there, which gave me kindlier feelings towards the place.

As before, we spent the night in a small house, which, since Ned's cousin was a tanner, smelt most vilely of tanning leather. However he received us kindly, and, like the aunt at St Morion, fed us free of charge. Again we were away long before dawn, riding through a bitter storm of rain and sleet, wrapped in sacks to keep ourselves warm.

By midday we had reached the town of Taunton, a very pretty city with thatched houses and many little gardens, now brown and wintry. Then, after passing through some well-cultivated farm-land, we came to a long dreary region of marshes covered for miles by grazing sheep, whose cries reminded me sadly of the plain round Villaverde.

Another long day went slowly by as the horses toiled along muddy roads at a pace just faster than a man could walk. At last Ned was obliged to acknowledge that we should not reach Bath that night; accordingly we stayed at a small and dirty inn which stood in a village called Chew. As we arrived in the dark and left in the dark I have no recollection of the place beyond the civility of the landlord who – since I had no money left, having spent it on food during the day – agreed to take my Spanish knife in exchange for a night on a straw mattress and a plate of porridge – a strange dish of crushed oats and water, such as would be given to animals in Spain!

Next morning, as daylight came, we reached a hilltop from which we had a prospect of Bath. I thought it a most noble-looking town. It is built in a valley, around a hot spring, and is not yet a hundred years old, having been built by a man called John Wood, so that people might live there and receive benefit from the mineral waters. Ned told me this, though what was in the waters he could not say.

When I saw those handsome houses, some of them snow-white, some already blackened by smoke, all arranged with such orderliness in rows and squares and curved crescents my heart beat fast indeed, and I said to myself,

'My father walked those same streets. Perhaps he often stood where I am now and saw this sight!'

Ned asked me where I would wish to be set down, as he was bound for the main market, which lies in the centre of the city. I told him The Rose and Ring-Dove Inn, and it was well that he had asked me beforehand, for this inn, he told me, lay outside the city, on the Bristol road, by a bridge that crosses the Avon river. He presently set me down there, having kindly gone somewhat out of his way to do so. In reply to my heartfelt thanks for all his kindness he said,

'Arr, lad, 'twas a pleasure to carry 'ee, 'twere like an eddication! I never laffed so much as at they songs o' yourn (once you had telled me the meanings), an' I'll carry 'ee again, an' gladly, any time as 'ee've a fancy to fare back to Falmouth! I come by every week – ask for me at Oliver's stall i' the market of a Friday marning!'

And so he cracked his long whip and rumbled

on his way, while I walked with a fast-beating heart into The Rose and Ring-Dove Inn.

This was a handsome building, large as a convent. It was timbered somewhat after the style of the houses in Llanes, and a beautiful sign, hanging in front, showed a red rose and a white dove, set against a green background. Behind the inn, pleasure-gardens ran down to the swift-flowing river, but there was little pleasure in them now: they looked most dismal with sodden grass and pinched brown roses hanging from the trellises.

In front, a gravelled yard was full of coaches, large and small.

I ventured into the main entrance-hall, and hesitated there, feeling foolish and scared enough; here I stood, in my damp, salt-stained clothes, without a penny in my pocket, my only belongings a bundle of papers, a piece of black plume, and a few brass buttons – why should I expect anybody to welcome me? And how should I set about making inquiries?

It took me a long time to pluck up my courage; for, thought I miserably, once I have made inquiry here, if no one is able to give me any information, then I am at a stand indeed! I have come all the way from Villaverde to this spot – at what a cost – supposing I find here no clue, no means of going on, then I am undone. And so is Sam.

So, trembling inwardly, I loitered in the main hall of the inn and looked about me. The point where I stood was like a busy cross-roads – doors were all the time opening and shutting, bells were ringing, waiters were scurrying back and forth, carrying trays with coffee and rolls (for it was yet early); boot-boys darted by with clean pairs of boots, barbers' boys with hot water and razors, and the barbers themselves with bags of powder; washerwomen stumped past with bundles of clean linen, horns blew outside the door, and messengers pushed through with bags of letters.

In all this busy commotion no one seemed to regard me, and yet, somehow, I felt myself an object of scrutiny. Turning my head, I noticed an oldish man, dressed in black, sitting on a bench, who seemed to observe me very fixedly and attentively. This disturbed me, for his black dress reminded me of the alguacil in Oviedo, so, all of a rush, I accosted a pretty chambermaid as she skipped by, and asked her if she knew any person by the name of Brooke, who lived in this inn, or somewhere not far away?

Giving me one brief disdainful glance she snapped out,

'Never heard of 'em in me life – nobody o' that name here!' and ran on her way.

Now I was utterly discouraged, not daring to make inquiry of anybody else, lest the haughty chambermaid should pass by again and overhear me; I was about to wander back into the rain-washed inn yard, had not the elderly man at that moment risen from his seat and walked over to me. I saw him come with apprehension; yet his aspect did not seem threatening. Indeed as he approached me, his face seemed to hold a look of cautious hope.

He said to me – his voice was most gentle and polite:

'I beg your pardon, my young sir – I am a little hard of hearing; I believe you were inquiring for Brooke?'

'Yes, sir!'

Now my heart bounded up. Seeing him close to, I felt sure that he was not an alguacil. Perhaps he was related to me! His face was lined and thoughtful, with a look of kindness and intelligence; he carried a flat black hat in his hand, and wore a clean white band round his neck.

'Might I inquire *your* name?' the gentleman next asked me courteously.

'Yes, sir, it is Brooke, Felix Brooke. I am come from Villaverde, in Spain, to inquire for the family of my father, Captain Felix Brooke. Can you perhaps – ?'

But before I could finish, the gentleman had both my hands in his, and, exclaiming, 'Oh, my dear, dear boy!' he was shaking them up and down as if he could never leave go of me.

'The moment I set eyes on you,' he was saying, 'the moment I saw you I felt sure you must be your father's son! You have such a look of him! Oh, I am so rejoiced that you came here! I was so afraid that you would not!'

'But, sir – were you then expecting me?' I asked, very much surprised. Wherever I went, it seemed, people knew beforehand that I was coming!

'Yes, yes!' he said. 'We have – *I* have been hoping to see you these three weeks past – oh, but filled with such apprehensions as to what perils you might be encountering – offering up so many prayers for your safety – thanks be to God who has brought you safely here!'

He let go one of my hands and wiped a tear from his eye, saying, 'Forgive me! You look so like your father – it brings him back, so, to see you!'

Quite bewildered by this speedy and unexpected change in my fortunes, I hardly knew what to say, but giving me no time, he exclaimed,

'You are cold and hungry I daresay – you are very likely half-starved! Come – come quickly, my dear boy, come with me – ' and he half-dragged me from the hallway down a passage to a stable-yard at the back of the inn, where he called loudly,

'James, James, I have him, I *have him*! James, where are you? James! Set to the horses at once!'

A little brown man shot out of the stables, did a kind of caper of delight, then disappeared, to return leading two chestnut horses harnessed to a glossy four-wheeled wooden carriage with glass windows in front and at the sides.

'Here we are, here we are!' said my elderly companion, and bustled me to the carriage. 'See, see, James, I have him – is he not the Master Felix of twenty years ago? To the very life?' And to me, 'This is James Merriwether, who taught your father to ride his first pony.'

'And rarely he shaped at it – he rode like a gipsy,' said the little man, thrusting out a gnarled

314

brown hand, 'And I'll warrant you'll be the same, my young master, for you've a horseman's upright back and flat thigh – or my name's not Jem Merriwether!' and he, too, shook my hand up and down as if he could not bear to stop.

Then I was almost lifted into the carriage – which, I learned later, was called a chaise – Merriwether took his place on the box, and the black-clad man climbed in beside me.

We started off at a rapid trot, taking the road away from Bath, and bowled along by the river, which here wound beside a great flat meadow full of brown cattle, below a wintry wooded hillside.

'Sir,' I said, 'please explain to me for I am wholly puzzled – were you expecting me to come to that inn?'

'Indeed we were, my boy, and had been for weeks past! But then, the day before yesterday, we had intelligence by post from the Customs Officer at Falmouth that a boy named Felix Brooke had been saved from a wreck, so our expectations – may I say our *hopes* – had become more immediate!'

'But who did the – Sir, may I please know whom I have the honour of addressing?'

Being quite ignorant of whom he might be I used the politest Spanish mode of address, and my companion broke into laughter.

'Indeed you may, my dear boy,' he said in a friendly tone. 'But there is no honour in the case! My name is Thomas Burden – the Reverend Thomas Burden; for many years I was your dear father's tutor, and I am also your grandfather's chaplain.'

Another grandfather! I thought. And then – like Father Tomas – but what a difference!

'Then, Senor Burden – if my grandfather does not live at The Rose and Ring-Dove – how did word reach you?'

'Why, your grandfather has been advertising for you – or at least, his man of business, Mr ffanshawe, has – he had left word at all the Channel ports – '

'But why has he been advertising *now*?'

I was even more puzzled than before. Why should this English grandfather begin to advertise for me after twelve years? Or had he been doing so all through my life?

But how did he even know of my existence?

'Why advertise now?' said Mr Burden. 'Why, because we had a letter from your Spanish grandfather, the Conde de Cabezada – a most dignified, proper letter, I may say – explaining that you had left your Spanish home, and he had reason to believe you were coming here.'

'But how did *he* know where to write?' I was more and more amazed. 'He could not have received my letter yet. He did not even know that I had an English family. I did not know it myself, for sure!'

'Ah, I am no hand at telling a tale!' exclaimed Mr Burden apologetically. 'I have it all topsy-turvy! He knew, of course, because when your great-aunt Isadora died – '

'*What?*' I gasped. 'She is *dead*?'

I do not precisely know why, but this news came as a most mortal shock to me – I turned cold from head to foot, the very marrow seemed to drain from my bones. That she, who had wished and caused me such harm, should suddenly be *gone* – disappeared into the shadows – how can I explain what I felt at hearing this? It was not fear, but a kind of dark sadness. I had hated her so fiercely; now she was gone; what avail to hate her any more?

'Are you ill, my boy?' inquired Mr Burden anxiously. 'You have gone very pale?'

'No – no, thank you, senor; I am not ill; only the shock – it is so strange. – How did my great-aunt die?'

'It seems there were some prisoners lodged in your grandfather's house at Villaverde, on their way to trial – '

I nodded, having known of this from Senor Smith's letter.

'And your great-aunt went up to visit them – it was thought, with charitable intentions of giving them counsel or religious instruction: but she caught a malignant fever from one of them, and died of it within a week.'

Another cold shiver went through me as I thought of that scrawny, wiry old body stretched out on a bed of sickness, tossing in fever; great-aunt Isadora had always been so vigorous and strong, she had never known a day's ailment . . . I felt as if the fever had entered my own bones.

'On her deathbed,' said Mr Burden, 'she made a confession that greatly shocked your grandfather the Conde. It seemed that she had always hated your mother, and hated *you* equally, from the moment of your birth. So, when, three years ago, I wrote to your grandfather – '

'You wrote to him three years ago?' I exclaimed in amazement.

'I should go back earlier in the story; I am making a sorry tangle of it,' Mr Burden lamented. 'Four years ago there came into my hands a letter from your father – '

'From my *father*? *Four* years ago?'

Hope flashed up in me like a comet; then sank again as Mr Burden said sadly,

'It was written before he died; ah, poor fellow, he was so injured in the wars that he could hardly scrawl, and the address was so ill-writ that the letter wandered half over England before it reached us. And then we could not read it! Will you believe me, Felix, when I tell you that it took me a year's patient labour to decipher his writing, and even then I do not believe I could have done it if I had not been a student of strange scripts, Coptic, Sanskrit, Arabic, and others?'

'Indeed I *will* believe you, Senor Burden,' I said with heartfelt truth. 'For I have myself some papers in his writing, and the only words I could decipher, from start to finish, were the ones naming the Rose and Ring-Dove Inn, by which means I was able to come here.'

Then, filled with joy, I cried out, 'If you can read

my father's writing, Senor Burden, can you help me to understand these papers?' And I pulled out the little packet in its waterproof wrapping.

'It will be my happiness to help you,' said Mr Burden, receiving the packet from me with gentle hands. 'Ah, I see you have your father's book also – he was so fond of that book! He would have it with him always – he thought it one of the shrewdest and best-writ tales he had ever come across, and often said he wished he might meet the lady who wrote it – '

'But then,' I puzzled, going back to his tale, which still seemed all snarled up like a tangle of worsted, 'what happened after you read my father's letter? What did it say?'

'Why, it told of his marriage, and your birth, and your mother's death, and your poor father said that he feared he himself had not long to live. And he gave the name and address of your grandfather in Spain. So then we wrote at once to the Conde de Cabezada, asking for news as to what had happened to your father, and about yourself and saying that, if the Conde agreed, you should be sent over here to receive an English education. – But it seems that your great-aunt Isadora managed to intercept this letter so that the Conde never knew of its arrival. They found it among her belongings after her death. – And your great-aunt Isadora wrote a false letter here, saying that you had died of a fever. Your English grandfather was much grieved at this intelligence, and wrote no more. Your great-aunt Isadora must, I fear, have

319

been a very wicked woman,' said Mr Burden in a tone of moderate condemnation.

'She wanted her own grandson to inherit Villaverde,' said I. 'My cousin Manuel. And I suppose she feared that, as soon as Don Francisco knew that I was legitimate, he would wish to keep me.'

'Disgraceful,' murmured Mr Burden to himself. 'Disgraceful behaviour. However, she has gone to her rest now and made her peace with God; it is not for us to condemn her.'

I did not really see why she should not be condemned. She had caused much harm and unhappiness.

'If she has made her peace with God,' I inquired, 'does that mean she has gone to heaven?'

It did not seem at all fair to me that *one* deathbed repentance should cancel a whole life of deceit and malice; and if great-aunt Isadora were now in heaven, I was not at all certain that I wished to go there. However I decided to discuss that with God at a later time.

Mr Burden said it was all a matter for debate; and then he smiled and said,

'Ah, you are so like your father!'

I was still pondering over his tale in which there seemed to be many gaps.

'I wonder how my grandfather Cabezada *knew* that I intended to come here and search for my English family? – I had said so to Pedro, but I had not told him where I intended to go.'

I wondered if great-aunt Isadora, on her deathbed confession, had mentioned bribing the

Comprachicos to decoy me on board the *Gui-puzcoa* and transform me by their terrible arts. If she had not confessed *that*, then she was still doomed to damnation. It made me shiver to think of her launching this hateful plot after me like a poisoned arrow, and then being overtaken by her own death before it had even been carried out.

I thought I would not mention this matter to Mr Burden.

He said, 'It seems that your grandfather the Conde received some intelligence about your journey. He had caused inquiries to be made after your departure, and had traced your progress part of the way. Then he had a letter from a priest in a village called Santillana, commending your bravery, and from that place he was able to follow your track backwards to a smith in Llanes, and a miller in San Antonio.' Mr Burden smiled, and added, 'There are probably not so many yellow-haired boys riding about north Spain, after all!'

I was quite surprised that my grandfather had taken such pains to trace me. But hoped, on reflection, that the reports he received of me on my journey would not have been too unfavourable.

Bringing my thoughts back to the present, I asked,

'Where are we going, senor?'

The chaise was now travelling along a smooth gravelled road between rough walls crowned with a curious iron-dark stone. Over to our left I saw a large and fantastic building, built of the same dark-coloured stone, and all crowned with cupolas and battlements, like a castle.

'Those are your grandfather's stables,' said Mr Burden, to my considerable surprise. They did not look in the least like stables.

'The way to them passes in a tunnel underneath this road,' he explained. 'And here are the park lodges.' He gestured at two small buildings with similar turret-work on the right-hand side of the road.

'Now we shan't be long, your lordship!' called back Merriwether, through an opening in the glass pane.

*Your lordship!* I wondered at this mode of address.

'Senor Burden – *who am I?* Please tell me about my English family?'

'But – ' He seemed astonished. 'Did your father, then, never tell you?'

The carriage turned to the right, passed through a gate between the two lodges, and began bowling along towards a dark mass of leafless oakwoods.

'My father?' I said. 'But I never *knew* my father!'

'Good heavens!' Mr Burden stared at me, wholly taken aback, it seemed. 'In all those years then – even at the last – he never divulged his identity? He was with you all through your childhood, and yet never revealed himself? Eh well – poor fellow – poor fellow! Doubtless he thought it best. He would always go his own way – there was no ruling him, or advising him!'

Utterly astounded at these words, I pondered

over them, while their meaning slowly shook and dissolved and settled into my understanding.

*Who* had been with me all through my childhood?

The carriage rattled through the belt of woodland, then emerged on the other side. Ahead of us rose a high, green grassy hillside, and at its foot, set between clumps of huge chestnut trees with massive twisted trunks, lay an enormous grey house – so long, so big, that it seemed like a whole village in itself.

'Do you mean,' I said slowly, 'do you mean, Senor Burden, that *Bob* was my father? Is that what you mean? Did *he* write this letter?'

'Why, of course – who else?' said Mr Burden. 'He wanted to watch over you as long as he could, poor dear fellow. – But now, here we are.' He added, more formally, 'Welcome to your grandfather's house, my lord St Winnow. Welcome to Asshe.'

'But who *is* my grandfather, Senor Burden?'

'His name, like yours and your father's, is Charles Felix Robert Lewis Carisbroke. He is the Duke of Wells and Taunton.'

The chaise rolled to a halt at the foot of a great flight of stone steps while I was still digesting this information.

# 11

I hardly noticed my surroundings, as Mr Burden
assisted me to alight from the chaise, and led me
up the great curving flight of stairs towards the
main entrance of the house. I was still utterly
stunned and perplexed by this news of my father.

If my father was Bob – why had he never
revealed himself? If Bob was my father – why was
my English grandfather a Duke? If Bob was my
father – why had he not *told* me about my English
connections, instead of leaving me an illegible
letter?

All these questions jostled together in my mind.
I stumbled along, hardly looking where I put my
feet.

At the top of the steps a wide terrace, with a
stone balustrade, extended on either hand, running
along the front of the house. Mr Burden glanced,
in a somewhat harassed way, to our right, where
two people were strolling, not far away. He said,
in a hurried, anxious manner.

'Ah – there is your grandfather. But perhaps it
will be best if you do not meet him just yet – '

He made as if to lead me into the house, but we

had delayed a moment too long, and the couple on the terrace came up to us. I saw a tallish, handsome man, with rather bulging eyes and curling brown hair – *he* could not be my grandfather – who carefully held the arm of a short, spare little personage, slightly bow-legged but elegantly dressed in a black silk jacket and pantaloons, with ruffles of the whitest lace at his neck and wrists; he wore an immense, comical, old-fashioned wig, out of which poked forth a sharp, wrinkled, suspicious old countenance, with a nose curved as sharply as an eagle's beak, and two bright, angry blue eyes. The eyes raked back and forth as if searching for enemies. They rested on me, darted away, came back again, left me once more . . . I saw with sorrow that they had no sense in them. They were the eyes of a child.

'Your grandfather is very old,' said Mr Burden in a hasty undertone. 'Do not allow yourself to be distressed by anything he may say. He is not quite in his right wits any more – '

My English grandfather stumped up to me, his buckled shoes and his black cane clacking impatiently on the pavement.

'Well, Felix!' he said sharply. 'I hear you have been playing truant, as usual! And your appearance is disgraceful sir – *disgraceful!* What kind of garments do you call those – ?' With his cane he jerked at my jacket – which was stained and threadbare enough, in all conscience. 'You look like a stable-boy – like a stable-boy, sirrah! Go and get changed immediately. How dare you appear

325

like this before me! Take a bath! And mind you are in time for dinner.' Then he turned on his heel, adding over his shoulder. 'You may send your brother Charles to me.'

'Y-y-y-yes, sir!' I said, angry because my stammer had come back – and very sad, also, because, if I had at any time framed hopes of what my father's father might be like, they certainly had not been anything like *this*.

'Lord St Winnow – this is Mr ffanshawe – your grandfather's man of business,' Mr Burden said, in the same hurried undertone, and the tall man made me a low bow, rapidly saying,

'Happy to make your lordship's acquaintance, I am sure!' before hastening away after his charge.

'Of course he took you for your father,' said Mr Burden, quietly, piloting me indoors, into a great black-and-white marble tiled hall with statues set about on plinths. 'And indeed, the likeness is remarkable. Poor man, his mind is all in the past.'

'Where is my father's brother Charles? The one he mentioned?'

'Your father's elder brother? He died at the battle of Waterloo.'

Just at that moment the sun came out, and a great shaft of light poured through a wide, high-up window, brilliantly illuminating the great marble hall. I stared about – at the brocade hangings, the suits of armour, the statues, the grand white staircase – feeling as trapped as ever I had at Villaverde. Here, it seemed, was the same thing all over again. Old people grieving for young ones who had been sent to their death.

'Why do men fight wars, Senor Burden?'

'Ah,' he sighed, 'if I could answer that, my dear boy, I should be the wisest man in the world! – But come, you are tired after your travels: Watchett, here, who is your grandfather's valet, will take you to your chamber. It is probable that there are still some clothes of your father's – or your uncle Charles – which may fit you; and if you have been on the road since dawn I expect you may be glad of a bath; and then I daresay you could eat a nuncheon!'

He smiled at me very kindly, as he offered me these remedies, and then moved away, saying, 'I will leave you in Watchett's care, and shall await you in the morning-room in half-an-hour's time.'

I thought what a piece of good fortune it was for me that *he* should be my English grandfather's chaplain. Suppose he had been like Father Tomas! What an arrival I should have had then!

I had not particularly taken to Mr ffanshawe.

Watchett, a stout, white-haired man, seemed friendly, however; he led me to a handsome chamber and there prepared me a bath in front of a great blazing fire of earth-coal. I was not used to so much attention and felt somewhat embarrassed by his services, but he left the room while I bathed, and presently returned with an armful of clothes, saying,

'I daresay these of your father's may fit you tolerably well, my lord,' and then put me at my

327

ease, while he helped me dress, by telling stories of my father's wild ways, how, as a boy, he spent all the time he could in the stables, and rode in horse-races at Newmarket, learned boxing of two great experts called Jackson and Mendoza, acted as whipper-in for his father's huntsman, and was rusticated from the university of Oxford for introducing a giraffe into the chapel of Christ Church College.

'Ah, he were a wild one, Master Felix were,' said Watchett fondly, helping me into grey breeches and a striped grey fustian coat with cut steel buttons – not in the first stare of fashion, I could see, but certainly far superior to my own damp and salty garments. 'But not an ounce of vice in him – heart of gold, Master Felix had.'

Buckled, square-toed shoes completed my attire.

'There,' said Watchett, arranging a white stock round my neck. 'Now you're as fine as fivepence, my lord! I daresay Mr ffanshawe will be taking you off to His Grace's tailor in Bath presently, but for a nuncheon at home, you will do very well. May I say how glad we are to have you among us! It's like a ray of sunshine to have a young face in the house again.' He gave me a warm smile and I felt that I had found another friend.

Mr Burden was waiting for me downstairs. I was relieved to learn that my grandfather would not be present at the meal; he, it seemed, ate by himself in his own apartments. Mr Burden led me to a dining-room where cold meat, fruit, cakes, and wine were laid out in golden dishes and crystal vessels. Mr ffanshawe was there, and a group of other men who were introduced by Mr Burden.

'This is Mr Willowes, your grandfather's secretary; and Mr Tyler, who looks after the estate; and Mr Bendigo, your grandfather's librarian; and Dr Larpent, your grandfather's medical adviser; and Mr Dinsdale who oversees the affairs of the house and garden; and Mr Tweedy the archivist.'

These men all acknowledged my introduction to them with perfect politeness; and glanced at me briefly, as if estimating me to be too young to be of any interest or importance. Mr ffanshawe, indeed, remarked that presently he and I must have a short conversation about business affairs; he was furnished he said, with a copy of my parents' marriage-lines, which had come to hand with my father's long-delayed letter; but he would be obliged if I could give him details of my age, place of birth, etc., for his records. That seemed to be his sole interest in me.

We sat down around a large table, were served by a stately butler, and all the men proceeded to eat a hearty meal, talking among themselves about the affairs of the estate, and quite ignoring me. When they referred to my grandfather, as they did from time to time, they alluded to him as 'His G', in slightly contemptuous, indulgent tones. – 'No use asking His G about that – better do as you think fit, Tyler. Sell off the bullocks and buy black-faced ewes.'

It soon became plain to me, listening, that my grandfather had nothing to do with the running of his affairs, that these men constituted the real power in the house.

Towards the end of the meal they began talking about me, however.

'Now that Lord St Winnow has returned, he had best be sent to school,' said Mr Willowes, a thin, dry, grey-haired man with gold spectacles halfway down his nose, glancing at me over the top of the spectacles in a severe manner, as if I were a bit of grit that had lodged in the works of a smooth-running machine. He went on, 'It is to be presumed that, as he has spent all his life in Spain, he is far behind in his studies. Mr ffanshawe, I leave it to you to select a suitable establishment where his lordship may be prepared for Eton and Oxford.'

Mr ffanshawe said, 'I had already been considering that point myself; I think Pulteney's Academy in Bath will do very well. Mr Burden, I am sure, will be good enough to examine his lordship and discover his capabilities and attainments; and, Mr Tyler, if you will charge yourself with outfitting him, I fancy he may be despatched to school within a week or so. I will communicate with the headmaster of the Pulteney immediately. Let us see – he will need clothes – books – a box for his things – a horse – furnishings for his room – '

I felt rather astonished at being thus briskly disposed of; they seemed to be dealing with me as if I were a parcel. I could not complain that they bore me any ill-will or behaved unkindly; indeed, as I presently discovered, they were all men of honour and discharged their duties with the utmost

330

diligence and regard for the good of the estate. It just had not occurred to them that my wishes need be considered.

But then, I acknowledged to myself, I was not at all sure what my wishes *were*. How could I decide whether it was better to be sent away to school, and meet some English boys, or to remain here and be snapped at by my mad grandfather?

Then a thought came to me which made the blood run quick in my veins.

I said,

'Mr ffanshawe, have I any money?'

He stared at me rather blankly, as if the great gold ornament in the centre of the table had suddenly piped up and asked him a question.

'Eh? I beg your pardon, Lord St Winnow? Money?'

His expression was so comical that I almost laughed.

'Er – I believe Lord St Winnow wishes to ascertain whether he is possessed of *funds*,' remarked Mr Tyler, a red-haired man who looked like a foxy horse, or a horsey fox.

'Eh – well – well – I could advance your lordship half a guinea,' Mr ffanshawe conceded.

'No, thank you; I don't mean that,' I said civilly. 'I meant, is there any money here that belongs to me?'

'Why – why yes,' said Mr ffanshawe, looking as if all this were most improper. 'A sum was laid aside for your lordship, by the terms of your late father's Will, to be administered by Trust, er –

invested in the Funds – bringing in an income of some three thousand pounds a year – '

'So, as I haven't spent any of it since I was born, there must be a great deal of it by now?'

'I would not say a *great deal*,' said Mr ffanshawe fastidiously, 'not a *great deal*, but a reasonable sum, yes, my lord, to be administered on your behalf at the discretion of the Trust, until you are of age.'

'And what is the Trust?'

'The Trust? Why, that is the persons designated to administer the funds.'

I felt as if we were going round and round in circles.

'Yes, but who are these persons?'

'Why, Mr Willowes, Mr Tyler, Mr Bendigo, Mr Burden, Mr Dinsdale and myself.'

'Very good,' said I. 'Then, if you please, Senor ffanshawe, I wish you will have five hundred pounds from my monies despatched to Truro jail, for Mr Sam Pollard, who is imprisoned there unjustly for debt, part of the sum to pay off his debt, and the rest to be used by him as he chooses.'

'*Five* hundred *pounds*? – I trust your lordship is speaking in jest?' said Mr ffanshawe after a pause. 'Five hundred pounds, I would have you know, is a very considerable sum of money.'

'I am quite aware of that, Mr ffanshawe,' said I. 'Sam Pollard is a friend of mine who risked his life to help me, travelling in a ship full of dangerous criminals, and he accompanied me to England, where he knew that he might expect to be flung into jail. I wish you will send the five hundred pounds to Truro at once, if you please.'

The eight men all stared at one another.

'This is very untoward,' said Mr ffanshawe.

'Unprecedented,' said Mr Willowes.

'Exceptional,' said Mr Dinsdale.

'If the boy really owes his life to this person – ' said Mr Tyler.

'But how can we be sure of that?' said Mr Willowes. 'A young person cannot possibly judge of such a case. The boy may well have imagined the danger.'

'Young persons are easily imposed upon,' agreed Mr Bendigo, a dusty little man with red-rimmed watery eyes. 'The man in Truro jail may well be a character of the lowest order.'

'I think it would certainly be our duty to look *most* closely into the credentials of the fellow in the jail before we disburse any money,' said Mr Dinsdale.

'Five hundred pounds, your lordship, cannot be laid out as if it were half a guinea,' said Mr ffanshawe.

I began to feel my temper going, as I thought of Sammy Pollard lying in Truro jail – which I imagined like the calabozo in Oviedo – while these old roosters ate their dinner off gold plate and pecked my patience to pieces.

Then I noticed that Mr Burden was smiling at me sympathetically, so I made a great effort at control, and said,

'Mr ffanshawe, you spoke just now of purchasing a horse for me; how much would such an animal cost?'

'Why,' he said, 'I suppose one might be procured for a couple of hundred guineas.'

'And my clothes and furnishings – how much will they cost?'

'About the same, I daresay – a little more.'

'Very well. Pray give me that money in cash, Mr ffanshawe, and I will undertake to buy my own clothes, very much more cheaply, and my own mount. I am accustomed to ride a mule, which I can obtain for a twentieth of that sum, and I will send the rest to my friend.'

Their faces lengthened, their mouths opened, and they looked at one another in utter dismay.

'Ride a *mule*? Lord St Winnow ride a *mule*?' said the foxy Mr Tyler in tones of strong disgust. 'That is quite out of the question!'

'But it is not out of the question that I should neglect the friend who saved my life at the risk of his own?' I said with some heat.

They all looked at one another again, and Dr Larpent, a well-set-up, good-natured, clever-looking man, said,

'Perhaps if Lord St Winnow were to step aside into the library a moment, the Trustees might convene a formal meeting and discuss the matter quietly. I am sure they can find some means of settling this affair to everybody's satisfaction.'

Glancing at him, I was surprised when he gave me a friendly wink. Thawing a little, I replied in a dignified manner,

'Certainly; I will be glad to retire to the library.'

'Lynton will show you the way,' said Mr Burden, smiling at me, and the stately butler did so.

The library seemed much more promising than that of my grandfather at Villaverde. Many of the volumes in the well-stocked shelves were plays, novels, or poetry. I wondered if they had belonged to my father or my uncle Charles, and if I might get permission to take some of these books away with me to school.

Then, in a glass-fronted case, I discovered a number of musical instruments – flutes, pipes, a fiddle, a viol, a rebeck. Full of delight at this welcome sight, I opened the case, pulled out a set of pipes, and began to softly play one of the tunes that Sam and I had composed, which we had called 'An Air for the Bad-Tempered Mule, with Various Variations'.

The ripple of the notes soothed my anger and filled me with a calm, steadfast resolve to see that Sam received the money somehow. My first indignant notions – of taking one of the gold dinner-plates, riding off with it to Bath, and pawning it – died away; I thought to myself, 'Come, Felix! You have made your way here, you escaped from Oviedo jail and from the shipwreck and the Comprachicos – by God's help; do not lose trust in Him now.'

Sure enough, after ten minutes or so, Dr Larpent came into the library. I was playing away and did not hear him at first until he said, 'Ahem!'

I looked up to see him smiling at me. He said,

'I have always been told that your father was a very gifted musician, and now I believe it.'

This statement gave me a complicated pain, which I did not wish to examine, so I said,

'Did they decide about the money?'

He began laughing. 'Yes, they have it all arranged! Poor fellows, you must make allowances for them. They are only just beginning to realise what has happened to them. They have run everything in their own way for so long – since your grandfather fell into his dotage – five or six years now – but do not worry, they will come around in time! They are really a set of good fellows, only a little stiff in their notions.'

'So what is to be done?' said I, a little stiffly myself.

'There is an agent for your grandfather's estate in Exeter, since the Duke owns considerable properties in the West Country. This agent will be instructed to travel to Truro and assign the necessary funds to your friend.'

'I suppose they want to make certain that my friend is not "a character of the lowest order",' I said hotly. 'Well, they will find that my story was true in every particular and my friend is a very good, honest man, who has been villainously ill-used.'

'Then you have no cause for anxiety,' said Dr Larpent cheerfully.

Mr ffanshawe soon came in to confirm this, and to ask if I wished to despatch a note to my friend in Truro. I noticed that he now treated me more seriously than he had done before, and looked at me directly, when addressing me, with a certain respect in his manner.

I said I should indeed like to write a letter to my friend, and, as there were pens, ink, and paper in the library, I sat down to do so at once. With my heart in my pen, I wrote Sam that I had succeeded in finding my kin, that they were rich and powerful, and that I was therefore able to send him means to free himself from debt, which I was happy to do, as it was only a tiny and partial payment for all he had done to help me. I begged him to apply to me here, or to my grandfather's agent, should more help be needed. And I wrote, 'I know that you will be anxious to return to Spain with all possible speed, for Juana will be so anxious about you. Any money left over is for your passage. I do not ask you to delay your departure. But still – if you *should* require to stay in England for any reason – I hope you will come to see your Friend.'

I folded the paper and sealed it with my grandfather's seal (a fountain springing from the turrets of a castle) then gave it to the messenger who was waiting to ride with it to Exeter.

Having achieved this filled me with relief. Mounted on a good horse the man could easily reach Exeter within the day; by next day the money would be in Truro, and Sam released from prison. I would not be quite free of anxiety until I heard from Sam himself that this was so, but meantime

I felt much eased, and in a mood to learn more of this great domain where I found myself.

Looking through the library window and seeing Mr Burden strolling on the terrace, I went out to walk with him.

'Is it all arranged?' he said kindly. 'Is the money on its way to your friend?'

'I hope so!' said I. 'Senor Burden, are you at leisure? Can I ask a kindness of you?'

'Of course, my dear boy! I am entirely at your disposal.'

Accordingly I pulled out my father's papers, which I had transferred to the pockets of the striped coat that had once been his, and said,

'Senor Burden, can you read these to me? For I cannot – I cannot understand why my f-f-fa – ' I stopped, took a breath, and began again, as Mr Burden quietly waited, 'I don't understand why he *pretended* to me all those years! It gives me a pain to think about it. And I am hoping that this paper explains why he did it.'

'I think I can understand why he did it,' said Mr Burden quietly. 'But let us see.' He looked about us and said, 'At the end of this terrace there is a little loggia which receives the afternoon sun. I think we shall be warm enough there for half an hour.'

So we settled ourselves in the small stone shelter, which looked out on to the grassy rolling park, with its grazing sheep and deer.

Mr Burden took the papers and studied them in

silence for some considerable time. I did not ask him questions or try to hurry him; I waited.

At last, very slowly, he read out the contents of the letter:

'My dearest boy: I shall be gone when you read these words. Forgive me for not speaking them to you aloud – I will try to explain how it all fell out. You see, when I was young, I was a wild, impatient boy. Charles is fourteen years older – he was always well-behaved and I was always in trouble. Many, many times, Felix, you remind me of myself! When I was sent home from Oxford university my father was so angry that we had a terrible quarrel – he said he never wished to see me again. So I left home and enlisted in the -th under the name of Ensign Brooke. I was happy in the army and soon won promotion. Then, when I was with General Moore's army in Astorga, I met your mother – she was being educated at a convent there – I loved her at first sight, she loved me, and we made a runaway match of it. This was in 1808. Oh, she was beautiful! It cheers me to think of her. Strange that I write this letter in the house where she lived. I wrote to my father that I had married her, but had no answer from him. I supposed he was still too angry to reply. I planned to take Luisa to England – I was sure when he saw her he would forgive us. But then she became ill – she was expecting you –

and had to return to Villaverde, for General Moore's army was retreating; she could not accompany me. Little did we think that we would not meet again in this life. Then I was wounded, so badly that for months I lay like a dead man in a mountain shepherd's hut, cared for by kind people who said I reminded them of their lost son.

'At last I was well enough to crawl, and I crawled over the mountains to Villaverde. That took many more months.

'Arrived there, I found that you had been born, and that Luisa had died. Receiving that news was like my death knell; I did not think I had very much longer to live myself. I discovered that no letter had ever come from my father. Nevertheless I swallowed my pride and wrote again, sending our wedding lines and telling of your birth. That letter, too, remained unanswered. Meanwhile I could not bear to reveal myself as Captain Brooke, as Luisa's husband, and ask for the charity of the Cabezadas. They did not even believe that we had been married – or that I came of a good family – how would they receive me, penniless, crippled, cast off by my father? But as Bob the groom they were prepared to receive me and give me house-room. And thus I could be near *you*, Felix, and see that you were healthy and thriving, even if treated somewhat harshly. My poor boy! Many a time I have longed to reveal myself, but that would be to involve you, a child of four or five, in a daily deceit – or to shame you before all – I could not do it. All I could do was to pour my love on you in small ways, see you grow strong and active, rejoice in your good spirit.

'I shall ask Bernardina to give this to you when you are grown, as I do not think I shall last much longer, and death may take me suddenly when it comes. Dear boy, when you are a man, I think you should make an attempt to be reconciled to my family. Perhaps my letters to my father miscarried – or perhaps he will have died by this time and Charles come into the title. Charles is a good fellow and he would take you in – he always had a kind spot for me. He is clever – not like me – all I wanted was horses and music and fighting. And your mother! I shall soon be with her.

'So, Felix, when you are grown, go to England, go to the town of Bath, take the road that runs westwards to Bristol past the Rose and Ring-Dove Inn, and that will lead you to Asshe. And there, I am sure, for my sake, the family will welcome you.

'My dear boy, I have been a simple fellow all my life, but you, with your mother's spirit in you, have the makings of something more, I am sure. Do well – live bravely – choose the best things – be happy. And you will spare a kindly feeling for your loving

Father.'

Mr Burden's voice shook as he read aloud the last lines. I looked up with blurred eyes, and saw that his face was working. Silently, he handed me back the pages, and I bent my head over them.

Now that I knew what the contents were, I was just about able to make out a word here and a word there.

Mr Burden presently said,

'Now do you understand why he did not tell you?'

'Yes, I do,' said I slowly. 'He felt unable. But oh, I wish he had not! It is as if he had been play-acting to me, all my life.'

Mr Burden reflected a while, then said,

'Try to think of it in this way. – You speak English very well. But perhaps you are more fluent in Spanish? Perhaps that is the language in which you do your thinking?'

I did some thinking, found that it was in Spanish, and said yes.

'And yet,' he said, 'you are able to hold a conversation with me in English – luckily for me! Since, I blush to confess it, I have no Spanish.'

'Yes, sir – but what has that to say to anything?'

'Your father made use of the only language in which he *could* speak to you – that of Bob the groom? Do you see? But because a person is speaking in a tongue not his own, that does not make what he expresses in it any less true, or less loving.'

I thought I understood a little of what he meant, and said that I would try to think of it in that way.

But I still felt a sore sadness within me, which would take long to heal.

Then I asked,

'Senor Burden?'

'Yes, my dear boy?'

'How did you know that I would be coming to the Rose and Ring-Dove? And giving the name of Brooke?'

'Because the priest at Santillana wrote of your intentions to the Conde your grandfather. And he wrote to us.'

'I see.' I felt somewhat awestruck at the workings of providence which, it seemed, playing back and forth like a shuttle on some great loom, had woven this web between England and Spain without my being in the least aware of it.

What could be the purpose of this mysterious pattern? And what part had I in it?

Just then a clock somewhere overhead chimed the hour of three, and Mr Burden, glancing at me kindly, said,

'You have much to think about, my dear boy. And I, too, have work to which I must apply myself. I am writing a history of the Carisbroke family. – I began it for your grandfather but since he, poor man, is no longer able to profit by it – since he has given up reading – it will be my pleasure to finish it for you.'

I thanked Mr Burden for his thought, and looked about me rather dismally, wondering what to do with myself in the house of Asshe.

Here I am, I thought, at the end of my journey,

and what do I find? An angry old madman, a house even more silent than Villaverde, an estate that is conducted like a merchant's counting-house by a group of lawyers and business-men; I am neither wanted nor needed. Asshe, indeed!

But then I thought: I had better wait patiently and see what God had in store for me.

Mr Burden, as if divining my thought, said,

'Believing that you might like to see over some of your estate, I told Jem Merriwether to bring round one of your grandfather's riding-horses and escort you wherever you care to go. Your grandfather (who, like your father, was a famous horseman) still has some fine mounts in his stable. – And I know that Jem has a longing to talk to you of your father.'

We returned to the main entrance where, sure enough, Jem awaited me, riding a black mare and leading a most beautiful fiery little chestnut, not large, but so graceful and spirited that he looked ready to bound clean up the great flight of steps, did Jem let go of his bridle.

So I thanked Mr Burden, and rode off with Jem across the park.

'Eh, I thowt as much!' said Jem after a few minutes. 'Ye've your father's seat an' your granfer's hands – proper owd wizard 'e be in the saddle to this day, though 'e be flown in 'is wits. Now what manner o' mounts would you have had in Spain, then, Master Felix?'

In no time I was telling him all about Villaverde, and he was telling me all about my father's pranks when a boy; and soon my soreness was somewhat healed. For I saw, firstly, that Jem had loved my father and grieved for him when he left – and now, too, I knew where my father had learned the 'language' in which he had spoken to me in my childhood. It was from Jem! And perhaps, I pondered, even as I told Jem about the bad-tempered mule, and how she had saved me from the morass ('Arr!' said Jem. 'Wunnderful clever beasts, mules be!') – perhaps it was because my father had received more love from Jem than from the Duke, his own father, that he had chosen Jem's language in which to speak to me.

We rode through great russet drifts of dead leaves in the beech-woods, and along by the river, and then up, along a grassy crest of hill from which Jem said, we could see five counties, and the hills of Wales in the distance, across the Bristol Channel.

'I'll be putting up some jumps for 'ee tomorrow, Master Felix,' said Jem hopefully, 'and then we'll have 'ee out hunting, come Christmas!'

His face fell when I told him that I was being sent to school in Bath, but he sighed and said,

'True 'tis, there bain't enough young company for 'ee here. Still, 'ee'll be home for the holidays, I dessay.'

I said I hoped so, and thanked Jem for the ride.

Back at the house I found my way to my chamber, where Watchett had laid out more clothes for me, and then I dined with Mr Burden and the rest of my trustees – Dr Larpent, Mr Dinsdale, and Mr Tweedy had retired to their respective homes.

During the meal Mr Burden told me something of the history of the Carisbroke family – how they had come to England with the Normans in 1066, and how they had been granted this manor by the Norman king, William the First, and how, since the house owned by the previous Saxon lord was but a smoking ruin, it had by its new owner been given the name of Asshe. And he had married the Saxon land-holder's daughter, whose name was Aelfrida, and from that day on, four out of six in the Carisbroke family had her small stature, flax-fair hair, and bright blue eyes.

Indeed there were many portraits of them hanging round the walls, as I soon saw – short, fair-haired, blue-eyed men astride of their horses or with hawks on their wrists – a great number of them as like to my grandfather as one pea is to another.

And like to myself also.

Is it not strange then, that, remembering how alien I had felt to the portraits of the lanky, black-haired Cabezadas, I should now feel so homesick for Villaverde?

After the meal I asked Mr Burden if I should visit my grandfather again for a while, and he said yes. But the Duke was playing with a box full of shoe-buckles, sorting them and stirring them, picking out one, looking at it, and putting it back. He glanced up at me and said irritably,

'Go away, boy, go away! I have never cared to have boys about me – tiresome, noisy, fidgety, ill-conditioned pests, all of them!' And back he went to his buckles.

Mr Burden told me softly, as we walked away, that my grandmother had died shortly after the birth of my father so that he, like myself, had never known his mother. And my grandfather, grieving for his wife, had shown scant patience with the younger of his two sons, leaving him mostly to the care of his tutors.

After I had cheered myself with a little music I went up to bed, for I was both weary and sad. But yet I could not sleep. I lay tossing in my great bed, in my great chamber, hearing nothing, for there was a solemn hush in and around the great house, as though all life had come to a stop there.

How shall I endure it? I thought.

And to God I said, Why did You bring me here? What is to happen now? Please help me to understand all this for I am very unhappy.

I remembered a little song that Sam would sometimes sing laughingly,

> Ay, Dios de mi alma!
> Saqueisme de aqui!
> Ay! que Inglaterra
> Ya no es para mi!*

* Ah, God of my soul
Take me from here
Alas, England
Is not the country for me!

347

# 12

I spent a week at Asshe, until my trustees considered me suitably equipped to go to school. Mr Burden escorted me into Bath several times, to buy clothes and schoolbooks, and furnishings for my room, and I was as much taken with this town at a close view as I had been by a distant one.

The streets were as lively as those of Oviedo – but very different – and there was such a variety of shops, and such remarkable things to be seen in the shop windows! In a bootmaker's window I saw a pair of boots immersed in a glass bowl of water, so as to show that the boots could not be harmed by wet; an apothecary's window had a collection of worms from human intestines, curiously bottled, testifying that patients had been relieved of these worms by the medicines sold within. There were plaster busts, painted to the life, displaying the newest forms of wigs (though most of the younger Englishmen do not wear wigs preferring their own hair); alabaster lamps, fine jewels, beautiful books, and birds in cages, reminding me of my dear Assistenta.

Since in some parts of the town there is no

carriage road, sedan chairs are used instead of carriages; these are made of leather, and are carried by two chairmen who wear large coats of dark blue. I would not wish to be carried in such a chair! for I observed that when it rained, the chairmen all come out, hoping for custom, and the chairs become wholly soaked with wet, outside and in.

Bath has many dogs, and Mr Burden informed me that many of them are turnspit-dogs; they are long-backed and short-legged; they are set in a wheel, and a hot coal with them, so the poor things cannot stand still without burning their feet; so they are kept upon the gallop until the roast is done, which may be two hours or three. This seemed very cruel to me. Mr Burden told me that one day, when all the dogs had followed their masters to church, the preacher spoke on a text from the book of Ezekiel regarding a chariot. When he said the word *wheel*, all the dogs in the church pricked up their ears in fright; at the second use of the word they uttered a doleful howl; and at the third repetition every one of them scampered out of the church with their tails between their legs.

Mr Burden was as kind as possible to me during the week, and so was Jem, who, as he had promised, built brushwood jumps for me in the park and encouraged me to leap my grandfather's horses over them, higher and higher. My rides with Jem were the pleasantest part of my life at Asshe.

Also I explored the great empty house with its pictures and its statues and its handsome furnishings. All was so neat, orderly, and silent that I found myself longing for the shrill voices of my great-aunts, with their clicking fans and rosaries.

I told Mr Burden the tale of my adventures on the way from Spain, and he, I suppose, told some part to the other trustees. For on the second or third day Mr ffanshawe, deciding, perhaps, that a boy who has survived such adventures could not be wholly stupid, began to explain to me about the workings of the estate, how the land was administered; how the tenants held their lands and paid their rents, and from what sources, tin mines, slate mines, timber, grain, and cattle, my grand-father's revenues were drawn.

Then my clothes were sent home from the tailors – black short jackets and long trousers, not unlike those I had worn in Spain – and I was pronounced ready for school. Watchett packed my box with the new clothes and Lynton made me up a box of provisions – currant wine, almond cakes, biscuits, fruit, and a great ham – 'For,' said he, 'we all know as how they starves young gen'lemen in them places!' And, after consulting Mr Burden, I helped myself to a number of books from the library.

'I should dearly like it,' said Mr Burden, 'if you would allow me to borrow your father's book, for I long to read it again – I will preserve it for you most carefully.'

Of course I said yes, and he recommended to me several novels, which, he said, he knew my father would have enjoyed and he thought I might also: *The Monk*, and *The Black Veil*, and *The Mysteries of Udolpho*, and *Northanger Abbey*.

Thus equipped, and with the horse that had been purchased for me led behind the chaise, I was driven into Bath on a dark rainy evening, and delivered to the Master of the Pulteney Academy for the Sons of Gentlemen and the Nobility, which establishment occupied a large blackened mansion at the foot of Queen Square,\* which is one of the handsomest squares in Bath, and full of houses as large as palaces.

The master, a Mr Alleyn, a lean, grey, gloomy man like a melted candle, received me civilly enough. I said a sad goodbye to Jem, who brought in my box, and then led my horse away to be stabled in a mews nearby. Then Mr Alleyn, having shown me my chamber, which was very tiny and right under the leads, since all the best ones had already been allotted (but with a pleasant view of the square), undertook to introduce me to the rest of the boys, who, at this time of day, were engaged in preparation of their tasks for the morrow.

He led me downstairs again to a large, bare room on the ground floor, from which, even before the door was opened, I could hear the most amazing noise, like all the parrots in Africa.

'That is the boys reciting their lessons,' said Mr Alleyn with his thin smile.

He opened the door and called out, 'Here is your new classmate, young gentlemen – Lord St

---

\* Queen Square built 1727–35.

Winnow. You may be excused the last ten minutes of preparation, in order to become acquainted.'

Then he left me with them.

Fifty pairs of eyes were fixed on me. Some of the boys, all seated at rows of desks, were smaller than I; most were my own size or bigger.

Addressing the boy nearest me, who had a pale spotty face, brown eyes, and a good deal of ink on his waistcoat, I said, 'How do you do?' that, Mr Burden having informed me, being the correct English way in which to begin an acquaintance.

'Hello!' cried a dozen voices. ''Tain't for you to speak, Johnny New! New bods don't speak here until they are spoken to.'

And a taller boy, who looked about fourteen, stepped up to me and roughly unbuttoned my jacket, ripping off a button in the process.

'New bods ain't allowed to go around with their jackets frogged up,' he said, scrumpling my hair and giving my right ear a tweak at the same time.

I was so amazed at this treatment that without pause for reflection I shot out my fist and knocked him flying. He fell to the floor, taking a desk with him, and the ink poured all over his head. From the way he yelled, you would have thought he had been cut in half. A general clamour of horror went up from the other boys; in the middle of which, the door shot open again, and Mr Alleyn hastened back.

'Boys, boys! Too much noise! What is going on?' said he.

'Oh, sir, the new boy has knocked down Fitz-warren!'

'What?' said Mr Alleyn, turning on me a most grave and reproving face. 'What is this, Lord St Winnow? Not two minutes in the school and already you are at fisticuffs? This is a bad beginning, indeed! I understand that you have just come from Spain, but I would have you understand from the start that we will not tolerate uncivilised behaviour here! No fights are allowed in this school. The penalty for infringement of this rule is to miss a meal, and that, I fear, must be your fate, St Winnow! No supper for you tonight. Now, boys, time for prayers!'

The desks which filled the great room were pushed to one side and the boys stood in rows while Mr Alleyn recited some prayers in such a rapid gabble that I could not understand him at all.

Meanwhile I was subjected to various minor annoyances – I was pinched, tweaked, jostled, my hair was pulled, my ankles were kicked, as the boys moved past me to their places. This, it seemed, was their way of welcoming a newcomer.

After the prayers, supper was served in the same room: pieces of oatcake, broken up, and a mug of coffee for each boy. I, being debarred from this, asked if I might go to my room and unpack my belongings, but Mr Alleyn said,

'No, St Winnow. Boys are not allowed in their bedrooms during the daytime. You may stay here

353

and continue to make the acquaintance of your classmates.'

This process consisted of their all firing questions at me, which I answered as best I could.

'Where's your father, new bod? Where's your mamma?' I said they were both dead.

'What were you a-doing in Spain?'

But my answer to this was drowned by the jeering voice of a pasty-faced boy with jam on his collar, who called out;

> Winnie Winnow is a Dago
> Pipes his eye and lives on sago!

which verse won instant popularity and was taken up by the whole roomful of boys in a loud chorus.

'Winnie Winnow!' they shouted. 'Winnie Winnow! By gob, he's a frog! He eats fried worms! He only washes once a year!' and other stupidities.

I tried to ignore their insults, as I was not allowed to fight them; stuck my hands in my pockets, and thought of the far worse dangers which I had come through: the terrible people in the mountain village, the threats of the gente de reputacion and the alcalde; the shipwreck and the Comprachicos. But the prickling annoyances of those boys were tiresome beyond belief, and hard to disregard. They shouted, 'Take your hands out of your pockets, new bod! New bods ain't permitted to put their hands in their pockets! Ya, boo, Johnny Dago!' and so on, until I was nearly mad with irritation, and heartily relieved when an under-master, or usher, named Mr Crackenthorpe, came into the room and rang a bell which meant that it was time for bed.

It was strange to lie in my narrow cot and listen to the sounds of the town outside: I was amazed at the night-long clatter of the coaches over the cobbles, the cries of chairmen, the hourly call of the watch; not till nearly dawn did I fall asleep, having much on my mind, and then I was woken by the dustmen, with their bells and chant of dust-ho!, the porterhouse boys and milkmen, each with different cries; so I came down to breakfast scarcely more rested than I had gone up.

Breakfast consisted of a liquid which they called coffee, but which tasted to me like brown water; thin slices of bitter bread, toasted, with a little butter – and countless more insults and jeers from the other boys, to which I did my best to turn a deaf ear, having no other recourse. I longed to set about them and knock them all flying.

One boy, more good-natured than the rest, who told me his name was Lord Fred Beauchamp, informed me that the teasing would die down in a month or so.

'They always give it thick to a new bod for his first half, you see! That's the rule. But if you take care not to do any of the things that are *fango*, then it'll die down quicker.'

'What is fango?' said I.

'Why, fango is – is anything that ain't done – like keeping your jacket buttoned, you know, or walking with your hands in your pockets, or using the front stairs; you must always use the back ones, unless you are with the Beak. And don't try to go near the fire – only praetors may go there.'

'Who are the praetors?'

'Why, the monitors – the big ones – you'll soon learn their names. You must always do what they bid you. And you must learn the lingo of the school.'

'Why, what is that?'

He told me that the boys had their own words for many things, such as *dobbo* for book, *milky* for master, *prog* for food, *prad* for horse, *mallicko* for bed, and *going up Jenkins* for going to the toilet stool. New boys were supposed to learn these words and have them perfect by the end of a week. I said I thought this stupid; why should I take pains to learn such childish rubbish when there were perfectly good English words for the things? But Beauchamp told me that unless I did so I should be sent to Coventry.

'Sent to Coventry? What is that?'

'Why, no one will speak to you!'

'That would not worry me in the slightest degree, since they all talk like six-year-olds. In fact I should prefer it.'

The masters' rules were even more trivial and irritating than the boys' rules. We might not leave the building unescorted; we were forbidden to venture forth into the streets of Bath unless one of the masters accompanied us. We might not ride our horses, except two by two, at a sedate trot, once a day, for half a mile out into the country and back. We might not smoke – not that I wished to – or keep dogs, or talk, save at stated times, or sing in our bedrooms, or play musical instruments, or wear coloured cravats, or read novels except after eight o'clock in the evening, or attend cock-fights, or make purchases from the shops in Bath, save on a Saturday, when there was a half-holiday, and then again one of the masters had to accompany us and we might not go off alone. Never have I encountered so many senseless rules! It seemed most of them had been invented to forbid acts that I had never thought of committing.

Also there were many more things that were *not done*. Fred Beauchamp advised me about these too.

'It ain't done to mention your sister, St Winnow. So, if you have one, keep her dark!'

'I have not got one, but what a piece of imbecility is this?' I said, thinking of Nieves. 'If I had one, why should not I mention her?'

'Oh, it ain't fango to talk about girls. Girls are totty-headed things!'

When it came to the lessons, I was surprised to find that I was tolerably well up with the rest of the boys, and even ahead in some respects. Father Tomas had taught me well, it appeared; I had something to thank him for. Only, the boys all laughed at me, because I pronounced the Latin and Greek words in a different way from theirs; they were highly entertained by my *false quantities*, as they called them.

I said, what did it signify how the words were spoken, so they were the right words? And who knew, anyway, how the ancient Greeks or Romans *had* spoken them? But Mr Alleyn, who taught these languages, told me I must learn the English way to pronounce them, or I would never be allowed into Oxford. Remembering that my father had been expelled from that place, I was not at all certain that I wished to go there. Certainly I did not wish to go if it was anything like the Pulteney Academy for the Sons of Gentlemen!

Oh, how can I express the tedium of that month! I felt I had sooner be in jail at Oviedo – I had sooner be aboard the *Guipuzcoa* with the gale blowing up – I had far, far sooner be back at Villaverde, ducking the blows of Father Tomas and riding my bad-tempered mule over the stony prado.

Although the boys' teasing did presently abate somewhat I could not make friends with them.

They were too childish! Their whole lives seemed concerned with petty friendships, petty quarrels: *linko*, they called these, and *bello*: 'Say, have you heard, Townshend is linko with Bellingham, now, and he's gone bello with Desborough; they aren't speaking since Des borrowed his Latin crib and spilt ink on it!' 'Hey! Fotheringay is linko with De Vere – Fothers had a box of prog from home and the two of them ate it all up together!'

Their talk was all of this idiotic kind, until I could have died with boredom.

Even more ridiculous was the way they went on about some of the masters. These were decent enough men, Mr Crackenshaw, Mr Dingley, and Mr Wells, though I do not think any of them would have been much use aboard the *Guipuzcoa* – but to hear the boys talk about them you would think they were descended from Phoebus Apollo, the God of the Sun! They had another word, *socco*, for their feelings about the masters.

'Did you see how Mr Dingley smiled at me when I was giving my recitation? I am quite socco about him! I shall die if I don't sit next to him at dinner.'

So the long dull days wore on, until the boys began to talk of how they would go home for Christmas.

And what shall I do? thought I. Return to Asshe, to hear tales of my father from Jem, and of the Carisbroke family from Mr Burden, and watch my grandfather playing with his shoe-buckles?

One Friday morning I had risen early, before the rest of the boys, and stood idly in the big dining-room, looking at the black trees and blackened houses in Queen Square, where a thin snow was commencing to fall. I watched the post-man in his royal livery of scarlet and gold, hurrying from house to house, announcing his arrival with his loud double-knock. At last he approached the Pulteney Academy, and, as he did so, I suddenly had a strong feeling – I *knew* – that he carried a letter for me.

Rap-tap! went the knocker, and, as the man-servant was still upstairs, taking hot water to all the boys, I quietly went into the front hall and collected the letters myself, though I knew that it was considered disgracefully fango to do such a thing.

Sure enough, not one letter for me, but two! — both sent on from Asshe — the first I had received since I had been at the school.

Laying the other letters on a small table, I ran quietly up the front stairs — another very fango proceeding but it meant that I was less likely to encounter anybody — and managed to get to my room unobserved.

There I read my letters.

The first was from Sam, in a round, sprawling handwriting that seemed exactly like him.

'My dear old Mess-Mate! Forgive your Pal for not having Writ before, I am a proper wretch but have been so busy with legal Doings as you can't imagine. I shall be grateful For Ever for your kindness in sending the money. When I am back in Spain, shall be able to repay Same & will lose no Time in doing so for Senor Colomas promised me a good wage. I set Sail for Spain tomorrow & tho Grieved not to see you agen, hope that, now you have found your Great Folk in England, Will not forget them in Spain & loving Freinds also, of whom your fellow-singer Sam is the foremost.

'Hearken, Felix, you cannot guess the marvellous Good Fortune your money brought me. Firstly I was able to pay my Debt to my uncle, so now I can visit England when I wish, without fear of Jail. And when I went to repay my uncle, what do you think I discovered? Why, he had reared up my little lad, my little Matt, that I thought was dead, and I have a son, a proper handsome little fellow of four years, the spit image of my Lily that's dead and gone! And he has learned to call me Farder, and the Magistrate telled Uncle Ebenezer 'tis my right to take him back to Spain with me – where I know Juana will Spoil him to death for she loves all children. Also, luckily, Uncle Ebenezer is in trouble with Customs over Run goods, so has no time to spare.

'Now, Felix, I am the happiest man in Cornwall this day, and if it had not been for you, I'd ne'er have come back to England, never known about this Treasure I found waiting for me.

'I am as glad as can be about your Great Kinsfolk, and 'twon't make a pin of difference as to how I feel about ye, for when two mates have been in danger such as we have seen together, they are knit for life, be they noble or Humble.

So no more now from your attached Freind,

Sam.'

Well, was not that a joyful letter to receive, and enough to warm the heart on a snowy morning! I was sad not to see Sam, of course, but rejoiced to my roots that matters had turned out so well for him.

What a strange thing, I thought, that he had a son all the time and never knew it. And I thought what a loving father Sam would make, how he would enjoy teaching young Matt all the things he knew himself.

I was glad he could take the boy back to Llanes, where Juana and little Conchita would be sure to welcome him and play with him.

Boys ought to be with their fathers, I thought.

I said a prayer of thanks in my heart to God for arranging Sam's fortune so well, and another one, asking for a safe journey for him and little Matt.

Then I opened my other letter which, I now observed, came from Spain.

It was from my grandfather.

'My dear Grandson: I and your grandmother and your aunts have been rejoiced to hear, by a letter from the good Senor Burden, that you are safely arrived at the house of your English grandfather the Duque, and that you are now in school.

'Senor Burden will have told you of the wickedness of your great-aunt Isadora, and of her death. What can I say? I bitterly regret the injustice done to you during her life. Now I understand better why you left us, and the bad feeling that lay between you, that led to so much trouble for you and so many punishments, some of them, I fear, undeserved. But that is past now, and your great-aunt is dead, and I hope you can find it in your heart to

362

forgive us. We miss you greatly – the house seems very quiet without you.

'We heard of your adventures on your journey from the good priest at Santillana, and it rejoices me that you endured perils and difficulties with the spirit of a Cabezada – and of a Carisbroke! Senor Burden has written me the history of your English family.

'We shall be hoping, your grandmother and I, to hear the last part of your journey's adventures, and how you finally reached your grandfather's house.

'Pray, my dear grandson, write us a letter as soon as possible.

'And perhaps – perhaps – some day you will find it in your heart to come back.

I send you my most esteemed greetings,

Your Grandfather.'

After I had read this letter I sat holding the paper for a long time. I saw in my mind's eye the great white slopes of the sierra, as viewed from my window; I saw the cobbled stable-yard, the grey-and-damask saloon, the chapel with its red light, the little stone stair where Bernardina had died. I saw Bob's little room – I could never think of him as Father, he would always remain Bob to me. How far away he seemed from me now, how close he had seemed – even after he had died – at Villaverde.

Before I had noticed it, my mind was made up. I looked about the little room. There was not much I wanted to take. I had some gold sovereigns – enough to buy a warm jacket and a set of pipes. The rest of my belongings I packed into the box, and attached a note to it, directing that it be sent back to Asshe, with my horse.

I could write to Mr Burden and Mr ffanshawe later, explaining. I did not think they would be too surprised. Some day I would come back – but not just yet.

I ran down the stairs at top speed, even faster than I had run up. In the hall I encountered Fred Beauchamp, who said,

'Hey, old feller, where are you off to? It's just on breakfast time!'

'I have an errand in the town.'

'In the *town*? Are you queer in your attic? Old Alleyn will be in a rare tweak when he finds out!'

'I don't care!' said I, and slipped out of the front door. Running along the snowy streets to the market, I thought, I can travel back with Ned as far as Falmouth. I can work my passage on some ship to Santander or Bilbao – I know enough to do that now. Or, if they are full-handed, I will pay my fare. I can reclaim Assistenta from the convent, and the bad-tempered mule from the monastery; I can visit Sam and Juana and little Matt and Conchita and Senor Colomas in Llanes. Happy thought! I can spend a little time with Nieves and her family in San Antonio. Things will be better between me and Grandfather – now I shall be able to talk to him and tell him my adventures. And – if providence is kind – which perhaps is more than

I deserve – but I have been very lucky up to now – perhaps when I get back to Villaverde, old Gato will still be alive, and when I go down to the stable-yard he will be waiting there, and will come to rub his head against my leg . . .

Book **2** in the FELIX TRILOGY

# BRIDLE THE WIND

*If you're an adventure addict then you'll love BRIDLE THE WIND – it's un-put-downable!*

*Here's a taste of what's in store...*

*Shipwrecked, imprisoned and then haunted by a ghoulish premonition – brave Felix may be down on his luck but he'll never, ever give up...*

'*Oh*, but I don't want to die!'

And then, a second time, putting the fear of death, such as I had not felt, even through the shipwreck, into my own heart, '*Oh – but – I don't – want – to – die!*'

Petrified, I stared all around me. From where could the voice possibly come?

Trembling uncontrollably, I looked upward, and now, just for a moment, it seemed to my dazed senses that I could see something - some *body* - suspended from one of the arching boughs overhead, that I could see a thin form swinging, dangling at the end of a rope not three feet above me... It faded, melted, and was gone.

*Book 3 in the FELIX TRILOGY*

# THE TEETH OF THE GALE

*G**rab a copy of the thrilling finale of THE FELIX TRILOGY. It's an action-packed read – so hold on tight!*

*Pulses race when brave Felix leads a rescue mission with his sweetheart, Juana. It's a deadly dangerous task – will Felix keep his head and return a hero?*
*Here's a tingling taster...*

'Juana! Keep very still!' I called hoarsely.

My heart seemed to fall clean out of my body into the gorge below. There she was, defenceless, in deadly danger, and here I was, strung on two ropes over the gulf, with my gun strapped out of reach, useless on my back; however fast I moved, I would never be able to get back in time to save her if the bear flew at her.

The massive bear turned, at the sound of my voice, and eyed me intently. I joggled frantically on the rope, to hold its attention.

'Bear! Bear!' I yelled. 'Look at me! Look at me on the bridge. Come and get me, bear! Here I am!'

**THE FELIX TRILOGY** by Joan Aiken from Red Fox
| | |
|---|---|
| *Go Saddle the Sea* | ISBN 0 09 953771 0 |
| *Bridle the Wind* | ISBN 0 09 953781 8 |
| *The Teeth of the Gale* | ISBN 0 09 953791 5 |